THE GIRL ON THE SHORE

By
ROSANNE L. HIGGINS

To my sisters, Heidi and Eileen, and my brother, John. May we continue to laugh with and at each other for many years to come.

Chapter One

Maude laid quietly in bed, waiting for her heart-beat to return to normal, reviewing the details of the nightmare that had just released her from its clutches. The room was dark against the heavy drapes that held the morning sunshine at bay. Time travel dreams were always problematic, and returning to the present was uncertain. The furniture in her bedroom matched the period in which the house was built, nearly two hundred years before. In the dark, the American Empire four poster bed and massive chest of drawers gave the room an uncertain provenance. Given that Maude's vivid dreams often focused on the mid-nineteenth century, she often awoke uncertain if she had returned from it.

Those dreams provided Maude with chillingly accurate pictures of her home city of Buffalo, New York, during the period. Historically verifiable details confirmed the past was communicating with her during these dreams, helping her to understand the unique connection she had with the city during that earlier period. This latest subconscious vision was a disturbing depiction of both past and present events. Maude had recently experienced a traumatic event reminiscent of an earlier time in Buffalo. She was still, evidently, trying to reconcile it in her mind.

This morning's dream started in the nineteenth century with Martha Quinn, a physician, desperately looking for her husband Johnny, who had fallen into the Commercial Slip, the entrance to the Erie Canal. Without warning, both the time and the characters changed, and it was Maude, in the twenty-first century, plunging into Lake Erie in search of her husband Don, two very similar events coming back to haunt her, linked forever, but they were separated by more than a century. Both events directly affected her. In her past life as Martha Sloane, she had lost her husband that night at the entrance to the canal. In the present, Maude's husband had survived his fall into the lake. Closing her eyes in the small, dark bedroom, she recalled the details vividly.

Martha's nephew, Daniel, had beseeched their help when Felicity, his fiancée, had been kidnapped by Mason Leonard, the keeper of the insane asylum. Her husband Johnny, brother-in-law Michael and Daniel had surprised the keeper and his henchman as they tried to escape by canal boat. She arrived at the dock just as the confrontation had begun. Martha's attention was diverted by the skirmish in the water. Two men had actually fallen into the slip. She knew one of them had to be her husband, which meant that the other was Mason Leonard. One man, she couldn't tell which, was struggling to gain control of the other, who was trying his hardest to push his aggressor under the water.

"Help him, Michael!" she screamed to her brother-in-law.

She ran along the dock for a better look, scanning the water's surface, frantically searching for her husband "Where is he?" Martha cried. "Where's Johnny?"

In the way of many time travel dreams, the scene abruptly, yet smoothly shifted with the passage of nearly a century and a half. The fleet of sailboats anchored in the marina clearly belonged to the present. Now Maude became both the actor and the observer in her dream.

She was frantic as she dove in, breaking the surface of the water. It was impossible to see anything in murky lake water at night, but she immediately went back under in desperate search of Don. She could feel the weight of her wet clothes dragging her down as she struggled again to resurface.

There was a disturbance in the water that Maude could feel rather than see, like someone was thrashing arms and legs. She swam closer and a panicked hand grabbed on to her arm. She tried to shake it off, but then she realized that one of the men who had fallen into the water had pinned the other to the pylon of the dock. He was unconscious and the other man was stuck beneath him.

Maude did not know the identity of the man who grabbed her, so she grabbed the arm of the unconscious man and dragged him to the surface after the other man had been set free. It became more difficult to tow the unconscious man and she realized that the other man was grabbing for his arm. Whether he was trying to help or hinder her, Maude did not know, but when all three of them broke the surface, only two of them gasped for air.

3

Maude opened her eyes, unwilling to risk the return of that terrifying feeling every time she awoke from this nightmare. Johnny had died that night in the Commercial Slip, but Don had survived his ordeal in the lake over a century later. In her dream, one of the men had died, but Maude couldn't remember who. She always woke before she could determine which husband was lost to her, the one from her past life or the one from the present. The confusion over which century she awoke to only increased her anxiety

"Hey, Maude, it's me. I'm here." Don had seen his wife wake up in this state more than he was comfortable with in the months since they had confronted a jewel thief at the outer harbor marina. They had each arrived at the marina independently, Don to catch the thief who had stolen from one of their most valued clients, and Maude to save Don from the same fate that Johnny Quinn had suffered all those years ago. However, Maude's plan was foiled soon after she arrived on the scene. Lying in wait, Don saw the thief, Lester Northrup, leading Maude and her friend at gunpoint down the dock. He had leapt off a moored sailboat to tackle the man, sending them both into the water. It was true that the incident was eerily similar to the death of Johnny Quinn more than a century ago, who had met his death trying to save a young woman kidnapped by the keeper of the insane asylum. Don knew how Maude's dream ended and that he needed to remind her Johnny had died in 1870, while Don had survived his ordeal just a few months ago.

"You're here; thank God you are here." She turned and allowed herself to be folded into his arms.

Don held his wife as her heartbeat returned to normal. There was nothing else to say now that she knew he was safe. They were soulmates, not just in the sense that they were deeply in love, but real soulmates who had been husband and wife across many lives. Maude and Don Travers had been Martha and Johnny Quinn in another life. That life was also in the city of Buffalo, New York, but during the nineteenth century. Martha and Johnny had met as children in the Erie County Poorhouse and had grown up together when they were fortunate enough to have left that place. Martha became a physician at the insane asylum, and Johnny owned a dry goods store on Main Street. In the present day, Maude and Don lived and operated their antique business in that very building on Main Street where the dry goods store had been.

A few years ago, Maude and Don would have thought the events they had recently experienced were the stuff of fiction, not their real lives. It was a lot for anyone to grapple with. Don thought they should talk to someone, either together or separately.

"*'I have dreams about the past, and I recently learned that my husband and I were also married in a past life. Oh, and I can touch a human skeleton and get visions about what life was like for that person.'* You don't think a therapist would take us seriously, do you?" she had argued when he first suggested it.

"How about talking to someone at Lily Dale?" Don countered. The Modern Spiritualist community was close by and offered a perspective that would undoubtedly be more receptive to their issues.

Maude had befriended an elderly woman from Lily Dale who had been helping her to understand this unusual connection she had to the nineteenth century, but poor Charlotte Lambert had been dragged into the confrontation at the marina with the thief Lester Northrup for her troubles. Maude was reluctant to impose upon her again after all that had happened.

"I'll figure it out." That is what Maude told him every time her husband had suggested she seek help to understand her recurring nightmare, but Don wanted his own answers. While they had a few years to grow accustomed to Maude's unique relationship with the past, only recently did they understand Don's connection. Maude had dreams of the past before, and those dreams always contained accurate historic details. The fact that she was having a recurring dream and awoke not knowing which of her two husbands had survived was troubling because he wondered if it was prophetic. Was he meant to die at the marina? Had the messages from the past interfered with the present?

* * *

Later that morning, Maude found herself headed to the very place she had been reluctant to go for help. She slowed the car down as she turned off route 60 and on to Dale Drive in the small town of Cassadaga, New York. She was minutes away from the Modern Spiritualist community of Lily Dale and the urgent news for which Charlotte Lambert had summoned her. The call from her dear old friend had caused Maude to drop everything that morning and make the hour-long trek from Buffalo to Lily Dale. Charlotte was a psychic medium and her advice, observations and speculations regarding Maude were profound and life-changing, when the two women finally made sense of them.

The problem with Charlotte, and many other psychic mediums, was that the information coming through from the other side was seldom rich with detail or context. Individual practitioners often have very specific means by which they communicate with the spirit world. Some see flashes from the physical world, actual visions, while others receive information in the form of shapes or colors, and still others interpret the unseen world through sound or smell. The lucky recipient gets a straightforward message like 'Your grandmother is here and she doesn't like the man you had dinner with last night.' More often, it goes like this: 'I'm getting an older female energy, a maternal energy. Does this make sense to you? She seems upset...'

The conversation goes on from there as the message is decoded. The recipient who trusts the process and the messenger attempt to offer explanations in the way of people or events that seem to fit the clues. Those who are skeptical withhold information, assuming a legitimate psychic medium should already know. Faulty reasoning, Maude thought. If the messenger was a stranger, how would they know the particulars pertaining to any family member of the recipient? Although it often left her frustrated, Maude was one who trusted both the process and the messenger, and so she hopped in the car and drove all the way to Lily Dale to hear what Charlotte Lambert had to tell her.

"You poor dear, rushing all the way here. I didn't mean to frighten you." Charlotte met her at the door of the Victorian cottage she lived in year-round. Lily Dale was busiest during what they called the camp season, the summer months when the earliest Free Thinkers of the late nineteenth century gathered by the lake to exchange ideas on a wide variety of topics, including women's rights and religion. Outsiders thought these discussions were, at the very least, unconventional, but to some they were considered blasphemous. However, Charlotte cherished the off-season and was willing to brave the isolation and harsh winters by Cassadaga Lake for the tranquility of the Leolin Woods, where she spent countless hours regardless of the weather, in quiet meditation.

Maude gave her a wary smile. She wasn't exactly frightened; however she knew whatever was to be learned over tea with this wise old woman would take her further down a path she was thus far reluctant to go. "Don't be silly. I was overdue for a visit." Charlotte's expression indicated that she was not fooled, so Maude gave in. "I'll admit I was surprised you wanted to see me right away."

"I am sorry to have sounded so dramatic." Charlotte ushered her into a parlor that looked like it hadn't changed since the cottage was built in the late nineteenth century. Her great-grandmother came to Lily Dale as a child. There was no safer place for a gifted child of color. The house had been passed along in her family, each generation producing an heir with highly developed inner senses. "I do wish you lived closer."

The other thing passed through the family was the sense of safety and security felt in the close-knit community of Lily Dale. Charlotte remembered well the Civil Rights movement of the 1960s and what life had been like for people of color before that. Her family and others like her had always been accepted and respected in Lily Dale, and she seldom left the gated community.

"No worries. I was happy to get away from the shop." Maude took a seat and reached for the cup and saucer that sat atop the fine lace tablecloth brushing against her knee. "So, what have you got to tell me?"

"Well, last night I was walking through the woods and I was joined by a woman named Mary. She was wearing early nineteenth-century clothes, nothing fancy; she wasn't a woman of leisure."

Maude knew that Charlotte was not talking about a living person, but rather a spirit. "Do you think she is connected to me?"

"Yes, I do. She showed me images of the sea, a small thatched cottage on a remote island, and a red horse pulling a wagon over a stone bridge. I think she was from Ireland," Charlotte told her.

"I know I have ancestors who came from there, but I never did get around to finding out anything about them," Maude told her.

"She may not be your ancestor, dear." Charlotte looked at Maude with eyebrows raised, waiting for her to catch up.

"I don't understand." As soon as the words left her mouth, she realized that wasn't true. "Oh, wait, this woman was somehow connected to Martha." Maude made no attempt to hush the audible sigh at the end of her statement. A visit to Charlotte usually had something to do with Martha Sloane Quinn, a nineteenth-century physician who had lived in both Buffalo and Lily Dale. After all, it was through Charlotte that Maude learned she had been Martha in a previous life.

Maude had come to realize that the research started in graduate school would become her life's work. A project analyzing the ledgers of the Erie County Poorhouse helped complete her doctorate in anthropology, and had also connected her to Ciara, Patricia and Martha Sloane. When Maude left her career in academia to open a business with her husband, her connection with the poorhouse and this family was not severed. She had no idea that the building where she and her husband Don had started their antique business (and now lived in as well) only brought her closer to them. As the details of their lives manifested themselves through dreams and research, Maude's relationship to this family deepened. With this connection also came the realization that Maude had some gifts not previously revealed. She could conjure up accurate details from the past in her dreams. With Charlotte's help, she pieced together the clues she received. Between the dreams, historical research and a few whispering bones from the poorhouse cemetery, Maude began to understand the lives of the Sloane sisters in the burgeoning city of Buffalo. Orphaned on the journey emigrating from Ireland, the girls had no choice but to seek refuge in the county almshouse when they arrived in Buffalo. Each sister rose above her humble beginnings. Ciara worked tirelessly to help the poor, Patricia became a teacher, and Martha a physician.

It was such a gift, this window into the past, especially for an anthropologist. Because of this unconventional means, however, Maude couldn't share outright what she was learning with the scholarly community, and instead wrote fictional accounts of the sisters and their experiences in nineteenth-century Buffalo. It provided enthusiasts of Buffalo's history a glimpse into an era that had been largely previously unexplored without her having to document her sources. It was also a way of chronicling all that she was learning about herself in both her past and present lives.

The most startling revelation was that Maude's husband, Don, had also been Martha's husband Johnny in his past life. They were truly soulmates and might even follow each other through eternity. That realization should have provided comfort, but through past life regression, Maude had learned of Johnny's death at the hands of Martha's nemesis just in time to save her own husband from a similar fate. While she was grateful beyond words to have Don with her, she remembered all too well the emptiness and despair Martha felt when she realized Johnny was gone. Maude carried those feelings with her all these months later, and with them the fear of wondering what might happen next. Try as she did to distract herself with the work of the business she shared with Don and her research and writing, she could not shake it. More recently, Maude no longer had dreams that chronicled the past. Instead she had the same recurring nightmare that only left questions she was afraid to ask. A message from or about Martha was not something Maude was ready to deal with just yet.

"What did this woman have to tell you? Wait a minute; is she here now?" Maude asked cautiously. The appearance of spirits from her past had occurred before during visits to Charlotte. Maude took a few deep breaths to relax and see whether she could sense the presence of this spirit.

Charlotte watched as Maude made the effort to connect with this unseen companion, pleased that she was open to the experience. After a few minutes, the blank look on her face indicated that Maude's effort was unsuccessful. Charlotte then answered her question. "Yes, she is here now."

"How does that work, exactly? How can this woman, whom I have never met, know to contact me through you?" Maude was asking partly out of curiosity and partly to delay further communication with the woman named Mary.

"The love connection is boundless; it is not unusual for someone from the other side to go to great lengths to try and make contact. This woman loved Martha very much. I felt the maternal energy the minute I realized she was with me in the woods."

"So, are you saying Mary is Martha's mother?" Maude asked.

"I wasn't certain last night, but now that you are here I am convinced of your past relationship," Charlotte told her.

"What is so urgent that Martha's mother needs to speak to me?" Maude braced herself for the answer.

"Well, I'm not sure exactly. As I said, she just keeps showing me these images of the sea, the cottage on the remote island, and the horse-drawn wagon on the bridge." Charlotte closed her eyes in concentration. "Along with these images, I am feeling a sense of dread. Something unwelcome is connected to that location."

It was Charlotte's calm confidence when she delivered a vague message that often rubbed Maude the wrong way, although she knew the old woman did not mean to irritate her. Charlotte had long grown comfortable in her own skin and had encountered thousands of confused people in a lifetime of mediumship. She delivered the message; that is all she could do. It was up to the recipient to make sense of it.

"You think the images she showed you are of Ireland?"

"Well, I can't be sure. I've never been there, but I've seen parts of it in the movies and in pictures and it looks like it could be Ireland to me. The family came from Ireland, didn't they?"

Maude knew nothing of the life of the Sloane sisters before they came to America. Although she created a backstory to use in her novels, those details were the furthest thing from her mind faced now with the spirit of Martha's real mother. "Can you describe what she's showing you?"

Charlotte nodded confidently. "I'm seeing large cliffs, several in a row. It's like I'm seeing them from a ship. They are huge and the waves are crashing all around them." Charlotte closed her eyes and concentrated on the images Mary was providing.

Maude shook her head, having no idea where these women were trying to direct her. "I've never been to Ireland either and I'm even less familiar with the countryside than you are."

"She's very insistent, dear. Could we get an atlas or something? What about the computer?" She turned and began speaking to the empty space beside her. "We don't know what you mean." She turned back to Maude, but her focus was inward. "Now she's showing me the equivalent of mental snapshots of the island. It is large. From the sea, you can tell it is the largest of three." Closing her eyes again, she continued. "It is very old, ancient by American standards, and at the mercy of the sea and the wind by the looks of it. Still I don't think there were many neighbors. She passed only a few cottages on the way to the boat that would take them off the island."

"What do you mean about passing cottages and leaving the island?" Maude was becoming interested. "Is she showing you a specific event or just a series of images to help us figure out where she came from?"

"Both, I think," Charlotte answered. "Anyway, she's shown me all she needed to. She's gone now."

"Just like that?" Maude still didn't really understand communication with the spirit world. "She just popped in to flash a few images and now she's gone?"

"Oh, no dear, she's been with me since I first met her last night. She must be satisfied that you received her message because she has been very persistent. That is why I wanted you to come right away if it was possible. Her persistence was starting to get on my nerves."

That last comment made Maude laugh out loud. "Well, I guess I have received her message, but I don't understand it. Why did she show you those images? They mean nothing to me. I have never been to Ireland, assuming Ireland is what she was showing you. It could be England, or any number of other places. I also don't know anything about Martha's family before they came to America, so I don't know how to begin to understand this."

Charlotte reached for the teapot and refilled both of their cups. She smiled, handing the cup back to Maude, knowing once again they were embarking on an important journey together. "Well, this should keep you busy for a while."

"Very funny. I don't have time to go on another wild goose chase. I've got a new book coming out and things have been getting busy at the shop. I really can't focus on this right now." Maude continued to complain as she pulled out her notebook and began to carefully transcribe the experience with Charlotte and Mary, stopping her tirade only long enough to clarify certain details of Mary's message.

Maude knew there would be no peace until this latest mystery was solved. Her experiences unraveling Martha's life had provided her with the insight and inspiration to write two novels. Perhaps there was a third shrouded in the mist surrounding the thatched cottage on the remote island, facing the large cliffs of presumably another island.

* * *

Instead of driving directly home, Maude made a detour to Canalside, a downtown destination honoring the city's industrial heritage. The season wasn't quite over yet, and Maude thought a bit of paddling around in the water of the inner harbor might help her digest what she had learned from Charlotte. Besides, there was no hurry to get back to the shop. Christine, her part-time employee, had agreed to stay until the store closed. Don wouldn't be home until after dinner and her sons were scheduled into the early evening as well. There was no line at the rental hut so late in the afternoon and she was on the water in no time.

Maude's kayak glided smoothly along the surface of the water. The grain elevators loomed at the edge of the river, just across from the Commercial Slip. It was a haunting reminder of earlier revelations that she still hadn't reconciled. Buffalo's inner harbor was probably the last place she should be looking for peace of mind, but it was impossible to stay away. The idea that somehow the water would have the answers she was looking for kept her coming back, although it had yet to reveal any new secrets.

Just a few months ago, Maude had been enjoying a lovely spring afternoon with Don, kayaking on the river when she had a vision of the past combined with a chilling feeling that something terrible was going to happen, or maybe already had. She would learn soon enough that it was both. The experience on the river conjured the shadow of Johnny's death in the Commercial Slip. It wasn't until she underwent a past life regression that Maude learned those details and had been able to use this knowledge to save her husband from a similar fate at the hands of Lester Northrup.

"You tend to be surrounded by the same cast of characters in each life," Charlotte had once told her. *"Negative karma will follow you until you do something to break the cycle."* Maude had learned that not only was Don her husband in a past life, but Lester Northrup, her nemesis in the antique business, had also been her nemesis in a past life. Evidently there had always been some man in her circle, a professional acquaintance, who grew to resent her. That umbrage would lead to an act of desperation on his part that required the intervention of her husband, who ultimately died trying to protect her. Maude wondered how many times that scenario of bad karma had played out until she finally saved Don's life.

Negative karma will follow you until you do something to break the cycle. It was over, of that Maude was sure. This time it was Lester who died in an underwater struggle. So why was Martha Sloane's mother hovering around Lily Dale with a message for her? Was there more negative karma? Perhaps another spirit who was desperate for her story to be told?

It was Frederika Kaiser who had started it all. The widow from the poorhouse had been brutally beaten by her husband in life and her body nearly stolen to be illegally sold as a medical school cadaver in death. Her spirit had provided Maude with vivid glimpses of the abuses she suffered in life each time Maude touched her skeleton. Using the journal of Ciara Sloane Nolan, the first matron of the Buffalo Orphan Asylum, Maude was able to fill in some of the details of Frederika's story.

Unable to share these revelations with her colleagues at the university, she wrote her first novel of historical fiction.

Every time she had completed the unfinished business of those on the other side, some new and life changing detail was revealed. Maude realized that in addition to visions brought on by contact with historically significant items or places, she had vivid dreams with incredible historical accuracy, and she could undergo past life regression, led into a hypnotic state in which the past was also revealed.

These abilities still had not fully revealed why all this was happening to Maude. She was meant to tell their stories, complete the business they had left unfinished during their lives and recognize the connections between people in the past and those in the present. What remained unanswered was why Maude Travers was chosen for all of these.

Charlotte had once suggested that it might be her duty in this incarnation. Looking out over the empty river, Maude called out, "What do you want from me now?" Resting her paddle across the top of the kayak, she floated for a while. It wouldn't have surprised her at all if there had been a response to her desperate plea. When there was not, she felt compelled to continue. "It's not bad enough that I'm caught up in all of this, but now, so is Don."

Learning that they were soulmates had oddly created a distance between them. At first Maude just thought he was trying to process it all, and giving him some space to do so was the best decision. Now she was not so sure. Recalling their conversation just last night reminded her of how things were changing between them.

Don had glanced up from the book he was reading as Maude climbed into bed. "I won't be home until late tomorrow night. Can you pick up Glen from football practice?" It was not unusual for him to make such a request. He had always picked up the boys from school, but with each son pursuing different high school sports, their schedules were no longer predictable and sometimes conflicts arose.

"Yeah, no problem. I thought you were staying in town tomorrow?" Maude was accustomed to her husband travelling in pursuit of vintage and antique lamps. Don drove all over the northeast to estate sales, antique fairs and flea markets. He also scheduled several days each month at home to work on repairs and installations of the treasures they bought and sold. Lately he was away more often than not and Maude was looking forward to having him around.

"I got a call earlier in the week about an estate in Watertown, so I wanted to get up there before anyone else got wind of it," Don told her.

That was it, no other explanation or apology for springing additional travel on her at the last minute. That lack of consideration was becoming the norm. Until recently, they had worked seamlessly as a team in the running of their business and the raising of their two sons. Now that the boys were older, coordinating schedules wasn't as problematic as it had once been, which could explain the increase in Don's traveling. Still, Maude wondered if there might be other reasons for his absence.

They had spoken seldom of past lives or karma since the incident by the marina, where Maude and Charlotte Lambert had been held at gunpoint by Lester Northrup, and Don was almost killed in the struggle to rescue them. Maude wondered if her husband's patience and understanding of all she had been going through had finally reached its limit after that terrifying night.

How on earth would she tell him about her visit with Charlotte this morning? There was evidently another twist in the path they had been thrust upon by the whispering of Frederika Kaiser's bones, and, for the first time, Maude was uncertain if Don would follow her.

Maude looked at her watch, and realizing her time with the kayak was nearly up, she dipped her paddle back in the water and turned around. The river had failed to provide any wisdom or insight into her problems. "Looks like I'm on my own," she mumbled and paddled toward the dock.

Chapter Two

Having fully acknowledged herself as a coward and willing to live with it, Maude went to bed as soon as both of her sons were safely home. Don had texted that he would be home by nine o'clock. With any luck, she would be asleep and they would not have to share the details of their respective days. Don would be in the workshop the next morning by the time she got the boys to school, so there would be no time to catch up before she had to open the shop. Her experiences with Charlotte earlier that day would keep until she better understood them. It wasn't like she was purposefully keeping anything from him; she was just waiting for the right time.

With that reconciled in her mind, Maude turned her thoughts to the unusual message from the spirit of Mary Sloane. *"The love connection is boundless; it is not unusual for someone from the other side to go to great lengths to try and make contact,"* Charlotte had told her. It seemed somehow sad to Maude that Mary Sloane was so desperate to give her that message. Was it the love for her daughters that drove her to Lily Dale or something else? What was this woman's unfinished business? As Maude drifted off to sleep, that sense of sadness permeated her dreams as she journeyed in her mind back to the past.

* * *

Buffalo, New York, Spring 1880

The carriage made its way into the city having traveled along the Buffalo Road from Cassadaga throughout the better part of the day. Martha could have taken the train - it would have been faster - but she needed time to think and Alva had graciously offered to accompany her. Her nephew Daniel, and his family had left the day before, when word first arrived of his father's death. Martha's son Robert had ridden all night to deliver the news.

The passing of Dr. Michael Nolan was the end of an era both among his very extended family and for the city at large. In 1835, he was among the first graduates of the Geneva Medical College. Michael resisted the idea of establishing a lucrative practice in the flourishing city of Buffalo, and instead chose to serve the city's most vulnerable members. It was at the Erie County Poorhouse that he met Martha and her sisters, who had sought refuge there when they first arrived in the city. They had lost their parents and youngest sister to a shipboard illness on the journey from Ireland, and had gravitated to a few of the kinder inmates. Michael would marry Martha's oldest sister, Ciara, and take in a rather large extended family of paupers and orphans who had befriended Ciara, Martha and their middle sister Patricia in the poorhouse.

Michael became a highly respected physician and citizen over the years, holding a seat on the city's Board of Health and acting as Dean of the Medical College at the University of Buffalo. He served as a father and as a mentor to young Martha, who was just four years old when she left Ireland. He took fatherly pride in seeing her become the city's first female physician. It was Michael's good standing in the Buffalo Medical Society that helped secure Martha a position as the house physician at the insane asylum of the county poorhouse. Martha worked there healing the minds and the bodies of the inmates for two decades until the tragic death of her own husband, Johnny Quinn.

Johnny had also been an orphan at the poorhouse when he and Martha met as children. He was one of the inmates fortunate enough to follow Martha and her sisters to the farm on North Street when Michael and Ciara married. Although they grew up side by side, their relationship had never been that of a brother and sister. They were soulmates, although it took a while for each of them to accept that they were meant to be together. Just after Martha finished medical school they were married and lived happily for twenty years above the shop Johnny had inherited from Michael's parents. When Johnny died, Martha was devastated. With her son Robert to run Nolan's Dry Goods Emporium, she moved to the growing community of Spiritualists in Cassadaga.

While Martha had known most of her life that she was bestowed with the rare gift of the second sight, she had no idea the range of such gifts and that there were others who possessed them as well. With Johnny gone, she could not face the life they had shared in Buffalo alone. Under mentorship of clairvoyant healer Alva Awalte, Martha learned that some of these special people found their way into the county insane asylums, easily disposed of by those who feared or didn't understand them. Realizing the dangers posed to gifted individuals, she knew she must help protect those who were unable to do so for themselves. Her decision to move to the lakeside community and join the Spiritualists of the Cassadaga Lake Free Association was as much out of the need to safeguard the vulnerable among them as it was to develop her own gifts in the hopes of making contact with her beloved husband.

In the quiet solitude of the lakes of Cassadaga, Martha realized her own abilities were not limited to the second sight. She found that under the guidance of Alva and some of the other Spiritualists, she could develop the ability to detect illness in the mind as well as the body. Through meditation, she achieved the ability to make a connection with those who had passed on, although those with whom she dearly wanted to communicate, like her parents and her husband, had little to say beyond the expressions of love and regret over having left too soon. For Martha, mediumship was a powerful healing agent and she relied upon it as much as she relied on the herbal remedies Alva had instructed her to make and use.

While living in Cassadaga, Martha befriended a Seneca man who was interested in the Spiritualists. He taught her to think of God in the trees, the air and the lakes. To respect the natural world and all those who lived in it helped one to be closer to God, he told her.

Martha's life on the banks of the Cassadaga lakes was vastly different than it had been in the city, but she cherished it.

Michael Nolan's death had brought Martha back to Buffalo, a place she hadn't seen in nearly a decade. His passing left her feeling empty inside, but in a different way than when Johnny had passed. All Martha had become she owed to Michael. He took her in and raised her as his own daughter. He saw her keen intelligence and recognized her special gifts, both as a healer and as a seer. He nurtured these things, rather than discouraging them. Michael put his own professional reputation on the line when there were still plenty of mouths in the house to feed in order to see her established as a practicing physician during a time when not many would seek treatment from a woman. He took her side against many a keeper of the asylum when they disagreed with what she thought was in the best interest of the patients there. Martha couldn't bear to reach Buffalo and see for herself that he was really gone.

As if reading her mind, Alva asked, "Shall we stop at the house on Division Street and freshen up a bit before we make our way to Linwood Avenue?"

Martha was silent for a moment, the only sounds coming from the carriage as it lumbered up Main Street. "I'm sorry, what did ye say?" She had been so deep in her thoughts that she did not hear the words of her good friend.

"I asked you if you wanted to stop at my house before we continue on to your sister's." Alva's voice was patient and kind. It was the voice she used with her patients, but in truth she was direct and excruciatingly honest with just about everyone else.

Alva Awalte had been the one to recognize the power in Martha's gift. A clairvoyant herself, Alva had spent much of her life helping those who had been demonized for their abilities. She kept the house at number 247 Division Street in Buffalo, where she had run a successful business as a clairvoyant healer for nearly thirty years before moving to Cassadaga with Martha. They had worked at the asylum together, Alva teaching Martha to extend her healing abilities beyond those of modern medicine. Together they saw many patients who were presumed insane because the circumstances of their lives had become overwhelming restored to full health and happiness. It could easily have been a life's work if not for the death of Martha's husband.

Alva had been a widow for several years before she met Martha, and knew the pain of getting up every day feeling only emptiness, and willing yourself to carry on. She had started Martha on her journey of becoming a Spiritualist and was determined to see her friend through this phase of her journey, and so left the business in the hands of her son and younger daughter and made the move to Cassadaga. With the city's most vulnerable patients in the competent hands of Dr. Nolan, Alva turned her attention to those in the lakeside community who were in need of her gifts.

Martha made the effort to extract herself from the past and put aside the feelings conjured up from her memories to put her friend's mind at ease. "Aye, Division Street first, I think."

Dear old Mrs. Metzker came out to greet them as the carriage pulled up to number 247. The woman was only a few years younger than Alva and had been her loyal housekeeper for decades. She and Mr. Metzker did not follow their employer to Cassadaga, instead staying to oversee the house on Division Street, which still offered safe haven for any who might need it, and to keep an eye on the business Alva had left to her children. "You are looking well, Mrs. Awalte," Bethany Metzker said as she opened the door to allow the women entry.

Alva nodded. "As are you, Bethany. Brian is better, I hope." Alva made frequent trips to Buffalo to check on her real estate investments and the few patients who still preferred to see her for whatever was ailing them. Her most recent visit saw Brian Metzker treated for rheumatism.

"He is an old fool but still does the work of a young man." Bethany smiled, proud that her husband was still able to be of service.

"He is indeed a fool; you both are. There is no need for either of you to work so hard. There are servants enough to do what needs doing."

Bethany ignored the gentle scolding and ushered the women into the parlor where the tea was already set out for them. "He'll have your things brought up to your rooms before you have finished your tea. Sit: I have news."

Alva reached for the teapot. "Nothing for you?" she asked Mrs. Metzker, noting only two cups on the tray.

Shaking her head, the woman said, "I have much to tell you. Had we not received word you were already on your way, Mr. Metzker would have sent for you." Turning to Martha, she added, "I was so sorry to hear about Dr. Nolan. He was an extraordinary man."

"Thank ye, Mrs. Metzker," Martha told her, "but please go on. What news have ye?"

"Yes, well, it was Dr. Nolan who brought this young girl to my attention. I'm quite sure he would have seen her released from the asylum himself had it not been for his passing."

In fact, Michael had been working up until his death. He suffered a heart attack just hours after he sent word to Division Street to inform Mrs. Metzker that Patsy, a ten-year-old negro child, had been admitted to the insane asylum. It was the child's age and the color of her skin that caught Michael's attention. He happened to be present when she arrived, having been called in to consult on a particularly horrific case of tertiary syphilis. It would have been hard for anyone not to notice the child's arrival. Patsy was restrained as she was dragged into the asylum kicking and screaming by two attendants.

Michael could see she was terrified. He had strong words with the keeper and had set off to have the same with the justice of the peace who had committed a child to the insane asylum when he suffered a massive heart attack.

Mrs. Metzker reached into the pocket of her skirt and withdrew a note, which she handed to Martha.

Mrs. Metzker,

I am leaving the asylum immediately to see the justice of the peace regarding the commitment of a young child. She is a negro child who was working with her mother at the home of Neala Ahearn on Pearl Street. What started as accusations of thievery turned into accusations of witchcraft. The child's fear grew as her mistress' temper flared. The pots on the stove began to rattle and boil over, frightening all present beyond reason. The power of animal magnetism is strong in such a young child. Please send word to Mrs. Awalte in Cassadaga right away. I will surely need her help with this matter.

Your most humble servant,
Michael Nolan, M.D.

Mrs. Metzker turned to address Alva while Martha read Michael's note. "We have seen this before. Gifted children are feared above all others."

"All too often, I'm afraid," Alva agreed. "The asylum has become a prison, the gifted in shackles so the ignorant can feel safe. They are fools, unaware that such power resides in all of us."

"Yet all of us can't control the world around us using the power within. Michael says she was able to bring the pots to boil and shake the pans on the stovetop," Martha reminded her. "The child is special, to be sure. Can ye imagine the sight of it? They believe they have cause to fear her."

Animal magnetism was often a topic of conversation between Martha and her mentor. Alva believed in the teachings of Franz Mesmer, an eighteenth-century physician who used the term to describe a force that existed within all living beings. With focus and training, it could be realized and utilized to manipulate the physical world. Martha had never been sure. She had seen with her own eyes what some people could do using what looked like the sheer force of their minds, like bend a spoon right in half, or lift a table off the ground, but that was just some people. Martha was certain that she was unable to do such things.

"I went to the asylum myself this morning," Mrs. Metzker reported. "The keeper agrees she is dangerous. He will only release the child upon the order of the justice of the peace."

"She is restrained, I'm sure," Martha commented, all the frustration of working in the asylum flooding back as she listened to the details of young Patsy's story.

"Her mistress was terrified after having seen her supper boil over the stove. She insisted Prudence, the child's mother, lock her in the pantry while she sent for the constable. Poor Patsy was removed from the house in shackles, according to her mother," Mrs. Metzker told them.

"The poor thing must have been scared to death." Alva had taken the note from Martha to read for herself. "It is not unusual for children to lack the ability to control such a gift, particularly under such circumstances," Alva commented. "No doubt they'll have her locked in a cradle on the third floor. There is no time to waste." The cradle was a particularly horrific devise used by asylums to restrain their most dangerous inmates. It looked like a crib, though not as deep, and with a lid which locked the patient inside. It was inhumane treatment for anyone, but unconscionable for a child.

Turning to Martha, she said, "My dear, please send my deepest sympathies to your sister, but I must get to the justice of the peace before that poor child is transferred to the Willard Asylum for the duration of her life." She finished her tea in one gulp and rose. "Come, Bethany, there is no time to waste."

The Willard Asylum was New York's asylum for the incurably insane. It was unusual for children to be sent there, but not unheard of. If this Mrs. Ahearn complained long enough, loud enough, and to the right person, the child could easily find herself committed there.

* * *

Martha allowed Brian Metzker to help her down from the carriage when they arrived at her sister's house on Linwood Avenue. It had been their house first, the house in which she and Johnny would have grown old had he lived. They had purchased it, but never had the chance to move in. "Would you like me to escort you to the door, Dr. Quinn?" Martha had carefully avoided this house for over a decade and now as she stood once again at the foot of the drive, she realized it would now remind her of the two most devastating losses in her life.

"Gran, ye're here at last. Thank the good Lord." Martha looked up and saw her oldest grandchild, Mary Alva, rushing toward her. Midstride, the girl remembered the somber occasion and slowed her pace, her white mourning dress barely moving as she covered the remaining distance.

Turning back to Mr. Metzker, she said, "Thank ye, but no. I'll be fine. If ye could just wait for a bit while I find someone to fetch my bags."

"No need, Gran. That'll be wee Rolland out right behind me to carry your things." She turned as her cousin, whom Martha hadn't seen since the funeral of his own grandfather and namesake five years previous, bowed politely as the situation demanded, rather than hurling himself into his auntie's arms as he might otherwise have done. "Now, just ye come right in. They're all waitin' to see ye."

Martha smiled as Patricia's youngest grandson took the valise from Mr. Metzker and led the way to the house.

A light breeze blew the black crepe ribbon hanging on the doorknocker as wee Rolland opened it for his aunt and cousin. The inside of the house was dressed for mourning. The heavy drapes were drawn closed and black crepe covered the mirror in the front hall against the long-held suspicion that the person who saw his reflection would be the next to die. The clock had also been stopped to mark the time of Michael's death.

It would all be removed immediately after the funeral. These rituals still seemed queer to Martha and she knew her sister only followed them to give her husband the courtesies the community expected for a man of his stature. In truth, Michael had thought it all quite absurd. It was not how things were done in the old country, to be sure. But they had long since left

Ireland, and Michael was a beloved and respected citizen of Buffalo deserving to be mourned by his peers.

The large hall and parlor were packed with mourners and it took some time for Martha to work her way through the crowd of friends and family to the back bedroom where she would find her sisters. It would be considered rude for other mourners to pay their respects to Ciara while she was in seclusion, but Martha's place was by her sister's side.

Ciara looked up as the door opened and Martha came in. "Ye're a sight for these sore eyes, sister!" She immediately enveloped Martha in an embrace that seem to wipe away the last four decades, leaving the physician feeling like a child again. Martha was immediately transported in her mind to the hold of the White Heather Princess all those years ago, when her parents and sister Katie had died from ship fever and she had sobbed in her oldest sister's arms. Soon she felt Patricia, holding on for dear life now as she had then. The three sisters just stood there and wept for a good long time.

When they finally parted, it was Patricia who spoke. "Now, here we are again, all back in Buffalo, widows this time instead of orphans."

* * *

Michael Nolan's life was chronicled by the eclectic mix of mourners making up his funeral procession. Directly behind the male members of the family (the women having stayed behind to prepare a funeral supper as propriety demanded) were his colleagues from the county board of supervisors, the area hospitals, and the university. Behind them, the friends and customers he had made through the dry goods shop his father had run for more than three decades, and his brother-in-law for twenty years after that. The shop was still in the family and not a day went by without someone asking after Old Dr. Nolan. At the very end of the procession were members of the working poor.

It was a long walk from the city to the cemetery in Cheektowaga where, as a parishioner of St. Louis Roman Catholic Church, Michael would be laid to rest. Those mourners without the resources to own or hire a carriage were only too glad to undertake the journey on foot. Many of them owed their lives to Dr. Michael Nolan. He had likely treated every one of them at some point in time, but for many his care went beyond that. He found them jobs, offered counsel during times of great loss, and defended the weak and weary against the justice of the peace, the keeper of the asylum, unscrupulous landlords, or any other person or institution who was unwilling to lend a reasonable ear.

Those people who arrived on foot would not follow the family into the cemetery or return with the rest of the mourners to the funeral supper. It's not that they wouldn't be welcome, for Ciara knew well the special place many of them held in Michael's heart, but she was still in seclusion and there was always the chance that some of the other mourners might express disapproval over their presence. Having no wish to be the source of trouble, they chose to honor Michael's memory from a safe distance.

* * *

Patricia's comment was on Martha's mind for the rest of the afternoon. That voyage across the Atlantic over four decades ago had forever changed their lives. Martha was so young when the family left their small village on Inis Mór, the largest of the three Isles of Aran, that there was little she remembered of the journey or why they had left in the first place. Sitting in the back room with their cups of tea, she asked, "Do either of ye remember much of Inis Mór?"

Ciara looked surprised to hear the question. Patricia took a sip of her tea and placed the cup back on the saucer before answering. "If I close my eyes, I can see the wee cottage we lived in plain as day. Do ye recall old Dearg?"

Martha closed her eyes, searching deep in her subconscious for an image and then seeing clearly the shaggy red horse. "Aye, I think I do! He had long whiskers, I recall, and they tickled my hand." Her expression changed as another less pleasant memory of the horse came to her. "Funny, now that ye mention him, I remember the sound of old Dearg crossing the bridge on the day we left the island. I had my head tucked under ma's arm the whole time, so I couldn't see a thing, but I remember the sound of the hoofbeats change once he got to the bridge, and I knew we'd soon be at cousin Patrick's and that he'd take us across the sea to Galway."

A flash of memory showed her the reason Martha had her head buried beneath her mother's arm. An old woman had approached the wagon as it lumbered up to the bridge, yelling something, but Martha could not remember what. The woman had frightened her, as did her mother's reaction to draw Martha closer. She quickly pushed the unpleasant recollection aside, not wanting to cast a shadow on their memories of home. "'Tis odd, I'd never thought of that day until now."

"Well, ye'd hardly remember it, would ye? I was seven and I recall very little of our life on the island." Patricia's thoughts wandered out loud as she struggled to bring back another small detail of her childhood in Ireland. She smiled, and almost popped out of her chair at the sheer joy of the memory she recalled. "Oh, I remember our wee cottage was full to burstin' and cousin Patrick had a penny whistle. There was music, and everyone was dancin'."

Ciara had been silent until now. She smiled, recalling the occasion. "That'd 'ave been at the new year." She thought for a moment before continuing. "You were five, I think, and Martha was just two. 'Twas da who gave Patrick that penny whistle. He got it in Galway." Ciara's voice dropped off, and it appeared as though she, too, was lost in the memory.

"Surely ye must remember how it was before we left?" Martha asked her oldest sister. Ciara was seventeen when they left Inis Mór and had become the guardian of her sisters after the death of their parents.

Occupied with her own thoughts, it appeared that Ciara had not heard the question, so it surprised Martha when she spoke. "No, not really. Just bits here and there, like Patricia." She was quiet for a moment, but then felt the need to addend her comment. "We had a time of it aboard the ship, if ye recall, and I've not had a moment since to spare many thoughts for the old country."

She didn't quite sound defensive, but moved to redirect the conversation lest her sisters pick up on her anxiety. "Well, that's enough talk of the past." Turning to Martha, she asked, "Can ye stay for a while, sister? I've got Patricia until month's end and I'd dearly love to have ye here as well."

The question took Martha by surprise. Of all the things that occupied her thoughts on the journey from Cassadaga to Buffalo, the duration of her stay was not one of them. "Alva was kind enough to accompany me, so I'll have to speak with her on the matter. I thought she would have been here this afternoon."

"Oh, I'm that sorry, sister," Patricia said. "She sent word from Division Street. She'll be here in time for the funeral supper."

"She must have had success with the justice of the peace," Martha speculated. "There was a child committed to the asylum yesterday."

"The wee lass Michael was trying to help?" Ciara interrupted. Michael had sent word to his wife explaining that he would likely be late for dinner on that fateful day. Ciara had received hundreds of such notes over the years, never dreaming that this time he wouldn't make it home at all.

"Aye." Martha went on to explain what little she knew about the situation.

"Imagine lockin' up a child in the asylum!" Ciara's anger was growing as she spoke, furious over the incompetence that had cost her husband his life. "People fear what they don't understand; 'twas no different back home." Memories stirred from their earlier conversation and the force of her temper had brought on that last comment. Ciara took a sip of her tea and hoped the others would let it pass without remark. To her relief, they did.

"Aye, those who fear the gifted pose a special danger to be sure. Will ye take the child back to Cassadaga with ye?" Patricia asked Martha.

"I would think so. Sure enough, her mother will never work again 'round here, and her father passed just last month." Martha speculated. "Aye, the child will be safer in Cassadaga."

Ciara had grown quiet again. She had said too much, even if her sisters had not noticed. She remembered well their lives in Ireland and the reason they had left. Their conversation had spooked her, and discussion of the child in the asylum had done nothing to quell the memories and regrets that now swirled in her mind.

Chapter Three

Buffalo, New York, 2016

Maude sat in bed methodically transcribing the details of her dream in the journal she kept beside her bed. Don wasn't lying next to her: it was just a fleeting thought that had passed through her mind while reaching over to the nightstand for her journal. She was relieved to be able to record these dreams without an explanation to her husband and didn't stop to wonder why he wasn't sleeping beside her so early in the morning.

An hour later, she was looking over her notes thoroughly confused. "This makes no sense. Why am I dreaming about three widows in Buffalo whose mother was long since dead?" When the lines on the page refused to yield an answer, Maude closed the notebook and returned her attention to the empty space next to her.

The rumpled comforter and sheets told her that Don had slept in the bed at least for some time during the night. Looking out the bedroom window into the alley behind the shop, Maude saw that his truck was there, so she got up and went looking for him.

ROSANNE L. HIGGINS

In the quiet of the early morning, Maude could hear the slow and steady breathing of her husband as she stepped out into the hall. Following the sound, she was not prepared to find Don seated cross-legged on the floor meditating. Quietly, she turned back toward the bedroom, but he spoke and she turned around.

"You don't have to leave. I'm done," he told her.

"You've been meditating?" It was impossible to keep the question out of her voice. It was also difficult to hide her surprise. He was usually up before her and she wondered how long this had been going on.

"Yeah, I thought I'd give it a try. You should, too; it's pretty relaxing." Without further comment, Don rose from the floor and kissed his wife. "Want some coffee?"

Maude silently questioned the logic of meditating to relax followed by the consumption of a caffeinated beverage. She could not hold back the urge to ask her usually laid-back husband why he needed to relax. "When did you start meditating?"

"I don't know…a few months ago, I guess."

As the coffee pot gurgled and sputtered, they each kept to their own thoughts waiting for it to finish. On any other morning, there would have been nothing awkward about the lack of conversation, but the idea that Maude was glad of it this morning made her feel guilty. She couldn't ask him about his day yesterday without having to share hers and she still wasn't ready to do that.

When the coffee pot gave a final hiss to announce it was ready, Don looked at the clock above the stove. "I'd better get the boys up."

40

"Yeah, I'll get some breakfast on the table," Maude replied.

The rest of the morning passed as it always did, in a blur as four people went about readying themselves for the day ahead. While Don showered, Maude took the boys to school and made a quick stop at the university on the way back to retrieve a notebook she had left earlier in the week. The alley behind her shop was blocked, so she parked on the street and entered the shop through the front door.

The bell above the door sounded as she came through to find her husband behind the counter. He seemed as surprised to see her as she was to see him.

"What are you doing here?" they both asked at the same time.

"Christine called in sick," Don told her. "I thought you could go back to bed. You haven't been sleeping well and I know you were up early again this morning. I had planned to take the boys to school this morning. I'd rather you not be driving when you're so sleep deprived."

Maude smiled, thinking of her journey yesterday to Lily Dale followed by kayaking around the Buffalo River, and wondering if she should be annoyed or pleased that Don was so overprotective. "I'm fine and as you can see, I made it there and back in one piece. What's wrong with Christine?"

"Food poisoning, she thinks. I didn't expect you so soon. I also didn't expect you to come through the front door." Don casually closed the laptop on which he'd been working as Maude moved to join him behind the counter.

"I didn't have any plans to work at the museum today." Over the last year, Maude had spent much of her time at the small museum that had been dedicated to the memory of the residents of the Erie County Poorhouse. Looking at the front door, she added, "The alley was blocked by a delivery truck, so I had to park on the street."

"Well, I've got everything under control here, so why don't you head upstairs and get some rest."

"I appreciate the offer, but I'm honestly not tired," Maude protested.

"Well, then, just go upstairs and relax. I've got this."

Maude got the impression that he was trying to get rid of her. On the other hand, she could go through her dream journal in private and even call Charlotte if she went upstairs. "Okay, but just for a few hours. I know things are piling up in the workshop."

Settled comfortably on the couch, with a steaming cup of tea beside her, Maude opened the notebook and began re-reading what she had transcribed earlier that morning. The details were already fuzzy; it would take several read-throughs to bring it all back.

* * *

Alva Awalte made her way through the remaining family milling about the parlor to formally pay her respects to Martha and her sister. "Dr. Nolan was a friend and an ally," she told Ciara. "We would not have been able to provide sanctuary to so many desperate people were it not for his help. I fear for the wretched souls in that asylum now that he has passed."

"My husband often spoke the same about you, Mrs. Awalte," Ciara replied. "We are grateful to ye for the work ye do, but also for the friendship ye offer my good sister. It's been a comfort to us that ye are in Cassadaga to watch over Martha where I cannot."

Overhearing her sister's remarks, Martha was a bit put out that Ciara thought she needed protecting. She did her best to push away the thoughts flooding her mind: arguments in her youth when Martha complained of Ciara's overprotectiveness, even when she was married with a family of her own. This was neither the time nor place for sibling rivalries. Entering the small room, she only said, "I'm that grateful for Alva's friendship as well. The good we have accomplished together could not have been managed without her."

Ciara's attention was diverted by her grandson, who had snuck into the room with Martha, giving Martha a chance to speak to Alva alone. "What of the young girl from the asylum?"

Alva could do nothing to stop the scowl forming on her face. "I don't know who is the greater fool, the constable or the justice of the peace! Arresting a child! The poor dear was terrified."

"She is powerful, is she not? Perhaps it was a good thing, her mistress calling the constable. Ye might not have known about her otherwise."

"Her gifts are many. We have your brother-in-law to thank for bringing her to our attention. I fear now that he is gone, our work will suffer, and so will a great many people."

That was something Martha had allowed herself to admit late the previous evening, when she was unable to sleep. It was more than just his family who would feel the loss of Dr. Michael Nolan. "Aye, I fear ye speak the truth of it, but this is neither the time nor the place to discuss the matter. Will ye bring Patsy and her ma back to Cassadaga?"

"I wanted to speak with you about that. I fear keeping them in the city any longer. Mrs. Ahearn, her accuser, has already learned of the child's release. She was furious. It is a matter of time before she finds a reason to send the constable to my house." Alva moved closer and lowered her voice. "I must get them away. She'll lose interest soon enough, I think."

"Will ye leave immediately, then?"

Alva took a moment before she answered. Martha was right, this was not the time or the place to discuss it, but she feared another opportunity to discuss the matter face to face would not present itself again. "Yes, I will see them safe to Cassadaga, and then I will be returning to Buffalo permanently. With Dr. Nolan gone, the gifted people who find their way to the city have no advocate."

It did not come as a surprise to Martha, although she did not expect things to move so quickly. "Do ye wish me to make the journey with ye?"

"That is up to you my dear, when the time is right. Your family has need of you now. When your obligation here is done, I will welcome your help should you wish to offer it, but I know your heart is in Cassadaga." Alva leaned forward to embrace her friend. Affection wasn't something she expressed often to those close to her, but she realized that this part of their journey together was coming to an end and they would see less of each other as time went on.

Alva expressed final condolences to Ciara before departing for the Southern Tier and her home by the lake. It was evident by the look on Martha's face as she watched her friend depart that she, too, had felt their paths diverge. Her interactions with Alva and wistful expression had not gone unnoticed by Ciara, who perhaps did not have the second sight, but had keen intuition nonetheless. "What's amiss, then?" she asked.

Martha hadn't seen her sister approach and quickly adjusted her features. "Oh, 'tis nothin'; Alva will be returnin' to Buffalo to continue her work on Division Street."

Ciara leaned forward, pulling her sister into an enthusiastic embrace. "Yer comin' home! I'm that pleased to hear it."

It was the day of Michael's funeral, the only father Martha had really known. How could she tell Ciara that she did not know what road she would travel next, or where it would lead?

* * *

The house on Linwood Avenue was full to burstin' for most of the month following Michael's funeral. Mary Karen, Patricia's only daughter, stayed on in Buffalo with her three sons while her husband returned to Albany. Ciara's son, Daniel, his wife Felicity and their four sons were also in residence. Although Martha's son, Robert, and his family lived in Buffalo, they were frequent visitors to the house while all the family was in town. It was both a joy and a distraction to have the children around, but the severe rain over the last week left them all indoors and in need of larger spaces.

The skies cleared just at the end of Ciara's period of seclusion, and she was pleased to set out with her sisters to the market, even if she had to view the city streets from behind a veil. It was worth conforming to traditional mourning fashion for a bit of fresh air and tranquility. The sounds of their grandchildren could be heard several houses over as the sisters made their way down Linwood towards North Street.

The women walked along in companionable silence, each enjoying the sunshine and the improved aroma that several days of heavy rains always brought to the city. Lost in their own pleasant contemplations, none of them saw the woman who had crossed the street headed in their direction.

"Excuse me!" The sisters each turned in the direction of the sound to observe an elderly woman approaching. The woman willfully disregarded social convention as she called out, apparently failing to notice that each of the sisters was wearing black.

Martha spoke first. "Good day to ye, ma'am. May we be of some assistance to ye?"

The woman looked to be of an age with Ciara, but not as steady on her feet. She leaned heavily on her cane, as if the journey across the street had cost her dearly. "Good day. I wish to have a word with ye, Mrs. Quinn."

"How may I help ye?" Martha asked.

The woman either didn't know or didn't care to use Martha's professional title. "I understand that you keep company with Mrs. Awalte. Might ye know her whereabouts currently?"

"I'm sorry…what did ye say yer name was?" Martha was aware that the women had not identified herself, which could mean that she did not want it known that she was seeking assistance from Alva. Clairvoyant healing was by no means accepted by the medical community or the community at large, and many people seeking help from Alva tried to do so anonymously. Still, given the recent events at the asylum and Alva's role in getting the child released, Martha wouldn't direct anyone to her friend until she determined the intent. Her caution was justified when the woman identified herself.

"I am Mrs. Ahearn, Neala Ahearn, and I wish to speak with Mrs. Awalte right away. My reasons are my own."

Martha could sense the tension in Ciara and touched her arm hoping that would be enough to keep her sister quiet. "I'm that sorry, Mrs. Ahearn, but I've not seen her this day."

"Pardon me, Mrs. Quinn, but I have been told that ye and Mrs. Awalte share a house in Cassadaga and that ye travelled to Buffalo together. Was I misinformed?"

Martha could think of no one among her friends or colleagues in Buffalo who would share such information with a stranger. It could only have come from the Justice of the Peace, who was likely bullied by Alva into signing the papers for the release of the young serving girl from the insane asylum. Alva had expected that the child's release would anger Mrs. Ahearn.

Martha stepped forward, raised her chin and looked Mrs. Ahearn directly in the eye. "I traveled here for the funeral of my brother-in-law. I'm sorry, but I can't help ye."

Stepping to the side, Martha attempted to continue her journey to the market, but Mrs. Ahearn laid a hand on her arm, forcing her to stop. She spoke quietly, so the other women would not hear her. "Be so kind as to give Mrs. Awalte a message for me. In the end, I will see her and the witch she is protecting locked up in the asylum, along with anyone who is assisting them!"

Unflinching, Martha said, "Good day to ye, ma'am," and turned to usher her older sisters past the angry woman.

"The nerve of that woman. Could she not see we are in mourning?" Patricia whispered, although they were more than a block away from Mrs. Ahearn.

"I confess, I did not think she would be so persistent," Martha commented.

"Nor so bold," Patricia added. "She approached you on the street and threatened you." Evidently Mrs. Ahearn's comments had been overheard.

"There's naught Mrs. Ahearn can do to me," Martha assured her sister. "The keeper of the asylum released the child into Alva's custody. I had nothin' to do with the matter."

"Are ye so sure she'll see it that way?" Patricia asked. "After all, the woman took the time to find out who ye were and then did confront ye here on the street, and all three of us clearly in mourning. I fear she is desperate to make sure that poor child is locked up."

Ciara, who had been silent thus far, nodded in agreement. "That woman is dangerous and you've no longer got Michael's good name to protect ye."

Martha sensed more than heard the anguish in her oldest sister's words. It would be easy to understand if Ciara held Neala Ahearn at least partly responsible for Michael's death. Perhaps the encounter was just too much so soon after her confinement. "Are ye feeling poorly, sister?"

"Aye, I fear that I am." Ciara looked down the street in the direction of the house, hoping her two legs would get her there. "I'll just return home and let the two of ye sort out the market."

"I'll come with ye," Patricia and Martha said in unison.

Ciara managed to convince her sisters that she would be fine by herself during the short walk home and immediately turned and walked away before they could argue the point. *Could that have been her after all these years?* She didn't dare express that thought out loud. If this Neala Ahearn was the same young woman she had known years ago on Inis Mór, she was indeed a danger to Martha. Only when she reached the solitude of her bedchamber did Ciara speak. "Oh, Michael, if ever I had a need of your counsel, 'tis now. What am I to do?"

Chapter Four

Maude closed the journal more confused than ever. What did Michael Nolan's funeral have to do with Mary Sloane's message? Still, the sisters had mentioned a place called Inis Mór. *They had left Inis Mór,* she thought, still staring at her own handwriting and hoping it would reveal more. "Wait! They crossed the sea to Galway." It was just an incidental mention in her first novel. Maude had chosen Inis Mór as the birthplace of her characters. She thought she had made it up. Apparently not.

"Finally, something I can work with." Maude spoke out loud as she went to retrieve her laptop. "Ah ha! Inis Mór is the largest of the Aran Islands on the west coast of Ireland." She found the link she had used to get some sense of the island for her first book. Scrolling down the page she continued to speak out loud. "The Aran Islands are across the sea from Galway, and also the Cliffs of Moher. Okay, now we are getting somewhere!"

The three tiny dots on the map at the mouth of Galway Bay represented the Aran Islands. The closest to the mainland and smallest was Inis Oir, pronounced *Inisheer.* The middle island was Inis Meàin, or

Inishmaan, and the largest and furthest out to sea was Inis Mór (*Inishmore*). Inis Mór must have been the island Mary was showing them.

"Okay, so I have a location. Now what? I still don't know why I am dreaming about three widows in Buffalo." As an afterthought, Maude added, "and who the hell is Neala Ahearn?"

A genealogical search of that name resulted in several people, none of whom could be reliably identified as her Neala Ahearn with so little information. "Figures," Maude mumbled, closing out the search program. It was very difficult to reliably identify women in the historical record because they did not own property and their name would change multiple times over a lifetime if they married more than once.

"Okay, so the family left Ireland. That's Mary's message. She is trying to get me to understand something about the day they left Inis Mór." Maude looked at her watch. "Damn it!" Somehow the entire afternoon had passed. Don must have assumed that she was sleeping and stayed down in the shop. Maude suddenly felt guilty for having deceived her husband. There was plenty of work to keep him in their workshop, but he had put all that aside to let Maude sleep. Only she hadn't slept a wink. She had spent the day trying to decipher a dream and still there was not enough information to indicate where Mary's message would lead them, assuming it would lead *them*. Maybe Don was through with the spirit world. She couldn't blame him if that were the case.

The rumbling of her stomach reminded Maude that it was nearing dinner time and that they were in desperate need of a trip to the grocery shop. "All this will look better after a home cooked meal." She put her computer and notebook away and went downstairs.

"Hey, did you get some rest?" Don asked, not the least bit put out that Maude had been absent from the shop all day.

"No, but I got a little work done and I need to talk to you about it. Let me just run to the grocery store and I'll explain over dinner."

"Fair enough. I have some things to finish up here. The boys have another late night tonight, so why don't you pick up a couple of steaks and we'll throw them on the grill."

Maude came home an hour later and immediately sniffed suspiciously in the air confirming the smell of pizza wafting down from their apartment.

"What happened to steaks on the grill?" She asked, handing two grocery bags to her husband.

"Well, I have a few things to tell you too, and I thought it might be best to just get to it."

Maude entered the kitchen first and saw that the table was set with real dishes instead of the paper plates they typically used with pizza, a bottle of wine, and two glasses. She turned to face her husband, who had already begun to put away the groceries. "What are you up to?"

She placed her purse on the counter and noticed suitcases in the hall. Resting on top of one of the cases were two passports with plane tickets tucked in each. "Surprise!" she heard Don say behind her.

Maude turned to face him once again. "Don Travers, what have you done?"

Don moved forward and plucked the tickets out from the passports, casually fanning himself. "You need a vacation. We both do. We fly out of Toronto tomorrow night."

"What? We can't just up and leave; besides, there are only two tickets. What about the boys?"

Don knew it would take a bit of convincing. In general, Maude loved surprises, but leaving their teenage sons alone for the first time and leaving the country with less than a day's notice was a lot to process. He put the tickets down, took her by the hand and led her back into the kitchen. Pulling out two chairs, he sat and motioned for her to do the same. "The boys have reached the age where they don't want to travel with us, or do you not remember our last family vacation?"

Maude smiled, recalling their trip to Philadelphia just a few months ago. "How could I forget. We were in one of the most historically significant cities in the country and I don't think they saw anything but the sidewalks. I was beginning to think they had their phones permanently attached to their hands."

"Yeah, and we had to be back in our hotel room by 8 o'clock every night so they could plug in and recharge!" Don readjusted himself so he could look Maude in the eye. "I did ask them if they wanted to come, but Bill's got exams next week and Glen's team made the playoffs. Mom and Dad are coming tomorrow night to stay with them. They'll be fine."

Maude shrugged in tentative agreement. "Assuming they don't drive your parents crazy, I can live with leaving the boys at home, but what about the shop? We just can't close for… how long will we be gone?"

"We'll be gone 10 days, and we don't have to close the shop. Christine will handle things while we are gone and the boys will fill in when they can."

Maude smiled, beginning to enjoy this interesting turn in her day. "How did you manage to pull this off right under my nose?"

"That was easy. I took full advantage of the fact that you have been totally distracted and completely exhausted." Don reached out and pulled her on to his lap. "Maude, you have to find a way to live with all of the things you're learning about your past life or you will completely miss out on what's left of your present life."

"Our past life, you mean. Don, do you realize that you could have died?"

"But I didn't."

"Yes, I know that, but don't you wonder what will happen next and whose life will be endangered because of it? Jesus, I got a phone call from Charlotte yesterday, and…" Without another word, Maude sprung up and ran into the hall.

"Sonofabitch! I knew it!" She held the plane ticket up, waving it at Don as he came in behind her.

"What? What's wrong?"

"Ireland. You've been talking to Charlotte, haven't you? I told her I was going to tell you when I understood more of what is going on."

Confused, Don took the plane ticket back and tucked it into Maude's passport. "I thought you'd be happy. We've talked about going abroad for years. I checked and we can even take quick trips to Scotland

and England if you want. It was just cheaper to fly in and out of Ireland."

This time Maude took her husband by the hand and led him back into the kitchen. She took the bottle from the table and poured two very generous glasses. "So, when did you talk to Charlotte?"

"I haven't spoken to Charlotte in months, but I'm guessing you have."

Maude took a long sip from her glass and over the next twenty minutes relayed her discussion with Charlotte.

"It sounds like she is describing the Cliffs of Moher and the Aran Islands," Don said when she had finished.

Maude stared at her husband dumbfounded. "How the hell do you have any idea what she was talking about?"

"Well, I have been secretly planning a trip to Ireland for the past few weeks, plus you wrote about the Aran Islands in your first book. That's where your characters came from, remember?"

It shouldn't have surprised Maude that Don had been able to immediately recall those details of her first book. He was always able to remember minutiae. Faced with the ghost of Martha's actual mother in Lily Dale, thoughts of the characters in Maude's books, or the presumed fictitious details of their lives had not occurred to her until she recalled the details of her dream last night. Even when writing her second book, Maude often had to consult the first one to keep the details of the story consistent. It was just a story, wasn't it? "I really don't know anything about their actual life in Ireland." Maude's expression was thoughtful as she recalled what else she had written about the family and reconciled it with what she had learned from her dreams.

"It shouldn't surprise you to realize that much of what you thought was fabrication was likely true. Charlotte told you the woman's name was Mary; you named the girls' parents Ian and Mary Sloane."

Maude was quiet for long enough that Don finally spoke to break the silence. "We don't have to go. If you think this is the beginning of something you'd rather not unravel, let's just leave it. We can go some other place, far away from Ireland, or stay at home."

"It doesn't work that way, Don. You should know that by now." Maude drained her glass before she spoke again. "You meant for this trip to be a vacation, an opportunity for us to get away from all of this, but when we look at your actions in the context of what has been happening with me over the last two days, it seems like this trip is not a vacation. So, let me repeat your words back to you. We don't have to go to Ireland. If you're not up for this, we can go someplace else."

"Maudie, we are in this together. If you want to see this through, I'll be right there with you." He leaned over their wine glasses and kissed her.

Relief washed over her as she kissed him back. She rose from the table and walked back into the hall. Picking up the green suitcase, Maude rolled it towards the bedroom.

"What are you doing?"

"I'm not about to leave the country for ten days to seek out the mysterious places shown to me by the spirit of a woman I have never met without checking what you packed for me."

Chapter Five

More than twenty years had passed since Maude had flown across the Atlantic, and when they boarded the plane in Toronto the next day, she hardly recognized the first-class cabin as she passed through looking for her seat. Instead of fewer rows of more comfortable looking seats, there were pods where one could fully recline, sleep or watch movies on their own personal screen. It was even more surprising when Don pointed to the pods in row four and said, "This is us."

"You booked first class tickets?"

Don smiled, pleased he had surprised her yet again. "Sure, why not? I figured since we were traveling as a family of two instead of four, we might as well enjoy the trip." He was also hoping that the improved comfort would encourage his wife to sleep soundly on the plane and arrive in Dublin refreshed and ready for adventure.

The plan was successful. Maude was settled and dozing after the inflight meal. The small cabin of the plane formed a different image in Maude's mind as she drifted deeper into sleep.

* * *

Ciara had spent much of her time confined to her chamber since she departed from her sisters and walked home the previous day. She was grateful that being in mourning relieved her of the responsibility to play hostess, and with her sisters there to see to meals and the running of the house she could take time to think through her next move. Michael would have listened to her concerns and not been troubled by the secrets she had kept all these years, even from him. He would have protected her youngest sister from any threat still posed by Neala Ahearn, but Michael wasn't here now, and the safety of the family fell on her shoulders just as it had all those years ago when they first arrived in America.

Many years had passed since they were girls living in a remote island village, where there were no secrets and the good will of ones' neighbors could mean the difference between life and death. Not yet married, she was Neala Cleary then. Was this woman, Neala Ahearn, still a danger to Ciara's family? The threats to Martha indicated that she was. The woman had influence enough to find out who Martha was and where she was staying. Without Michael's protection, the woman might well be able to follow through on her threats. Perhaps it was time to draw someone into her confidence.

It took some time to assure Ciara's family that she was just fine and needed a bit of air. It took even longer to convince them that she was capable of taking a walk by herself. After reminding her son repeatedly that as a widow she was not expected to be accompanied when she left the house, Ciara headed out on foot to Division Street.

It was a good stretch of the legs between Ciara's home on Linwood Avenue and the Awalte residence on Division Street. Ciara thought herself a spectacle dressed head to toe in black crepe, with a veil covering not only her face, but almost the entire length of her body. She never did care for the social conventions of mourning, which seemed to have evolved in recent years to be a religion unto itself. Seeing other women adhering strictly to the wardrobe requirements of mourning, she felt pity for them in addition to a respectful sympathy for their loss. No other color could be worn except black for a year and a day. After that one could introduce a white collar and sleeves, and then lace trim or embroidery near the second year of mourning. During those final six months, a widow could begin to wear other muted colors like mauve, grey or lavender, but some women wore only black for the remainder of their lives.

It was true that she missed Michael dreadfully, but no amount of drab clothing would bring him back. Ciara wondered if other women pitied her as she walked the city streets, not over the loss of her husband, but over the necessity of suffering ridiculous restrictions simply because she was a woman. Men merely wore a black arm band or hat band. There was no period of seclusion, nor restrictions from attending social activities as there were for women. It was acceptable for men to marry within three months of the loss of their wife. The new bride was required to wear the proper mourning attire out of respect for the passing of the first wife. The idea of marrying again in three months or three years was not something Ciara could fathom, and she knew in her heart that, had the situation been reversed, Michael would have felt the same way.

Ciara wondered if other women thought these mourning customs absurd. To be sure there were some, usually women of means, who reveled in the attention, as if losing a husband elevated their status. In truth, many widows, even wealthy ones, were thrust into poverty after their husbands' death. Even if they had the skills to earn the wages their husbands had, they could not leave their children to seek a job outside the home. Although these women lacked resources to care for their children and keep a roof over their heads, they were expected to adhere to the proper mourning rituals. It was absurd. Ciara quickened her pace, not wishing to be out on display for one moment longer than was necessary to complete her journey.

Bethany Metzker answered the knock on the door almost immediately. "Mrs. Nolan, please come in. I do hope you are not here to see Mrs. Awalte. She is not presently at home."

"No, Mrs. Metzker, 'tis you I've come to see."

If Bethany Metzker was surprised at this request, it was well hidden under the accommodating nature of a loyal servant. She merely gestured toward the parlor and saw Ciara seated comfortably. "May I offer you my deepest sympathies over the loss of your husband. He was a great man, and Mrs. Awalte is very grateful for his assistance and support over the years."

"I thank ye, Mrs. Metzker."

"Now, Mrs. Nolan, what has brought you here to speak to a housemaid?"

Ciara appreciated the frank inquiry, although she knew well that Mrs. Metzker was not considered a housemaid by anyone residing at 247 Division Street, and took it to mean that she was free to be equally candid. "Yesterday my sisters and I had an unpleasant encounter with Mrs. Neala Ahearn. Do you know of whom I speak?"

"Yes. Martha came to call yesterday afternoon. I've sent word to Mrs. Awalte. It appears that Mrs. Ahearn is determined to see the child locked away."

Ciara was quiet for a moment, trying to decide what to reveal to obtain the information that she was looking for. "Had you known of Mrs. Ahearn prior to the incident with the wee lass?"

"No, I did not. You are concerned with the threats she made to your sister." It was not a question.

Ciara did not answer the questions directly, but instead began to tell a story she had kept to herself for over four decades. "I did know Mrs. Ahearn previously."

Mrs. Metzker listened carefully for the next hour while Ciara spoke of her childhood friend on a small island on the west coast of Ireland and how that friend had forced her family to leave the only home they had ever known. It was as if she were in confession, and with tear-filled eyes she ended her tale with the death of her parents and younger sister on the voyage from Ireland.

"My dear, you must not hold yourself responsible for what happened to your parents. They believed leaving was the safest option, given what you have told me."

"What now? Are we to move back to Ireland to be safe from that woman? I'm quite sure she was headed for my home when we ran into her on the street." Ciara picked up the veil that she had removed in Bethany Metzker's company. "Were it not for this, she would have surely recognized me, for I knew her immediately. Without the protection of a husband, what's to stop the whole mess from starting all over again?"

Mrs. Metzker considered the situation before she commented. "Do you fear her anger over the situation with the asylum or do you fear that she will recognize you?"

"There is nothing the woman can do to me. There never was anything she could do to me."

"If you worry for Martha, you must send her home. If Mrs. Ahearn fears the power of a small child, she will certainly think twice before seeking out Martha among her peers in Cassadaga. There will be no reason for the woman to bother you if your sister is not here. Besides, you are in mourning and within your rights to refuse callers should she have the nerve to show up on your doorstep."

Ciara contemplated Mrs. Metzker's advice as she walked home. Whereas her pace had been quick on the way to Division Street, it was slower as she made her way back to Linwood Avenue so that options could carefully be considered. She hated to part company with her sister, but could not risk stirring up the hornet's nest that was Neala Ahearn. Ciara stopped short, a solution presenting itself with stunning simplicity. When she had made up her mind, she continued, still at a leisurely pace, constructing her argument. By the time she reached home, Ciara was ready to make her case.

"I want to travel to Cassadaga with ye," Ciara told her youngest sister. "Every time I step out the door I remind myself and the rest of the world that I'm a widow. I want to go someplace where nobody knows me and nobody will whisper should I leave the house without a veil." It was really a brilliant solution to leave Buffalo, if just for a few months. She could grieve her loss in peace, far from the orbit of Neala Ahearn.

"'Tis a fine idea," Patricia agreed.

"Really, there is no reason both of ye can't come and stay for the remainder of the camp season," Martha suggested. She couldn't believe her good fortune. Ciara had been so preoccupied and upset, and Martha didn't have the heart to tell her that it was time to be returning to Cassadaga. Important things were happening, not the least of which was the demand of Theodore Alden that he be compensated for the use of the land they had been using for camp meetings. There was a group of Spiritualists who had moved to incorporate the Cassadaga Lake Free Society and purchase land for the group as an alternative to Alden's Grove. As one of the founding residents, Martha's presence was needed when the formal opening of the grounds occurred later that summer.

"Ye're pleased, then?" Ciara asked.

"Oh, aye. I think it's a grand plan. Ye can stay with me, or with Daniel." Turning to Patricia, she added, "With Alva gone there's room enough for Mary Karin and the lads, should they like to come along."

Patricia made no attempt to hide her enthusiasm. "That would be grand. Oh, I do hope Mary Karin agrees. The children would have a wonderful time on the lake."

"Can we be ready to leave tomorrow?" Ciara asked, ignoring the look of surprise on both of her sisters' faces.

Patricia spoke before Martha could organize a question in her mind. "Sister, ye've a house full of people. We can't just announce we're leavin' tomorrow. Mary Karin will need to send word to Albany and there's all the children's things to pack. I think we could be ready by week's end if we announce our plans at supper tonight."

Ciara had been prepared for this response and devised a reply of her own. "Aye, it will be difficult to get the whole group ready in such a short time." Looking at Martha, she continued, "I dearly wish to be away from here as soon as can be arranged. Would ye consider goin' on ahead with me, and the others will arrive when they are able?"

Martha assumed the encounter with Neala Ahearn - the woman who could be blamed, albeit indirectly, for Michael's death - had profoundly upset her sister. It was a relief to be going home, so there was no reason not to comply. "Aye, of course I will."

Multiple conversations erupted around the supper table when Ciara announced the news that she and Martha would be making the journey to Cassadaga the following day and that anyone who wished to join them down by the lake thereafter were welcome. In the end, it was decided they could not be ready in time for the morning train, so Daniel would take Ciara and Martha in the carriage as soon as they were able to depart. His wife Felicity, their children, and Patricia would travel by rail as soon as it could be arranged. Mary Karin and her family would return to Albany, having already been away too long.

* * *

Maude awoke disoriented as she often was after such a vivid dream. Taking stock of her surroundings, she wondered for a minute if she was in a spaceship. If that was true, Don was there with her. His familiar snoring was like a lifeline and after a few seconds of listening to it, she remembered that she was on a jet somewhere over the Atlantic. Quietly rummaging around in the dark for her carry-on bag, she found it and the journal she had stowed in the outside pocket. Turning on the small light, she began transcribing the dream.

Don lay there surreptitiously watching his wife. She was writing, so she must have had a significant dream. If there was something she needed to tell him, she would have turned to wake him, so he just stayed quiet and watched her work. There would be time enough on their journey to the west coast of Ireland to hear what she would eventually tell him.

Their vacation had turned into another quest. He felt different about this new twist in their path. Whatever Maude found out would likely have nothing to do with him. After all, Johnny had died in 1870.

Still, he felt connected to whatever they would learn while they were in Ireland.

They landed at nine o'clock a.m., Dublin time. Clearing customs and picking up the rental car took much longer than either Maude or Don had anticipated and it was nearly noon by the time they were en route to their hotel.

Don figured there would be a bit of an adjustment driving on the left-hand side of the road, but he hadn't counted on the different placement of street signs and traffic lights. It took over two hours to find their Bed and Breakfast in the town of Glasnevin, which was just a few miles from the Dublin Airport.

They had driven for about five minutes and blew through two red lights before Maude noticed that traffic lights were placed at the side of the intersections rather than overhead. "Stop!" she called just in time to avoid hitting the car that was stopped at the upcoming light. Even with the windows rolled all the way up, she heard the elegant Gaelic curse from the car behind them.

After a lengthy tour of Dublin, during which they experienced baptism by fire negotiating roundabouts while driving on the opposite side of the street at every intersection, they found their way to the outskirts of the city. "Okay, we're looking for Iona Park," Don told her.

"Yes, I know that, but some of the street signs are on the sides of the buildings, and some are on stone walls. I don't think the last two intersections we passed even had cross street signs. This is ridiculous." Maude was clearly frustrated. Even at a snail's pace, Don was driving too fast for her to locate the street signs, let alone try to read them. "We've passed that gas station twice now. Let's stop and get directions."

Don bristled at the idea of asking for help, but faced with the possibility of more time behind the wheel, he reluctantly pulled in.

It turned out they were just two blocks away from their B&B. It was at the end of a residential street lined with Georgian townhouses. In just a few minutes more, they pulled under the birch tree at the far end of the parking area.

"Shower, then food?" Maude asked her husband as she hauled her suitcase out of the trunk.

"Agreed, and if it's all the same to you, I'd prefer to walk around to look for a place to eat," Don told her.

"Sounds good. According to the B&B's website, it's about a twenty-minute walk to the center of the city."

Don snorted disbelief. "Twenty minutes if you know where you are going. Even on foot, I'm guessing that navigation will be a problem."

Maude laughed, nodding her head in agreement. "Okay, I saw a pub just up the street. Let's eat there and then explore. If we get completely turned around, we can always take a cab back here."

Their spirits were restored with a hot meal and a pint of stout. Don pushed his plate aside and took a satisfying gulp of beer. "So, I noticed you were writing in your dream journal on the plane."

"Yes, I dreamed about the Sloane sisters. I actually started dreaming about them before we left, after I met with Charlotte. They were reunited again after a long time. It was interesting: they started out in Buffalo as orphans and, in my dream, they were reunited as widows."

"All of them? Did you get any sense of the time period or how old they were? Martha lost Johnny around 1870, right?" Don immediately regretted bringing up the death of Martha's husband. The purpose of this trip was to turn Maude's mind away from intense grief she felt over the loss of Johnny, a grief Maude could not seem to shake, although it was so long ago, and in a different life.

"I would say maybe a decade had passed since my dreams of a few months ago. That would put Martha in her late forties. She had a grand-daughter that looked maybe about seven or eight years old." Maude paused for a minute, trying to recall the details that had been pushed from her mind by the hair-raising journey across the city earlier. "The sisters talked about when they had left Ireland. Ciara claimed not to remember much, but I got the sense that she was holding back. She didn't seem comfortable with the conversation."

"Any sense of how your dreams are linked to this trip?"

"Not really. There was brief talk of Inis Mór, but in the end the sisters decided to go to Martha's home in Cassadaga."

"Interesting. So, what's the plan for the week?" Don asked her.

Maude was confused. "I thought you had a plan! Haven't you been putting this together for a while?"

"I had a very loose plan, which was subject to change depending on what you wanted to do. I did a bit of checking while we were on the plane. We can head toward the Aran Islands on the west coast and take a ferry from Doolin - that's in County Clare - but we can't take the car with us to Inis Mór."

Maude gave her husband a suspicious look. "I know you, Don Travers and you didn't cross the Atlantic without at least booking a few places to stay, so why don't you tell me and then maybe we can make some adjustments."

"I booked a cottage in a little village called Puckaun. It's more or less in the middle of the country. Gene Kelly stayed there!" Don smiled, knowing she would be pleased to hear that. Maude had grown up watching old movies, and *Singing in the Rain* had been a favorite of her mother's. "The idea was to make day trips from there, but we don't have to do that if you are eager to get started."

"We got started the minute I arrived at Charlotte's cottage a few days ago," Maude reminded him. "How often do the ferries run to the Aran Islands?"

"Well, therein lies a potential dilemma. The only ferry that runs this time of year leaves at ten o'clock in the morning. We would have to get up pretty early tomorrow morning to get there in time."

"Well, then, the plan is to take our time tomorrow and drive to Puckaun. We can catch the ferry to Inis Mór the following day. That will give us some time to see a bit of the countryside along the way."

Don nodded. "That will work. I'll check around and figure out what to do with the car while we're on the island."

"No cars, huh? So, does that mean we're on foot while we're there?"

"Either that or we can rent bikes. There are a few options in terms of accommodations, everything from hotels to B&B's to camping. There's even something called glamping!"

"Glamping. Glamorous camping?"

"Sort of. Cabins are modeled after the ancient beehive stone huts that used to occupy the island. I'd say they have a different charm than some of the more traditional B&B's, but the price isn't bad," Don told her. "A downside to glamping is that we would have to buy and prepare our own food."

"Oh no, that won't do at all. Glamping is definitely out."

"I won't argue with you on that. Why don't we make a few calls when we get back to our room and see what we can find? Most of these places don't have websites."

"That sounds like a good idea," Maude agreed. "Maybe the woman at the front desk can make a recommendation."

It was just a few miles from the pub where they had lunch to Grafton Street. Full of lamb stew and beer, they thought it might be wise to walk around Saint Stephen's Green on the way to visit the shops there.

They entered the park through the grand stone archway at the foot of Grafton Street and immediately felt like they had traveled to another place entirely. The perimeter was heavily planted with trees to protect the park from the noise and pollution of the surrounding city. A forest of London plane, sycamore, birch, ash, hawthorn and laurel trees lined the path that followed a man-made lake, bisected at its narrow center by a stone bridge. The foliage that cascaded, climbed and creeped along its banks gave the impression that the lake was a natural feature of the landscape. The water birds seemed happy with their home, no matter how it got there. There were geese, swan, ducks and a few birds Maude could not name paddling around contentedly.

It was a beautiful day, though late in the afternoon on a weekday there weren't many people taking advantage of the fragrant gardens and pedestrian pathways the park had to offer. The only noises they heard were those of the creatures who made the park their home. Maude could see robins and wrens flitting about in the canopy. The occasional rustling of the undergrowth suggested that some kind of burrowing animals were scurrying about. Best not to know for sure, she thought.

"So, what do you think you'll discover on this journey?" Don asked.

"God only knows, but I don't." Anxiety, frustration and uncertainty all registered in her voice. Maude took a deep breath and directed her attention toward the paddling of ducks leisurely making their way across the pond in the hopes that the tranquil scene before her would offer some insight.

Don tried to keep the discussion moving in a productive direction as they crossed the stone bridge that lead to the Victorian flower garden in the center of the park. The ducks were swimming toward the bridge and they stopped to watch them pass under it. "I think it's safe to assume that both Mary Sloane and her three daughters are pointing you in the direction of Inis Mór, but the question is: why?"

"Yeah, it seems they were both focused on the time the family left for the States. I didn't really write much about that," she recalled. "I just said something about marriage prospects being slim for four daughters in such a small village and that they hoped for greater prosperity in Buffalo."

"Was anything said in your dream that might be of help?"

"I'm sure there was, but it is hard to say how. Ciara recognized a woman from her past, someone she knew on Inis Mór. In Buffalo, that woman had been responsible for a small child being sentenced to the insane asylum, but Ciara also blames her for the family's immigration to America. She's afraid the woman will recognize Martha, but I don't know why."

"Were you able to find any information on this woman?" Don knew his wife would have tried to find her in the historical record.

"No. It's so hard to track women in the historical record. In my dream, the sisters mentioned a cousin on Inis Mór. I guess I could see if there are any descendants still living on the island. It's small; there could still be some family in the area."

The bridge led to a large circular open space with manicured lawns, park benches and two large granite fountains at opposite ends. The beauty of the gardens filled Maude's senses, leaving no room for the Sloane family. Appreciative of all things born in the dirt, she methodically made her way around the circle, scrutinizing beds of geraniums, wallflower, and petunias for plants she did not recognize. Don followed, happily photographing any unusual plants Maude would try to identify later.

They returned to their room later that evening satiated and exhausted. Sorting through their purchases from Grafton Street, Maude set herself to the task of finding room for two hoodies, a scarf and a wool sweater in her small suitcase.

Don was finishing up his phone calls. The clerk at the desk had given him two recommendations for places to stay on Inis Mór. They had decided on a small farmhouse on the north side of the island. It wasn't exactly a B&B, but the owner had a spare room and let it out occasionally. "Okay, we are all set," he told Maude. "This was a great find. Mr. MacMahon's family goes back to the eighteenth century in that house."

Maude's smile was smug. "See, I told you it was a good idea to ask the girl at the front desk. Maybe Mr. MacMahon will have some information on the Sloane family."

Don agreed. "Well, if there are any descendants left on the island, he's likely to know them."

Later, Maude drifted off to sleep with thoughts of the Sloane sisters on her mind. Charlotte had suggested several times that she had the ability to summon her dreams. This was something Maude usually dismissed because after her last experiences in the nineteenth century, she was in no hurry to make any connection again. Still it might be useful to keep things moving along because their time in Ireland was limited. She relaxed, trying to recall her last dream in the hopes of picking up where it left off. With a silent request to her Spirit Guide for cooperation in this endeavor, she drifted off to sleep.

Chapter Six

Maude was looking over the map of Ireland as she and Don headed out of Dublin. If her attempt to conjure a dream of the Sloane sisters was successful the previous evening, she couldn't remember so much as a glimpse of it, which was just as well because her time would be best spent navigating their journey rather than transcribing and reviewing her notes. It had been easier getting out of the city now that they were familiar with the street name changes. Stone buildings soon gave way to stone walls separating green pastures as they made their way to Puckaun and the wee cottage Gene Kelly had stayed in.

It took just over three hours to make the journey across the country because they pulled over several times to photograph the cemeteries, churches and farmhouses along the way. At one point, they were stopped while a herd of sheep filed across the road on their way to a pasture on the other side.

"Good mornin' to ye! We won't be but a minute," the farmer called out as he led the sheep down the road. About fifteen wooly beasts complained as they made their way down the narrow road, annoyed by the disruption of their breakfast and by the yipping collies biting at their heels. While the spectacle was likely common place for the residents of County Tipperary, the two city dwellers from Buffalo were fascinated as they followed the herd.

"Slow down! You're getting too close," Maude ordered her husband as she hung out the window trying to keep her phone steady to document the migration.

Don stopped the car again as the front of the herd had made it to the gate and were slowly funneling through. The shaggy collies remained ever vigilant lest one of the sheep at the back of the line become impatient and decide to wander off. "Is that slow enough for you?"

Maude smiled as she slid back into her seat and watched the sheep file into the pasture. When the gate was shut and they were moving again, she reviewed the footage on her phone. "I can't wait to send this to the boys. I think Christine will get a kick out of it, too."

With the sheep out of the way, the remaining few miles went by quickly and they were still laughing about their adventure as they turned on the narrow lane that lead to a charming row of whitewashed thatched cottages.

"Glen would have loved to watch those dogs in action," Maude commented, "and Billy would have been calling them over to the car!"

"Yeah, I'll admit I'm feeling a bit guilty about leaving the boys at home," Don admitted.

"Since we are confessing, I'm actually relieved they're not here. This is not a typical family vacation. I agreed to this trip to get to the bottom of Charlotte's message from Mary Sloane. So far, I have been able to keep this part of my life from Billy and Glen. I feel like, if they were with us, I'd have so many things to explain that I'm not sure I understand yet. I'd like a better sense of why this is happening before I try and explain it to anyone else."

"I get it, but I think they're open-minded enough to understand," Don suggested. "Besides, we owe them some sort of warning in the event these abilities you have are passed down to one or both of them."

Maude hadn't considered the idea that her sons might have similar abilities. "Do you think they would even tell us if they had any weird dreams?"

"Probably not. They might not even notice them as unusual. You may have had dreams earlier in your life and not recognized them for what they were."

Worrying about whether or not Billy and Glen had similar abilities or if they would recognize them was not something Maude could add to her plate until she better understood her own experiences and the reasons for them. "Well, let's see if we can figure some of this out and then we can discuss what to tell the boys." Her comment was meant to put the subject to rest, but the seed had been planted in her mind and it would creep like an invasive vine into her thoughts despite any attempts to focus her mind elsewhere.

Their accommodations were situated in a small village consisting of several self-catering cottages, a grocery store, two pubs, and a Subaru dealership that stood oddly out of place against the rural landscape. Maude was delighted with their small whitewashed cottage, complete with thatched roof and red painted half door. She looked with a skeptical eye toward the main road as Don unloaded the car. "It doesn't look like there is anything in the way of a lunch option here." They had learned early on in their journey that most of the pubs didn't serve food.

"There must be something close by. Let's get settled and then we can stop in one of the pubs for a pint and get the lay of the land," Don suggested.

The slightly updated version of a traditional Irish cottage did not disappoint. The half door opened into a main room with a stone fireplace, and a stairway leading to a loft. It was simply furnished with a hutch adorned with traditional blue ware china, a small table, sofa and chairs on either side of the fireplace. Moving toward the back of the house was a modern kitchen, toilet and shower. Of the three bedrooms available, Maude chose the loft, smiling as Don lugged up the bags without complaint.

"I'd say you have earned yourself a pint," she told him when he descended the stairs out of breath.

The closest of the two pubs was just a few steps beyond their door and they entered to find it mostly empty but for the three patrons seated at the bar and an elderly woman behind it. Maude and Don took two stools toward the end. The three patrons were having a lively conversation that was difficult to make out given their thick accents and the speed at which they spoke.

"'Tis Friday, after all, and the faeries are most powerful on a Friday," the barkeeper told them, as if her comments would put an end to whatever they were arguing about.

"For feck sake, Sheila, don't be talkin' to me about yer faerie shite," the youngest man told her. "We're livin' in the twenty-first century!"

The old woman behind the bar turned to Maude and Don to include them into the discussion. "The faeries are a peaceful folk and they don't care for the hurlin' to begin with, but on a Friday, they get up to mischief more so than usual."

Another young couple was seated at the bar. The woman turned to Maude to offer an explanation. "Dublin won last night, and our Peter here is none too pleased."

When Maude looked confused, the other man stepped in to explain that the sport of hurling was like a religion in the rural parts of Ireland. Peter had been rooting for Galway. She had a feeling she was starting trouble, but couldn't resist asking anyway. "Why don't the fairies like hurling?"

"They are a graceful folk and don't much care for the violence of sport," the bartender told them.

The couple then gave them a brief description of the game. "It sounds a bit like lacrosse," Don observed, "But I suspect there's more contact than what is allowed in the States."

Peter had grown impatient with the talk of faeries. "They didn't lose because of faeries! They lost because their passing game was shite!" With that, he slammed his empty glass down on the bar and left.

"Ach, don't mind him," Sheila told them, taking stock of her two new customers. "Tell us about yerselves. Yer from the States, then?"

They spent the next few minutes telling Sheila and the other couple about Buffalo and receiving a few recommendations for a quick meal. Maude's mind returned to the fairies, and although she was hungry, thought that Don wouldn't mind waiting another hour or so. "So, tell me more about the fairies."

"Have ye no faerie folk in the States?" Sheila asked. Not waiting for an answer, she continued. "We call them the Sidhe in the Irish. They are a race between angels and man, gifted with special powers. They've beautiful palaces of crystal and pearl beneath the sea, where they live a life of joy and beauty, never knowing disease or death."

The young woman, Michelle, took up the story from there. "The faerie folk are beautiful, with flowing yellow hair. They were once angels in heaven, but were cast out for their pride."

By this time, Sheila had taken a stool behind the bar, settling in to tell a long story. "'Tis on Fridays that they have special powers over all things. On that day, they carry off the prettiest of the young girls to become the brides for the faerie chiefs. The children of a Sidhe and a mortal mother are beautiful and clever, and often endowed with special powers. After seven years, when a mortal wife has grown ugly, they are returned to their home, possessing a special knowledge of herbs and secret spells in compensation for their capture."

"The Sidhe look with envy on the most beautiful mortal children," Sheila continued, "and have been known to steal them away, leaving ugly changlings in their place." She paused and lowered her voice. "Only fire can break the faerie magic and return the lovely child to mother's arms."

Over the next hour, Maude and Don learned about the faerie folk. They loved beauty and luxury and were contemptuous of economy and thrift. People shouldn't stay up too late because the faeries like to gather around the smoldering embers of the hearth after the family has gone to bed. One must never completely drain their cup, for the faeries would enjoy a bit of wine as well. They are a clean folk, and the wise mortal leaves a bowl of water for the faeries to wash.

"So, ye see, the Faerie folk are most powerful on a Friday," Sheila told them, as the conversation circled back around to the sport of hurling. For Sheila, that was explanation enough for Galway's loss.

"She's a treasure, is Sheila," Michelle told them when the old woman had left the bar to fetch more ice. "She's worked here since she was fourteen, seventy-odd years as a barmaid and still strong as a bull."

Don asked the question that Maude couldn't find the words to inquire tactfully. "Does she really believe in fairies?"

To Maude's relief, Michelle didn't seem offended by the question. "The faerie stories go back centuries here in Ireland. Growing up in a small village like Puckaun, she'd have surely heard them from her gran and her gran's gran, as I did myself," she told them. "It's not so much a belief as a tradition at this point, part of a simpler way of life that's mostly gone. It does no harm, after all, to leave a bit of ale in yer glass."

"I'll bet she has some fascinating stories to tell," Don said of Sheila over dinner later that evening.

"Yeah, can you imagine working over 70 years? That would put her in her mid-eighties at least. Did you see her hauling those buckets of ice from the cellar?"

"She's stronger than I am," Don admitted.

"It's too bad we're leaving tomorrow," Maude said. "I could have easily spent an afternoon talking to her."

"Well, the journey has just begun," Don told her. "Let's look at Sheila as the first of many interesting people we hope to meet along the way."

Chapter Seven

Maude and Don set out early the next morning toward Doolin, where they would catch the ferry to Inis Mór. In some places, the roads were so narrow that Maude could not keep her window open because the foliage growing along the stone wall would surely have poked her right in the eye. After about forty minutes of crawling along they nearly met their end when another car came speeding toward them.

"Shit!" Don managed to slam on the breaks as there was no place to swerve to avoid hitting the oncoming Fiat. "Now what?" He turned to Maude, who had nothing to offer in the way of advice, but checked the security of her seatbelt just in case.

The driver of the other car appeared unfazed by the ordeal. After a quick wave out the window, she backed up at a pace Don couldn't believe until she reached a drive just barely visible about one hundred feet behind her. There she maneuvered the car in with admirable skill and waited patiently for Don to pass. "I wonder how often that happens?" He mumbled as he pulled away.

"I'm not sure I want to know," Maude answered.

After another hour and a half of treacherous narrow country lanes, they reached the port of Doolin, secured the car in the parking lot, and boarded the ferry. Heading out to sea was like sitting on a roller coaster with no seatbelt. Luckily, Maude and Don loved roller coasters and turned their faces toward the wind as the boat was tossed carelessly around the sea. Other passengers didn't appear to enjoy the experience and were reluctant to give up their white-knuckle grip on the benches even when the erratic motion of the boat ceased. It took a bit of coaxing, but Don managed to convince the woman sitting next to him to move aside for just a minute so he and Maude could get up and walk around.

"Did you dream last night?" Don asked cautiously as they made their way toward the bow.

Maude looked disappointed. "No, at least I don't think so. I'm still trying to make sense of my dream on the plane. Ciara got very distressed when she recognized a person from their past, but how far back this woman goes, and why she might be a threat to Martha is still a mystery. It's so frustrating. I don't understand the connection between the Sloane sisters in 1880 and Mary Sloane's message in Lily Dale. I'm not a DVD player; I can't just rewind to the spot in history that I need."

"Have you tried?"

"Of course, I've tried." There was an edge to Maude's voice which was not lost on her husband. In pursuit of what unfinished business she was currently undertaking on behalf of the spirits, Maude's dreams revealed clues in their own time. There was always some help from the historic record in the way of journals, ledgers or newspapers. Here in Ireland, she didn't know where to turn for more information and she said as much to Don.

"Well, I've done a bit of reading on the subject and it may be possible for you to access the same information from your dreams through meditation."

Maude turned to him with brows raised. "You have?"

Don knew his wife well enough to detect a bit of accusation underneath her surprise. The best move was to explain with confidence. "Yes. I know it's frustrating to have to wait for information to be provided to you in dreams, so I did a little research of my own and I think you can access the same information through a kind of meditation." Don glanced at her quickly before continuing. She was listening, always a good sign. "Also, if I'm being honest, I'm feeling a little left out. Whatever this is about affects me too. If you can share what you're learning with me, maybe I can help. Maybe some detail will jump out that you might otherwise overlook."

Maude was silent for a few moments while she processed this latest revelation. "Let me just see if I understand what you're suggesting." She shifted a bit to better see Don. "You want me to achieve a meditative state in which I'm able to make a connection to the people in the past and explain to you what I am seeing while I am seeing it?" Don nodded and she continued, "I appreciate your confidence in my abilities, but I think you might be reaching too far here."

"I don't think I am. I spoke to someone and he taught me how to guide you through it." Don knew that last comment might take the conversation in a completely different and unproductive direction.

"You talked to someone?" Maude's tone indicated she was willing to reserve judgement until further details were offered. "Care to elaborate?"

Don looked her directly in the eye. "You talk in your sleep."

"I...what?"

"You talk in your sleep. The first time you had that nightmare you mumbled 'it's not over.' I had a feeling we would be going down this road again and I wanted to find a better way to help you though it."

Maude was stunned and couldn't decide whether to be concerned or angry. She settled for asking more questions. "You heard me say something out of context from a dream and didn't think it was important to ask me about it? Was that an isolated incident, or do I babble in my sleep often?"

"I only heard you talking in your sleep that one time. I did ask Charlotte about it when you didn't appear to remember it the next day and she didn't feel comfortable talking about it without you being there. I wanted to try and understand before I told you, so Charlotte referred me to another person in Lily Dale for some guidance." He stopped for a minute to assess her reaction, which indicated that she would continue to hear him out. "Anyway, she introduced me to Rodney, Rodney Wake, and I visited with him a few times over the last few months."

There was a long silence while Maude tried to reconcile what he was telling her with his recent out of character behavior and increased time away from home. When the quiet stretched out longer than was comfortable, Don spoke again. "Look, Maude, I'm only trying to help you figure this out. It's hard to watch you going through something this big and not be able to help in some way. Are you willing to try this with me?"

Was he talking about past life regression? She had done it before with Charlotte, who was a certified psychic medium experienced in mediating a mental journey into one's past. Don had done more than a little research if he felt confident enough to guide her through something similar. It would have taken extensive training for Don to learn how to do it, which meant he must have visited Rodney Wake more than a few times. Clearly that was a discussion for another time.

It would be easy to disguise her fear by becoming angry at her husband for consulting Charlotte and this other man in secrecy, but in fairness, Maude had, on more than one occasion, dismissed the old woman's claims that she had more control over her abilities than she had currently realized. The truth was that she was grateful that Don was willing to try and understand the things of which she was terrified.

"So, does your sudden interest in meditation have anything to do with this?" There was only the tiniest bit of accusation in her question.

Don smiled, grateful she was willing to understand and accept his help. "Yes. Meditation has taught me how to connect with Spirit and how to ask for and accept help while I'm trying to navigate all of this. This is scary for me, too, but I think we can pull it off together. What do you think?" He decided to leave out the part that he had never actually guided another person through the kind of meditation he was suggesting they attempt.

Maude was not accustomed to hearing her husband talking this way. She thought he wanted an end to all this supernatural stuff, yet he had devoted himself to learning more in an effort to help her. As the ferry approached the shore of the tiny island where they hoped to find the answers to their questions, Maude realized how lucky she was.

The ride toward shore was a disappointment compared to their exit from Doolin. The sea was calmer and a few sailboats sat anchored in the bay, waiting for their day to begin. As the ferry drew closer, Maude studied the scene before her. There were pony carts patiently waiting to offer transport around the island. A shack offering bicycles for hire was crowded with school-aged children. She had read that the school on Inis Mór offered summer classes in Gaelic and wondered if these children were part of that program. There were others leisurely making their way up the few streets that lead away from the pier, perhaps to the restaurants and shops that provided a living for the island residents.

Maude felt a sense of familiarity that was both soothing and unnerving. It almost seemed that if she spoke to any one of these people, they would know her. Underneath those feelings of comfort and anxiety was an urge to find out more. The sense that she was connected to this island and its people was palpable and needed to be explored.

"Alright. Let's find a quiet place on the island. Maybe being here will help me tune in, in some way."

Relief spread across Don's face. "You read my mind. See, you're already better at this than you thought you'd be!"

As people trickled off the ferry they were swamped by islanders offering a variety of services, including guided tours of the island, accommodations, dining and a few places to stop in for a pint. Maude and Don made their way through the crowd to find a man sitting patiently in a pony cart holding a sign that read *Travers*.

"Mr. MacMahon?" Don called out to the man, who looked to be about ten years his senior.

"'Tis I, James MacMahon, and would ye by chance be Mr. and Mrs. Travers?" MacMahon climbed down from the cart and extended his hand.

"We would!" Don replied, shaking the hand that was offered. "This is Maude, and I'm Don."

"'Tis a pleasure to meet ye both. Now let me just take yer bags and we'll be on our way." The cart was smaller than the others Maude saw lined up along the road, but fit the two of them and their luggage comfortably.

"Thank you very much, Mr. MacMahon." Maude had to raise her voice a bit to be heard over the clip-clop of hooves on the paved road. "We didn't expect you to meet us at the ferry."

"I'd be well pleased if ye'd call me Jamie. I figured ye'd have yer bags and it's a ways yet to the house." MacMahon had turned around to answer, confident that the sturdy pony would stay the course. "I keep a motorcar in Doolin, but Dílis here takes me 'round when I'm on the island." He went on to explain that the pony's name meant *faithful* in the Irish.

"You don't live on Inis Mór?" Don asked.

"I'm what ye Americans would call," he paused for a moment to think of the term, "semi-retired. 'Tis a family home here on Inis Mór, and my gran still alive and well at the age of ninety-three. I come at the week's end and when the room is let to lend a helpin' hand."

The road was as narrow here as it was on the way to Doolin, and Maude was captivated by the wildflowers cascading out of the crevices in the stone walls. "Are those bleeding heart?" Maude asked.

Jamie turned and looked closer at the wall. "Aye." Realizing her interest in all things botanical, he began identifying the various shrubs and grasses whose twigs were used to make baskets or brooms. "We used to pick raspberries just beyond this hill when we were young," he said, pointing beyond the stone wall.

"How far back do your ancestors go on this island?' Maude asked him.

"Aye, we've been here since my great gran's great gran, longer than that, maybe. 'Tis much the same as it was then, is Inis Mór." Jamie pointed to the maze of stone walls that divided up the rugged terrain. Each of those enclosures was a separate parcel of property. Most were just big enough to build a small home and to plant a subsistence garden. A few of the parcels had one or two cows or donkeys grazing contentedly. It seemed even today, many of the residents of Inis Mór kept to the traditional way of life.

"Are there many of the old families left here?" Maude could have just asked outright about the Sloanes, but she knew somehow it would be considered rude to do so. It was important to get to know her hosts before she interviewed them.

Jamie shrugged. "There's a few of us yet, I suppose." He took a moment to adjust the reins he held casually in one hand. "So, what brings ye to our wee island?"

Maude had been expecting that question and had formed an answer that closely resembled the truth. "I'm doing some research for a book." She quickly told him of her university position and of the poorhouse project she had been working on. "Anyway, I've written two works of fiction based on my research and I'm here working on the third."

"Oh, so ye're a writer. Will I know any of yer work?"

"Likely not. My books are not well known outside the city of Buffalo, New York."

"Well, ye'll have to send us a copy of yer new book when it's completed. Gran still loves to read and she'll be well pleased to tell folks that ye did stay right in our house while ye were writin' it."

Maude laughed. "I'll do that."

The cart turned onto another narrow road that divided a barren and rocky landscape on either side of it that was different from the fertile landscapes they had passed on the way to the ferry in Doolin. It seemed that Jamie anticipated questions about the unique terrain because he began to speak about if before his passengers had a chance to ask. "Practically every field in Aran is man-made," he told them. "They worked like slaves, to be sure, the earliest settlers did, breakin' up the big rocks. They hauled in seaweed, sand, crushed rock and the like to spread over the fields until they were suitable for planting." He waved his hand around, drawing their attention again to the maze of stone walls that were evidence of the efforts he was describing. "Not much will grow in such inhospitable soil, still we produce rye grass for thatch, oats for the stock and ourselves, and cabbages, potatoes and onions enough. 'Tis a hard livin' to work the land on these islands."

"Now, mind ye, 'twas no easier makin' a livin' from the sea. Back then there were fisherman, of course, and kelpmakers. They gathered seaweed and dried it to extract iodine for medicine, which they sold in Galway. Some were sealers, or fowlers," Jamie turned to make sure he was understood. "They hunted the seals and the seabirds, don't ye know, for their eggs and feathers."

Jamie held their attention for the entire journey, adding flavor to his historical lecture with family stories. As he spoke, the limestone gave way to green pastures. Dílis continued along the road for a few more minutes and then turned without prompting down a narrow drive. The scene was right out of a travel brochure. Bordered by low stone walls, the earthen drive separated two pastures larger than they had seen thus far. On one side, a few cows grazed lazily with no interest in the approaching cart. For nearly two centuries, Jamie told them, fine calves had been the pride of this farm, and mainlanders came from far and wide to purchase them. Now they just kept a few to honor the family's fine tradition. The occupants from the other field whinnied and trotted over to greet their sister while she guided the sturdy cart to the small barn that was behind the house. At the top of the drive was a house a bit grander than many of the humble cottages they had passed along the way, yet still looked at home against the wild sea.

Maude was delighted and jumped out of the cart as it slowed to a stop. "You have horses!"

"Aye. Those are Connemara ponies, fine riding horses. The larger one is called Cecil and the smaller one is Brutus. Now Dílis here is what ye call a Tinker's horse. Ye see her like among the Travelers. It'll just be a minute while I send her away to join them." It was easy to see that sturdy wee Dílis was well suited to the Gypsy life compared to her more elegant companions.

"What can I do to help?" Don asked as he exited the cart and removed the bags.

"Ye've done it, so ye have," he said, pointing at the bags. Jamie looked toward the house as the back door opened. "There's Gran now."

"Welcome to our humble home," Dorcas MacMahon called as she came out to greet her guests. A strong voice and balanced stride gave the impression of a woman who felt much younger than her advanced years. Jamie stopped what he was doing to make the proper introductions.

"Thank you. We are delighted you had a room available for us," Maude told her.

"Aye, well, I do enjoy a houseguest now and again. I must say it's been some time since we've had visitors from the States, hasn't it, Jamie."

Jamie nodded as he continued the process of unhitching Dílis.

Mrs. MacMahon beckoned them to follow her. "Do come in and we'll have some tea and ye can tell me all about yerselves."

The women started toward the door and Don turned to deliver another offer to assist in detaching Dílis from her cart. "Away ye go," Jamie told him. "I'll join ye presently."

They entered the house through the back, directly into the kitchen. The room was a charming mixture of old and new, including weathered stone floors, a porcelain sink, cast iron Aga stove, microwave and dishwasher. "Now, let me just put the kettle on and then I'll show ye to yer room," Gran MacMahon said as she walked toward the stove.

Passing through the hall outside of the kitchen, Maude could see a comfortable sitting room on one side and a more formal living room on the other. "You have a beautiful home, Mrs. MacMahon," she commented as they climbed the stairs.

"'Tis kind of ye to say, and please, call me Dory."

When they were situated in the cozy sitting room with a tray of tea and brown bread with butter and jam before them, Maude felt like she had known Jamie and his grandmother all her life. The conversation flowed easily as they got to know each other. Dory laughed as Don told them of their adventures navigating Dublin and the herd of sheep that delayed their trip to Puckaun. "Aye, well, ye'll have no such troubles here in Inis Mór. We've but a few roads on the island." With a wink of her eye, she added, "Ye may see yer fair share of sheep, though."

"We thought we might rent bicycles to explore the island," Maude told them.

"Ye could do that, but seein' as ye've an eye for a fine horse, I'd let ye have Brutus and Cecil, should ye have a mind to ride somethin' without wheels," Jamie offered. "They could both use a good stretch of the legs."

"I think we'd enjoy that. Thanks," Don said. They were both accomplished riders, although neither had been in the saddle for a few years. Seeing the delight on his wife's face, Don decided to keep to himself that they would likely regret pony trekking around Inis Mór the next day when their legs were unable to carry them down to the breakfast table.

"That's settled then." Dory looked at Maude with anticipation. "Jamie tells me ye're a writer and that yer research has brought ye here."

"Yes, I'm working on a novel." Maude took a few minutes to tell her about the Erie County Poorhouse and the Sloane sisters. "My understanding is that they were originally from here. Do you know the name?" She noticed the spark of recognition on Dory's face at the mention of the name Sloane and was relieved that neither of the MacMahons asked how she knew that the sisters had come from Inis Mór..

"Aye, the Sloanes have been here longer than we have, I daresay. If yer wantin' to know more about the Sloanes in America, ye must talk to Fianna Griffin, Fianna Sloane Griffin, that is," Dory told her, pronouncing the woman's name as Feena.

Maude could not believe her good fortune, a Sloane descendent still living on the island. "That would be wonderful. Do you think we could arrange to meet her sometime tomorrow?" She hoped the request wasn't too forward.

"Well, she's not so young as I am, is Fianna, but she does love visitors just the same. I'll send Jamie 'round this afternoon and see if it can be arranged."

Maude remembered that Jamie had mentioned that his grandmother was ninety-three. If Fianna Sloane was older than that, she wondered what, if anything, the woman might recall about her family history.

"Aye, she may be older, gran, but she is as agile of mind and body as ye are yerself, and well ye know it." Whether Jamie could read the concern on Maude's face was uncertain, but his comments were a relief regardless.

"Aye, that she is. That's clean livin' and the sea air, so it is. Though, now that I think on it, what good has it done the pair of us? We've outlived our husbands and our families have all left the island for greener pastures, so to speak." She paused, looking at Don to include him in the conversation. "That's the way of it on Inis Mór. 'Tis a hard life here still and few of us are born to it. I raised two fine daughters here and one son, Jamie's pa, and they all left to make a livin' on the mainland." There was a resignation in her voice bred deep in the bone. She had accepted long ago the same realities of her ancestors; most people were not suited to the isolation and hard living of the Aran Islands.

"Agh, listen to me moanin'. Ye'll think I'm feelin' sorry for myself. The truth of it is, I'd have no other life, and so it's true of the others that stayed. We value the old ways here. To be sure, we'd have not survived so long as we have without them."

Later that afternoon, Maude and Don, each astride their elegant ponies, set out to do some exploring. They were riding single file down the narrow road, feeling no need to chat as they took in the scenery. Maude was thinking of their conversation that morning on the ferry and trying to chase away the doubt that was beginning to creep into her thoughts. Don seemed confident that he could help direct her into the past. He had taken the time to learn how, so she needed to have faith that he would guide her through it. She came out of her thoughts abruptly as Cecil came to an unexpected stop. Brutus had stopped ahead of him in front of an old cemetery.

"I think we should go in and take a look around," Don suggested. "Maybe we can find the headstone of an ancestor that will give you a closer connection to Martha and her family."

"Great idea. The cemetery isn't that big, so this shouldn't take long."

The small cemetery was enclosed within a stone wall atop a hill overlooking the sea. They tied the horses to a tree and walked in. Some of the graves were marked with grand Celtic crosses, and some seemed only to have small stones protruding up through the overgrown grass. They might have been broken or eroded over the centuries, but enough remained to mark the final resting place of the island residents. Beyond the stone wall just before yet another walled in pasture was evidence that the dead had proved too many for the space provided. There were a few modern graves there and room for more when the time came.

Toward the back of the plot were two rows of headstones bearing the name Sloane. The grave markers had been eroded by the relentless sea breeze, but they managed to identify the names of Jeanne and Patrick Sloane, both of whom had passed in the mid-nineteenth century. "Maybe they were married," Maude suggested. "Martha spoke of a cousin named Patrick in my dream. He took them across to Galway when they left here."

"Okay, I'd call that a pretty strong link to the events we're interested in." Don looked around the cemetery and up and down the road they had been riding on. They were alone. "What do you say we sit against the wall, over there, at the end of the second row of Sloanes and give this a try?"

They were both seated comfortably, Maude leaning against the wall and Don on the grass facing her, their folded knees touching. "Okay, just take a deep breath and relax. Do you remember when we left the ferry? As we rode down that road, away from the dock, it was like passing through time. Think about walking slowly down that road. With every step you take, you go back further in time. Take a deep breath. The past smells different. What do you smell?

"Your aftershave. This isn't working, Don."

"Very funny. Take another deep breath. Feel the energy in this place. You've been here before; I know you can feel it. Just relax and connect with Martha's life here. Imagine the smell of driftwood fires carried along by the sea breeze." Don watched his wife take several deep breaths before she answered. "Can you smell it now?"

Maude was quiet for a long while, just breathing in and out. When she finally spoke, there was a distance in her voice. "Yes, there's an earthy smell too, like decomposing manure maybe, and roasting seaweed."

"That's great. What do you see?" Don asked her. He hadn't realized that his voice lowered, too, as if not to disturb her.

"The road beyond the cemetery curves. Just after the bend in the road there's a bridge." Maude stopped, as if she was listening to something. "Martha was right: the sound of the horse's hooves changes when it crosses the bridge." Her head moved, as if it were following the horse and rider who had crossed the bridge. "There is a small cottage down the road."

Don watched her brow furrow. "Tell me about the cottage?"

"I don't know, but I think we need to go and check it out."

In her mind, Maude approached the cottage. It was situated away from the road, surrounded by a stone wall. It was the color of natural stone, not whitewashed like the cottages they passed along the way to Doolin. The wooden gate creaked as Maude pushed it open to enter. Sounds of a struggle could be heard as she walked toward the door, the anguished moan forcing her to pick up her pace. She could hear women's voices.

"Now Mary, just ye rest for a bit until ye must push again. This babe is ready to come. It won't be long now." The old woman speaking gently to the sweat-soaked woman in the bed could be described as a hag by an unkind person. She was thin and crooked with age, stringy silver hair escaping her cap. Yet no one on the

island would dare to be so unkind. Old Mrs. Donohue was a respected, even feared member of the small community, having delivered most of the inhabitants on the island.

"It's Mary Sloane," Maude told Don. "She's having a baby." Looking at Ciara and Patricia who were seated quietly on the opposite side of the room, wide eyed and ready to do whatever might be asked of them, she added, "It's Martha, I think." Then more certainly, she said, "This is Martha's birth."

Old Mrs. Donohue motioned toward Ciara. "Come here, lass, and bring a damp cloth."

Ciara went to the basin on the dresser and wrung out a cloth. "Does it hurt, Ma?" she asked, gently patting her mother's damp face with the cool cloth. Ciara had also been present for the birth of Patricia and did not recall her mother struggling as much.

"A bit, dear. Don't ye fret. 'Tis as Mrs. Donohue has said. The babe will come soon."

The front door opened and another woman, who looked to be around the same age as Mary, entered. "I came as soon as Ian brought word," Jeanne Sloane called out as she hastily hung her shawl and made her way into the small bedchamber. "To be sure, the men are best left to themselves, so I thought I'd see if I was needed here."

Jeanne Sloane was the wife of young Patrick Sloane, Ian's cousin. Together with his three sons, Patrick would host Ian, who was certainly no longer welcome in his own home while his third child was coming into the world.

Jeanne took in the scene in the small chamber. "Well, it seems ye have things well in hand, Mrs. Donohue, as ye always do." Turning to Patricia, who looked both interested and terrified at the condition of her mother, Jeanne said. "Just ye come with me, lass, and we'll fetch some more water."

"Here comes another one," Mary whispered between clenched teeth. After three quick and shallow breaths, she let out a loud wail as she pushed her baby out.

"Dear God!" Jeanne heard the words coming from the bedchamber as she came back into the cottage. "What - what's wrong?" She came running in to see Mrs. Donohue gaping at the tiny infant in her arms. Patricia came in behind her, but Jeanne extended her arm to keep the child from entering the room. "Ciara, take yer sister and put on the kettle. Mrs. Donohue will be wantin' a cup of tea."

Jeanne hastily shooed the girls out of the room and then took a closer look at the babe in the midwife's arms. She took a quick step back and then made the sign of the cross.

Reaching into the pocket of her apron, Mrs. Donohue pulled out a small knife.

"May God give ye a steady hand!" Jeanne cried, and looked away.

"It must be done!" The old woman answered, and raised the knife to the baby.

"Something is very wrong," Maude told Don. "There's a membrane covering the baby's face."

"Can you see the baby clearly?" Don asked and Maude nodded. "Can you describe exactly what you see?"

With ruthless efficiency, Mrs. Donohue cut a slit through the membrane above the infant's mouth so she could breath. She carefully peeled the rest of it away and placed it on the nightstand.

Jeanne looked toward the nightstand and then made her way to the door. "'Tis the bible we're needin'."

"Aye," Mrs. Donohue agreed.

"The images are getting fuzzy," Maude told Don. With eyes closed, she lowered her head, willing the scene to come back. After a minute she opened her eyes. "Nope, it's no good. I can't see anything else."

"Let's just take the horses down the road and see what's really there," Don suggested as they both stood and wiped the dried grass from their pant legs.

"Okay." Maude wasn't sure what she was hoping to see, but mounted Cecil and continued down the road.

They followed the bend in the road and crossed the bridge. "So, is this pretty much what you saw?" Don asked.

"All except that." Maude pointed to a slightly deteriorating stone cottage with no roof that looked to be in the same location as the Sloane cottage had been. "It looks like no one has lived here for years."

"The house is in good shape," Don pointed out. "They may have just removed the roof so they didn't have to pay taxes." They had learned that was a common strategy of families who inherited old

101

properties whose upkeep was expensive to maintain. "Still, this is pretty good confirmation that what you saw was real," Don said, pulling a notebook out of his pocket and flipping through a few pages.

Maude was surprised to see that Don had been writing things down as she had been speaking. She reached out and Don handed her the notebook. Comfortable with Cecil finding his own way home, she knotted the reins and let them hang on his neck while she examined the pages.

"Wait. Do you want to go in?" Don asked. She pulled the horse to a halt, but continued scrutinizing his notes. He waited another minute before he asked, "Did I leave anything out?"

Maude scanned the pages again. "No, I don't think so. Something about the child's face being covered made them very upset."

"I'm not sure how you would research that from here. I doubt that Mrs. MacMahon has Wi-Fi back at the house."

"True, but this is exactly the kind of thing Christine would enjoy." Maude took out her cellphone to determine if there was a signal and was disappointed to find there was not. "Well, there goes that idea."

"Not necessarily. I bet we can use the land line at one of the pubs by the ferry landing if we offer to pay for the call."

Maude quickly calculated the time difference. "Yeah, that would work and we can grab something to eat while we are there. Let's drop the ponies off and head over on foot."

"Wait, let's take a look around."

Maude looked reluctant. "It's an empty, dilapidated cottage. There's not much to see."

"It is the cottage where Martha was born. C'mon, I wanna have a look around even if you don't."

"It's not that I don't want to see inside. We don't know who owns this property. We would be trespassing." The words sounded lame even as she said them. What was she really afraid of?

Don reached out and took her hand. "C'mon. I'm with you if anything weird happens."

Having her husband say it out loud made Maude see how ridiculous she was being. There was nothing to be afraid of. Weird things happened to her all the time. It was time to embrace it. She took a deep breath and squeezed the hand that held hers. "Okay, let's go."

There was no lock on the wooden gate, which Don took as a sign that explorers were at least not discouraged. "After you." He gestured for Maude to go through and followed, allowing the rickety old gate to swing shut behind them. Brutus and Cecil were happy to munch on the grass growing along the wall, unconcerned that their riders were trespassing.

There was no door and they walked straight into the two-room cottage. It was empty, but laid out like most cottages, with a main room for cooking, dining, and sitting in the evening. There was a small room off to the side and it looked as if there had been a loft above.

As soon as she entered the house, Maude felt connected to it. She wandered around, forgetting that Don was with her. There was no sense of foreboding. The house wasn't keeping any long-held secrets. The energy was clearly that of her ancestors. No one outside the family had ever lived any length of time in this cottage. It seemed to recognize her as one of them.

The remains of a modest stable could be seen out the back window of the small bed chamber. It was slightly downhill and not visible from the road. She tried to conjure the shaggy red horse Martha had described in her dreams. He was there, for just a minute, trotting up to the stone wall that backed up to what must have been a small kitchen garden. Was she really seeing Old Dearg, or just the image Martha had shown her in the dream?

Maude went back out to the main room, closed her eyes and took a deep breath. After a few minutes, she said out loud to herself, "Things were good here for Martha and her family. Whatever made them leave, it didn't find its way here." After a moment, she remembered Don had come in with her and looked to find him standing by the door. She repeated what she had said, assuming he had not heard it the first time.

Don smiled, pleased that she had been able to determine that by using her inner senses. "That's really great, Maude. You were able to make a connection here and learn some more important details."

"I didn't really learn any details. I mean I didn't have any visions or flashbacks of Martha or her family. I just get the sense that life was good here. It's just a feeling, really."

"Maybe, but you trust that feeling and that is progress. I'm glad you decided to come in here. I hope you are too."

Maude took another look around, her eyes resting on what would have been the loft area. Again, a sense of wellbeing overtook her, and she smiled. "Yeah, I guess I am."

Don could already feel that his short time in the saddle was going to come back to haunt him the next morning, and was happy to drop the horses off and continue on foot to the pub. "Maybe if we stretch our legs now, they will be more forgiving in the morning."

Chapter Eight

Maude was up the next morning at dawn and quietly made her way outside, journal in hand, to the patio overlooking the sea. Gingerly taking a seat near the small garden, she made the unilateral decision to allow Cecil and Brutus the day off and proceed around the island on foot. There had been no more dreams of the Sloane sisters in Buffalo or anywhere else since she arrived in Ireland. These dreams were still a source of confusion. The Cassadaga Lake Free Association had their first official camp meeting in 1880, giving her a time stamp on her dreams, so why was she conjuring the Sloane sisters during that period when their mother's message clearly indicated an event from before they left Ireland in 1835? Now the dreams had stopped. Had Maude learned all she needed to from the Sloane sisters of 1880?

The nightmares had stopped, too, and Maude wondered if the same reasoning was applicable. What was she supposed to have learned from that same recurring horror of losing her husband but not knowing which one? Perhaps it was her focus on this latest turn in the path, with Don at her side, that had driven the nightmares away. She feared the experience at the marina had put a distance between them and that Don would reject any further exploration into Maude's experiences with the past. Perhaps she feared that a part of him was truly lost that night in the river, but he was with her now, an active participant in this latest adventure. With those fears put to rest, Maude could focus on her latest dream and how it fit in to her experience yesterday at the cemetery.

"What about Neala Ahearn?" she mumbled, going over her notes line by line. "Ciara, Patricia and Martha in Lily Dale, is that important?" Since she began having insight into the past, Maude had never juggled two points in history before. It would not help to ask Charlotte. Even if it were easy to reach her, she would just tell Maude that Spirit communicated in its own way and time. One must stay on the path and complete the journey to understand.

Charlotte was full of common sense that was at times infuriating, but in the end critical to the completion of each journey. *You can have more control over your abilities if you learn to clear your mind and focus.* Maude had heard that line more than once. She had tried to focus her dreams the other night without success, but the experience in the cemetery with Don indicated that maybe Charlotte was right.

Reviewing the details of the cemetery experience in her mind against what she had read about making a connection with the other side, Maude formed some assumptions. With Don's guidance, she had connected to the energy of the location and followed it up the road to Mary Sloane's cottage. It seemed reasonable that her dreams of the Sloane sisters in Buffalo were different.

They were somehow a part of her, something to be recalled, rather than connected to. Could they really be summoned on demand?

Maude looked toward the house and then the barn. There was no indication that the occupants of either dwelling would be stirring any time soon. With eyes closed, she took a deep breath and began recalling the details of her last dream. Ciara had insisted on traveling to Cassadaga as soon as could be arranged. They had agreed to travel by carriage the next day with Daniel. Maude imagined the flurry of activity, hastily packed trunks being loaded onto the carriage. The house would be stuffy from the heat of the summer, and smell of polished wood and oil lamps. Spilling out from the hall to the drive, she could hear the farewells and reassurances from other family members that they would all meet up again soon.

"Your veil, sister," Martha reminded Ciara as they climbed into the carriage. "Surely ye'll wear the veil properly…"

Ciara scowled as she reached behind and pulled the covering over her face. "Aye, but just until we are outside the city limits, for surely nobody will know me once we're on the road." She honored social convention only so far. Traveling in a stuffy carriage enveloped in crepe was certainly not a pleasant way to pass the hours until they reached Martha's home. She allowed Daniel to help her into the carriage, and continued to complain while adjusting all the black fabric pooling around her. "I never could see the sense in all of this."

The cluster of people standing in the drive had caught the attention of Neala Ahearn, who slowed her pace as she approached the Nolan's house. Standing under a tree by the wrought iron fence that surrounded the property she waited unobserved, weighing the opportunity to confront Martha Quinn against committing yet another serious breach of etiquette in the name of discovering the location of the witch child whom she suspected of theft. Having convinced herself that the ends justified the means, Mrs. Ahearn started again toward the house, but stopped in her tracks as Martha moved slightly, revealing the woman fumbling to pull a veil over her face. "Dear God, it can't be," she hissed, moving further behind the tree so as not to be discovered.

Neala would have known Ciara Sloane instantly had she not been wearing a veil when they met on the street a few days earlier. There was silver threaded through her hair, but not much else had changed. Neala put the pieces together as she watched the carriage roll on to the street. There had been three women walking together. Ciara, Martha, "…and Patricia, of course," Neala said out loud as she watched the carriage pass through the gates. The younger sisters had been children when she saw them last. Neala remembered the letter that Patrick Sloane had shared with the other villagers the year after his cousin's family had left Inis Mór. Mary, Ian and their youngest daughter, Katie, had perished on the journey from Ireland, but Ciara had married a young physician and taken in her two surviving sisters.

"Well, ye seem to have done well for yerself after all, so ye did," Neala mumbled as she considered her next move. Seeing Ciara Sloane after all these years

presented more important problems than the child who had been released from the asylum. Still, perhaps both could be disposed of in the same stroke.

The family had all dispersed from the drive when Neala walked through the open gate toward the front door, only half sure of her plan when Patricia opened it. "Mrs. Ahearn, how may I be of assistance to ye." Patricia's voice was polite, but only just.

"I do apologize for the intrusion, Mrs. Um…"

"Mrs. Thomas."

"Mrs. Thomas, would ye by chance be Mrs. Patricia Thomas?"

"I would. If ye'll pardon me, Mrs. Ahearn, but my family is in mourning and I must get back to them."

Neala bit back a sly smile. "Yes, I am so sorry for your loss and I won't take but a moment of yer time. I've just come to apologize for my behavior the other day, but I see I've just missed Mrs. Quinn. Is she on her way back to Cassadaga? Perhaps I could send a note."

"No, that won't be necessary, Mrs. Ahearn. If ye'll kindly excuse me, though, I must get back to my family."

Patricia closed the door, not a bit concerned about her own rude behavior, and watched Neala Ahearn exit through the wrought iron gate. It would do naught but harm to convey the woman's apology to her sisters.

"Ciara Sloane, after all these years," Neala muttered as she continued walking toward Main Street.

"I dare say, ye'll catch a chill out here. Won't ye come in and I'll fix ye a lovely cup of coffee. It is coffee, isn't it? Most Americans take coffee, I find." Dory MacMahon pulled her sweater closed against the morning chill as she made her way out to the patio, "Oh, I've gone and startled ye. Did ye nod off, then?'

It took Maude a few seconds to pull herself from the past and remember where and when she was. "I must have," she lied. "The sounds of the sea must have lulled me to sleep."

"Well, I'll give ye a minute to get yer wits about ye again," Dory told her as she turned to go back inside.

Neala Ahearn, Ciara Sloane, Inis Mór? While it was still fresh in her mind, Maude opened her journal and hastily scrawled a few words. Maybe Fianna Sloane could help her to understand how these two women were linked.

"Are ye back in the right world, then?" Dory asked as Maude came in through the back door. Taking in the confusion of Maude's face, she added, "Our dreams often take us away when we sleep."

The truth of the old woman's words unsettled Maude, but she smiled and tried to shake it off. "It's starting to smell wonderful in here." She reached for the steaming mug that Dory was offering, inhaling the rich aroma. Taking in the cast iron pan on the stove already sizzling with sausages, she added, "Really, we don't want you to go to any trouble for us."

"'Tis no trouble. Ye've got a full day ahead of ye and ye must have a full belly to face it."

"Can I help with anything?" Maude offered.

Dory cocked her head in the direction of a wire basket on the kitchen table. "If ye have a mind to, ye can fetch some eggs from the henhouse out back."

Having spent a few summers at farm camp as a child, Maude was skilled in retrieving eggs from nesting hens. "I can do that." She plucked the basket off the table and headed out the door.

Thoughts of Neala Ahearn and her relationship to Ciara Sloane receded to the back of her mind as Maude made her way to the small stone outbuilding just a few feet away from the barn. She was greeted by a chorus of clucks and squawks from the six hens who knew the purpose of her visit. "Good morning, ladies. What have you got for me today?"

Reaching gently under the first hen, Maude felt a very warm lump. Extracting it slowly, she placed the egg in the basket. Repeating the technique five more times resulted in a total yield of 7 eggs. "Thank you, ladies." Maude held the full basket with two hands as she walked slowly back to the house.

The occupants of the barn sounded as if they were waking up as Maude passed by. Glancing through the door, she wondered who cared for the animals when Jamie was not here. It was true that Dory was in excellent health and more than capable of feeding the animals, but Maude couldn't see her regularly doing the heavier chores like mucking out the stalls. It probably wouldn't be polite to ask and the property and livestock looked well cared for, so she decided it was not worth mentioning.

"Ah, someone's given us an extra!" Dory exclaimed as she took the basket from Maude. "They're young hens yet, so we never want for our eggs in the mornin'. Just ye have a seat there and I'll freshen up yer coffee."

Maude was about to protest when Don entered with Jamie behind him. "I'll just be off then and give young Rob a helpin' hand with the mornin' chores."

Jamie said on his way out the door. Having never attended farm camp, Don followed in the hopes that he could be of some help anyway.

Well, there's that question answered, Maude thought as she watched Jamie head off to the barn. Gratefully accepting a fresh cup of coffee, she reluctantly took a seat when Dory assured her that further assistance was not needed.

"Ye'll be on yer way to see Fianna this mornin'. She'll be after feedin' ye as well," Dory warned her.

Feed them, she did. After a hearty breakfast with the MacMahons, Maude and Don made their way on foot to the home of Fianna Sloane Griffin, which was not the cottage around the bend from the cemetery. Fianna lived in the home of Martha's cousin Patrick, on the other side of the island. It was a long enough walk that Maude did not feel guilty about the prospects of eating again. Over a feast of sweets, Fianna shared her family's fascinating history.

"There were two brothers, ye see, Patrick and William born right here on Inis Mór, and their ma was a Scot, so she was. I come from Patrick's side of the family. They were the sons of Aiden Sloane, and his wife Branna, the first to come to Inis Mór. 'Tis quite the love story, that of Branna and Aiden Sloane, for he was a wanted man, having done his share to help Bonnie Prince Charlie reclaim the throne, for all the good it did, and she defied her parents and followed him into battle."

Maude was only vaguely familiar with the exiled Stuart kings and their attempts to regain what most Scots to this day referred to as their rightful place on the throne of Great Britain. "So, they came to Inis Mór…" She thought for a moment, "In the 1740s, I think it was. Aye, fled in the dark of night, so they did, and narrowly escaped the gallows." Fianna paused for dramatic effect before continuing her tale. "Ye'll be thinking 'twas because of Aiden that they fled, that, when it came down to it, he wasn't willing to give his life for the Stuarts, but ye'd be wrong. He was a canny man, was Aiden, and the English thought him dead even before the battle on Culloden Moor. Nay, the reason they left was because of Branna, so it was."

Again, she paused to let that revelation sink in. Fianna could tell a good story, and was well pleased to have an audience now. "Ye see, Branna was a powerful seer like her mother before her. 'Twas herself who had seen the bloodbath of Culloden, the battle that would put an end to the Stuart cause and the end of the clans in Scotland. Many women lost their husbands, their sons, their brothers and their fathers that day on Culloden Moor, but not Branna. She had pleaded with Aiden to walk away just a few days before the fateful battle. Well, Aiden Sloane was a man, and like any good man, he couldn't just walk away from a fight, but Branna begged him again and again. When that didn't work, she told him she carried his son, and would he leave the lad fatherless? In the end, Aiden's loyalty was to his wife and unborn babe."

Fianna took a sip of her tea before continuing her story. "Not wantin' to be branded a coward, Aiden chose instead to be thought a drunken fool. He was found by his wife face down in a stream, drowned for all anyone knew, except of course for Branna, who indeed knew better." Fianna chuckled, telling the story as if she had witnessed it herself. "Sure enough, Branna put on quite the show, angry at the other men for lettin' the man stumble off by himself, pickled in whiskey. The men were, of course, preoccupied with the battle to come, starvin' and outnumbered as they were. They paid her little mind, never even went to see the body for themselves. She and Aiden were able to sneak away, and nobody the wiser."

She stopped talking, apparently trying to recall some important detail. "'Twas a day or two after the battle when the two of them were found in a wee cottage about a day's hard ride from the bloody moor. Mind ye, Branna and Aiden were on foot, and her with child, so they couldn't travel as fast as a rider. Had it been the English soldiers who found them, the two would have been taken captive for sure, but as fate would have it, it was a few ragged survivors of the battle who did know Aiden Sloane and thought him dead."

Making sure her audience was riveted before continuing the tale, Fianna examined her tea cup and when she found it was empty, took the time to refill it. "Well, to be sure, they thought Branna had used her powers to raise Aiden from the dead. The men were injured, exhausted, and near starved. They were not in their right minds, and even accused Branna of having conjured an army of demons for the English, for how else could they have devastated the fearsome clans the way they did? The men made to hang the pair of them on the spot. Well, Aiden fought them off, stole their horses and the two fled in the dead of night, so they did. I daresay, had the men not been beaten and weary to their bones, the story may have ended differently, to be sure. As it happened, Branna and Aiden rode like the devil and didn't stop until they found their way here."

Don had been so enthralled in the story, he found that he was sitting on the edge of his seat. Nobody could embellish a tale like the Irish, except perhaps the Scots, and Fianna Sloane was apparently a combination of the two. "Wow, that's quite a family legend."

"'Tis the God's honest truth," Fianna spoke with a pride that had been passed down over the last three centuries. "Now, Aiden and Branna had two sons, as I said, William and Patrick. Patrick raised his family right here in this wee cottage."

The wee cottage had been enlarged and modernized over the years, but in general resembled the traditional Irish cottage. It was larger than the cottage Maude and Don had stayed in a few days earlier, and Fianna told them that a separate kitchen had been added in the 1950s. Prior to that they had been cooking over the hearth in the main room of the cottage, as their ancestors had done. The old stove had something delicious bubbling on it. Maude suspected it was lamb stew, and her stomach gave a rebellious rumble.

"Now, it's William's kin ye're after, is it not?" Fianna asked.

"Yes," Maude answered. "There were three daughters of Ian and Mary Sloane who survived the journey to America and lived in Buffalo, New York." She stated the information as if these facts had been uncovered during her research and not, as she previously thought, made up.

Fianna looked up at the ceiling, searching her memory for Ian Sloane. "Oh, Ian, he was William's son."

Maude did some quick calculations in her head trying to determine how Martha's father could have been the son of a man who must have been born in the mid-eighteenth century. "How old was William when Ian was born?"

"Oh, I don't know. He'd not have been a young man, though. It took time to find a wife back in those days. Island life was hard and many's the women who would have refused it. Most of our men married later than those on the mainland. As it happens, William and Patrick married two sisters from Galway. William's first wife bore him no children and died of the fever. Ian was the son of his second wife." Fianna reached over to the table beside her and retrieved an ancient looking leather-bound book. "All of us born on the island, up until my own three sons, have been recorded in the family bible." There was a sadness in her voice, maybe because the names of her grandchildren were not included. The fragile book looked to have several documents tucked away inside it for safe keeping, as was the practice in the past. She opened it toward the end, where a page of tidy handwriting revealed the Sloane family tree. Fianna pointed to the middle of the page and handed it to Maude.

With Don looking over Maude's shoulder, they examined the generations of Sloanes that had begun their lives on Inis Mór. "What's that written by Martha's name?" Don asked.

Maude held the page closer, but could not make out the tiny word. "I don't know." Handing it back to Fianna, she asked, "Can you make it out?"

Fianna adjusted her glasses and held the paper a bit further away. "I've never noticed that before, but I daresay, I've never really looked carefully." Shaking her head, she indicated that the writing was a mystery to her as well. "Perhaps ye should ask Father Cleary. He'll be familiar with how these records were kept by the old families."

After providing them with directions to the church and the best time to see Father Peter Cleary, who also was the island historian, Fianna looked out the window and noticed that the morning had faded to afternoon. "Ye'll be starvin', and me rattlin' on. I've got some letters to show ye, so just ye take a look at them and I'll fix us a bite to eat."

"Letters? From whom?" Maude knew better after Dory's warning not to argue that they were already full from their feast at tea and not in need of a meal just yet.

"The one thing ye will learn about the Sloane family is that we never toss anything in the bin. I've gone through the box over there," she pointed to the wooden crate on the floor, "and didn't I find some letters from your Ciara to Jeanne Sloane. Jeanne was young Patrick's wife; you'd call him Patrick junior." She motioned for Don to bring the box closer. "I'll let the two of ye sort through those. I've left the ones from Ciara on top."

When Fianna left the room, Maude just stared astonished at the crate before her. "I can't believe this!" Slowly, she reached in and pulled out a stack of letters bound together by a fragile string. "I'm afraid to even untie this. It looks like it's as old as these letters are."

"Well, someone's going to have to or we'll never know what they say," Don told her as he reached for the packet and gingerly untied the knot. "Let's try and organize these by date so we can read them in order," he suggested.

So many of the correspondences were too fragile to open. Back then, news from family in America would have been read over and over by friends and family back home, even months or years after it had been written. It frustrated Maude to focus only on the year 1880. So much of the Sloane sisters' history would have been recorded in these letters, but it would take weeks to properly read and document them all, and even longer to transcribe and study them.

After a few minutes of sorting, they identified two letters that were written from Ciara to her cousin Jeanne in the summer of 1880. Clearing her throat, Maude took the first letter and began reading aloud.

Chapter Nine

Mrs. Patrick Sloane
Oughill
Inis Mór , Ireland

June 2, 1880

Dearest Cousin,

I write in the English in response to your last letter, which was written in the same. I daresay, you are much improved in the writing of this foreign tongue from your previous letters. I am mortified to realize that it has been some time since my last letter. 'Tis with a heavy heart that I write now to tell you of the passing of my dear husband Michael. His own heart failed him while coming to the aid of a young lass who, without his intervention, would surely have languished in misery. We are three widows now, are Patricia, Martha and me. Patricia is a devoted grandmother, but it did not take much to convince her to accompany me and dear Martha back to Cassadaga Lake for a short while.

I'm sure I've told you of Martha's home by the lake. 'Tis a lovely village near Buffalo, in some of the prettiest country you'd ever want to see. The woods go on and on for miles. Tis like nothin' you've seen before, to be sure. The people here are called Free Thinkers by some, and Spiritualists by others. Many have special gifts, as Martha does, and see no cause to hide them. Others come from far and wide, seeking those with special gifts and pay dearly for the opportunity to be witness to miracles they perform. Why, I saw a man bend a spoon using just the force of his mind. There is a group of women visiting from Cape Cod- that's in Massachusetts - who can combine their power to raise a table up off the ground. Had I not seen these things for myself, I'd surely not believe them to be true.

More important than the special gifts these Spiritualists possess is the notion that women here are listened to with the same respect as many men. The Spiritualists hold picnics during the summer season, where other Free Thinkers from miles around gather to exchange ideas. There is music, and the most interesting lectures, where women speak of the importance of our roles in society. There are even women who seek to organize in order that we might fight for our right to vote. I daresay it would shock many of the folk at home, but so would so many other aspects of life here. Why, our dear Martha sits on the board of the Cassadaga Lake Free Association. The board of directors is an organization of people who make decisions about how this new community will be organized and managed. Would you ever believe it possible that our Martha is among them?

Dear cousin, I confess I seek to distract myself by telling you of our lives here, but there is something I fear I must share. There is more to the story of the young child who my dear Michael tried to help on the day he passed. She was a serving girl and a child who is gifted in the way of those who possess the second sight. The poor dear had been accused of thieving by her mistress. The woman had a fearsome temper which frightened the child. The power of her fear rattled the very pots and pans on the stove. The woman called her a witch. In the city, those who possess such powerful gifts are feared, as they are back home, and often locked up in the insane asylum. I know you agree that fear is unjustified. Thanks to my dear husband's efforts before his passing, and those of another kind woman, the child was spared that horror and is now safe here among the Free Thinkers, who do not fear such gifts.

You might think my tale ends there, cousin, but it does not, for I knew immediately the mistress who sought to have this poor child locked away the minute I laid eyes on her in the street. Had I not been wearing a veil, I daresay she'd have known me too. To be sure, I did thank God that she did not know Patricia or Martha, having last seen them as babes when we lived on Inis Mór. Dear cousin, the woman I speak of is Neala Ahearn!

I must confess that I was surprised to find she is now called Ahearn. It was Joseph Grady's eye she caught when we were young. I suppose it matters not, for my fear of the woman exists firmly in the present day, not in the past, although her behavior toward my family in the past informs my present distress. 'Tis not bad enough she still seeks to have the poor child she accused of sorcery locked away in the asylum, but I fear for what might happen should she discover that I live in the same city as she, and Martha not far from there as well. There is reason enough to fear that she could make the trip to Cassadaga in search of the child, for it is not far from Buffalo.

Oh, dear cousin, please do tell me that I am mistaken, and that Neala is yet on Inis Mór. If you cannot in truth tell me that, please tell me there is naught to fear from the woman.

With love,
Ciara

"Well, that didn't really tell us much," Maude groused, folding the letter carefully.

"Well, it confirms your dreams that Ciara feared this woman and that she had tried to cause the Sloane family harm," Don argued.

Fianna came into the sitting room. "Ye must be fair starved by now. Do come in and have a wee bit to eat before ye continue. These letters have been here all these years; they'll keep a bit longer, I think."

Maude and Don entered the kitchen to find a feast laid out on the table before them. Her suspicions were correct and three bowls of lamb stew had been set out, each with a mountain of mashed potatoes protruding out of the center. The stew was accompanied by a basket of brown bread and a crock of butter. Only now did Maude notice the aroma of fresh baked bread. They had been so engrossed in Ciara's letter, they hadn't noticed all the trouble their host had gone to.

"This looks delicious. Thank you," Don said, admiring the spread.

Mealtime conversation was limited to chitchat about the island and what Maude and Don had seen of it thus far. In her mind, Maude rejected several questions about Ciara's letter to her cousin, Jeanne, unsure how to ask them without sounding intrusive or revealing what she had learned from her dreams. The meal was delicious and plentiful, so much of the time around the table was spent in silence while each of them consumed it.

"There's bread pudding for later, so save some room," Fianna warned them.

When Maude and Don had finished eating, the day was nearly over. As much as they wanted to continue reading Ciara's letters, they could not impose further on their gracious host.

"Don't be daft," Fianna assured them. "I can't recall the last time I've spent such a lovely afternoon."

"We so appreciate your hospitality, Mrs. Griffin, but we have to stop by the pub before it gets too late and call our sons back home," Don told her.

"Ah, well, ye'll be missin' yer lads, I'm sure. Ye must promise me two things before ye leave, then."

"Of course," Maude agreed, "what can we do for you?"

"First, ye must come back so that ye can finish with the letters, and ye must promise to call me Fianna."

"We can certainly do both of those," Don assured her. "Would tomorrow be too soon?" He was concerned that the request would be too forward, but he knew Maude would be chomping at the bit to get back to those letters. "We are only here for a few more days."

"Not at all. Shall we say around the same time?"

"That would be wonderful," Maude agreed. "Thank you again for your hospitality and your wonderful stories."

Maude had given Christine the number of the pub they had called from the day before and had asked her to call them back at two in the afternoon Buffalo time if she had anything to report about Martha's unusual birth. They arrived in the pub just before seven, their time, and each ordered a pint while they waited for her to call.

"Is it me, or does Guinness taste better in Ireland? Don asked as he drained his glass. He was about to expand on his hypothesis when the phone behind the bar rang. As the bartender went to hand Don the phone, he pointed to Maude. "She'll want to speak to my wife, I think."

"Hi, Christine. How is everything? Are the boys driving my in-laws nuts yet?" Maude waited while Christine gave her news from home, turning to inform her husband as needed. "What did you find out about babies who present with a membrane covering their face?"

"Well, it was an unusual request, even for you." Christine had sensed the intrigue surrounding this request and was fishing for a few more details of her own. When none were forthcoming, she continued. "The membrane that can sometimes stay attached to an infant's face after birth is referred to historically as a veil or a caul, but it is really part of the amniotic sac. Those infants who present with it are referred to as caulbearers. It's very rare now, and was likely rare back then as well, although birth records for the period you are interested in are scarce. The folklore varies depending on which culture you're exploring, but is usually associated with the possession of otherworldly knowledge or abilities."

"In Celtic culture, the significance can also vary depending on where the phenomenon occurs. Caulbearers are thought to possess special gifts like the second sight. What can vary is how these gifts were perceived. Some seafaring cultures, for example, consider it a blessing. A caulbearer can warn of dangerous storms. The caul can be carefully removed and preserved. It might be stored away, like in a family bible, or carried by the bearer for good luck. I didn't have a lot of time to investigate, but depending on the time period, or the specific circumstances, caulbearers may have also been feared. The occurance of a few unfortunate events in which a seer is thought to be involved could change public perception quickly. If you want, I can e-mail you my sources," Christine offered.

"Yeah, that would be great. Thanks, Christine." Maude knew she would not be able to access her e-mail until they left Inis Mór, but if she could download the material on the mainland, she could review the details and maybe do a bit more research.

Don had ordered two more pints and handed one to Maude when she hung up the phone. "So, what did you find out?

Maude repeated Christine's brief explanation of caulbearers and recalled the reaction of the midwife just after Martha had been born.

"So, do you think the old woman didn't see it as a blessing?" Don mused.

"It's hard to say. She and Jeanne certainly seemed startled by it. I wonder if rumors of Branna Sloane's problems in Scotland followed them to Ireland."

"Maybe," Don agreed. "It is possible that people just realized her abilities on their own. It's a small island."

"Do you think Fianna would be willing to tell us more about Branna Sloane? It doesn't make sense that they would fear a seer in a community where so many of the people make their living from the sea. Maybe there was a specific incident that caused her neighbors to fear her."

"That's a great question. If Branna Sloane's second sight became something that the other island residents did not approve of or feared, it may be a family secret she is unwilling to share."

Maude took sip of her stout and considered her husband's insight. Fianna might very well take unkindly to probing questions about her family's history. Having spent the afternoon with a Sloane descendant, Maude's own family, albeit in another life, the family took on a different identity. They were no longer names listed in a ledger, journal or old newspaper. They were real people who may not want familial skeletons rattled. Perhaps Fianna had revealed all she was willing to share.

They would have to wait to learn more about Branna Sloane. Fianna sent word to them the next morning she was feeling a bit under the weather. "I hope we didn't wear her out," Don remarked as he joined his wife in her favorite spot on the back patio.

"I'm sure we did," Maude answered, placing her coffee cup on one side of the open spiral notebook in defense of the gentle sea breeze that was flipping its pages. "She's older than Dory and I don't think she gets much company." Maude tried not to feel too guilty over their prolonged stay with the old woman yesterday. Fianna did seem to enjoy it and they had learned some fascinating information about the Sloane ancestors which might be helpful in trying to understand Mary Sloane's message.

"So, what's plan B today?" Don asked.

Maude closed the notebook and placed the cup on top. "That is a good question. I've been sitting here trying to put all the pieces together. Looking at everything on paper, it just looks like a lot of random details across time. It seems reasonable that any special gifts Martha possessed were passed on from her great grandmother Branna. Somehow people became aware of her abilities, and feared them. Neala Ahearn had something to do with that, and Ciara was afraid that if she recognized Martha, it would happen again."

"It seems to me that you've put the pieces together very nicely," Don observed. "There are a few gaps, but you are on the right track, I think."

Maude blew out a sigh of frustration. "This whole thing started with a visit from Martha's mother, who apparently wanted to draw attention to the time when the family left Inis Mór. My dreams, which occur over forty years after that event, only offer small clues and are not easily accessed. I feel like they are significant, though."

Don listened and waited for her to finish before offering his opinion. "This may sound odd, but bear with me while I work it out. Maybe your brain is overloaded with trying to make sense of all these different sources of information. We may be overlooking another way to tap into this information that seems to be locked in your subconscious."

"I'm listening."

"Well, we have learned that much of the 'fiction' parts of your books turn out not to be fiction, Mary Sloane being a perfect example. You didn't know who Ciara's parents were or where they were from. You thought you made them up, but you didn't. You took the time to fact check your dreams, but not your novels. Maybe part or all of the fictional components really happened."

Maude thought about that for a moment. "Okay, assuming what you are suggesting is a possibility, how does that help me now?"

"Write your book. Maybe don't even start from the beginning. Martha and Ciara took off to Lily Dale. Start there, and see where the story takes you."

"Don, if I did that, there would be no way to tell if the details were true or not," Maude argued.

"True, but I think you will find that they are. These memories, for lack of a better term, seem to be locked up in your mind. They seem different from what we were able to discover in the cemetery the other day. In the cemetery you were connecting to some energy there, but your dreams come from inside you. They need to be retrieved. Some people argue that writing is a form of meditation. I've seen you while you are writing. The house could be on fire and you wouldn't notice. Get yourself in the zone and see what happens."

It made sense, and Maude could almost hear Charlotte giving her similar advice. "Well, I guess I could give it a try. What will you be doing today?"

"I don't know. Maybe I'll hang out with Jamie today."

Maude was fairly sure that Jamie spent a good portion of his afternoon in the pub where they used the phone. "Ha! Okay, but if I don't get very far with my book, I'm coming to join you!"

Chapter Ten

Maude opened her laptop and considered what she had learned so far about Martha and Ciara in 1880. She thought about the letter Ciara had written and the description of the Cassadaga Lake Free Association. There was a considerable amount of research on the history of the Modern Spiritualist community on her laptop, so Maude opened a few files to review her notes. Looking at some of the early photographs at the start of the camp season, Maude closed her eyes to imprint the scene in her mind. In a matter of minutes, her fingers were sailing across the keyboard.

> *"You that came up through the church are here, but you came up by the power of the God within you, and not by the help of the church. Unless you save yourselves, God Almighty will never witness your salvation."*

"Did I not tell you, sister, that Dr. Weathersby would speak of bold things. His words are considered blasphemy by many outside this community. I will not judge ye, should ye decide to return to the cottage," Martha assured Ciara as the charismatic man on the stage continued to speak.

Ciara looked around at the people seated on cut tree trunks made to serve as benches. There were over five hundred people spilling out of the House of Boughs, a tent frame with tree boughs, branches, flowers and vines covering it. They were riveted by the power of the man's words and did not seem outraged by his remarks.

> "The church makes the crutch necessary by creating the cripple. I do not believe that the crippling process was a benefit to anyone. The church creeds, with their restrictions, with the crushing soul bondage belonging to and enforced by them, has been, is, and only can be a nameless curse.

Even Prudence and her young daughter, Patsy, who had been quietly smuggled out of Buffalo, seemed to listen with an objective ear. They had been observing without judgment the Spiritualists of the Cassadaga Lake Free Society since their arrival a few weeks previous, and were cautiously beginning to think of this place and its people as home.

> "The church grasps the child with an iron hand and holds it in bondage. Forever keep away from your children that system of bondage that tends to crush spirit and hide the truth."

Dr. Weathersby's comments regarding children likely resonated with Prudence, whose daughter had been demonized in Buffalo by the very institution the man denounced. She did not understand Patsy's gifts, but refused to see them as a curse or a danger to others as Mrs. Ahearn had. Here in Cassadaga, they had been welcomed, the color of their skin irrelevant, and Patsy's gifts accepted without question. There had been great interest in Patsy's abilities, but Alva Awalte had made it clear that the child was to be left alone until she had sufficient time to recover from her ordeal in the Buffalo Plains insane asylum.

Ciara observed as Prudence craned her neck towards the stage, wanting to hear more of what Darius Weathersby had to say. Turning to Martha, she whispered. "Nay, I promised to keep an open mind, and I shall." As the words came out of her mouth, Ciara was silently grateful that Patricia had not joined them at the House of Boughs. She would not have been able to hear Dr. Weathersby's words without passing judgment. It was not out of any compelling need to supervise that Patricia had offered to accompany her nephews at the lakeside that morning. She could not help but interpret the words of people like Weathersby as an affront to all that was holy. It was one thing to enjoy a bit of a holiday by the lake with her family, but quite another to participate in the meeting of the Spiritualists.

Making no effort to suppress her pleasure at her oldest sister's thus far neutral reaction, Martha smiled and gave Ciara's hand a squeeze. It would take Patricia a while to understand, as it had Martha, that the Spiritualists had nothing against God. If only she was willing to listen, she might hear that the Spiritualists only rejected the restrictions placed on them by the Church, particularly regarding women. Women saw in

Modern Spiritualism their opportunity to be equals to men. Women were valued as partners, cherished for their wisdom and strength, which gave rise to a different kind of beauty that was equal parts gumption and compassion. They governed themselves by the wisdom of the God within them, not by the restrictive rules of their husbands or the church. In Cassadaga, women were free to express themselves intellectually, spiritually, and sexually.

Martha had never been able to give her heart to another man, but in the last year she had found a likeminded companion in Darius Weathersby. The relationship suited her because he spent much of the year traveling to the other Spiritualist camps. He had come to the religion in much the same way Martha had. The church had been no comfort to Darius after the death of his wife a few years ago. He had met a couple in Massachusetts who called themselves Free Thinkers. Darius accompanied them to a camp picnic at Lake Pleasant Spiritualist Camp, in Montague. He was immediately taken by the lectures focusing on the relationship between God and the individual, and how the Christian church can hinder, rather than help, that relationship. He gave up his medical practice in Boston and traveled around the East coast sharing his views and experiences with likeminded Free Thinkers.

When Darius came to Cassadaga, he and Martha provided each other with companionship and physical comfort, each understanding they would never take the place of the love lost to the other. Martha didn't have to explain this relationship to Alva, who had had a few companions of her own over the years, but what Ciara would make of Darius Weathersby was another question. Patricia would be shocked and outraged, that was certain.

"Dr. Weathersby is a dear friend. I was worried ye'd not take kindly to his words," Martha confessed.

Ciara gave her sister a thoughtful look. This man was important to Martha. Even if Ciara disapproved, which thus far she did not, he would have the benefit of the doubt for Martha's sake. "I must admit, I have heard others here say things more shocking than Dr. Weathersby. I daresay, while I may not agree with some of what is said here, it seems to matter not to those who say it. We are each free to hold our own opinions, which I do find I agree with wholeheartedly."

"Yes, sister, that is it exactly. We must listen to what is said, consider it, and then form our own opinions. None here will think less of ye for having a mind of yer own, least of all Dr. Weathersby."

Their conversation was interrupted by raucous applause that indicated the lecture was over. "Will ye stay for the music?" Martha asked Prudence.

"I do thank you, ma'am, but Patsy and I must be gettin' back now." Prudence had taken the position of housekeeper in Martha's and Alva's home, but had not yet grown accustomed to her new position. She was not treated like a servant, and was free to participate in the events of the camp meeting. It would take some getting used to, this ability to speak freely and express a dissenting opinion, not that she had any yet. The lakeside community was a wonderful place to raise her daughter, and Prudence would not jeopardize her change of fortune by becoming too familiar with her employers. "Are we expecting Dr. Weathersby for supper?"

"Not this evening, but Daniel's family will be joining us," Martha told her. She watched as Prudence and her daughter made their way through the maze of benches to the dirt road that led back to the cottage.

"Does she get on well with Felicity?" Ciara asked when they were out of earshot.

"Patsy? Aye, and I can think of no better person to help the child through her troubles," Martha answered. Ciara's daughter-in-law Felicity had suffered a similar experience nearly a decade before, when she had been sent to the insane asylum by those who feared her gifts. She was deaf, but could hear people's thoughts. Martha was sure Alva had Felicity Nolan in mind when she brought Patsy and her mother to Cassadaga. Felicity knew well the horror the child had been through, but also had benefitted from the charity of Mrs. Awalte and the Nolan family. Felicity was living proof that love and kindness could help mend a broken spirit.

Ciara noticed the expression change on her sister's face as Darius Weathersby approached. It didn't light up like it used to when Johnny called on her; it was more like a grateful smile. Maybe there was something between her sister and this man, but it wasn't love.

Under different circumstances, she would have stayed to meet the man, but Ciara still hadn't grown comfortable meeting people as Michael's widow. As soon as they had arrived in Cassadaga, she dispensed with the veil and morbid black clothing, but still wore the muted colors of a widow in the advanced period of mourning. Meeting new people, her loss so evident for all to pity, added a layer of humiliation to her grief.

It took some time for Weathersby to make his way through the crowd, so Ciara took the opportunity to make her escape. "Aye, well, Prudence will need some help gettin' the supper started," she told Martha.

Martha attention refocused on her sister. "Shall I accompany ye?"

Ciara shook her head. "Stay and visit with yer friends. I'll be fine." Before Martha could argue, Ciara turned and made her way through the crowd.

Martha might have followed her sister had it not been that Mr. Weathersby had reached her at the precise moment that her sister had disappeared in to the crowd. "Dr. Quinn, how lovely it is to see you again," he said, offering a seemingly platonic handshake.

"Good mornin' Dr. Weathersby. I did so enjoy yer lecture." She held his hand in both of hers, letting her fingers caress the length of his before she let go.

"There is yet some time before Mrs. Watson takes the stage and it is a glorious morning. Would you do me the honor of a short stroll by the lake?"

"I would sir, but my sister has come to visit and I do believe she has need of me at home."

His formal façade receded and was replaced by an understanding borne of experience. "I did hear of the death of your brother-in-law. Dr. Nolan is spoken of kindly here. They say he was a friend to the Free Thinkers and a fine physician. I am terribly sorry for your loss." His honesty underscored the change that had occurred in their relationship in the past few months. "Perhaps your sister is less in need of your company and would value a few hours in peaceful solitude?"

As Martha considered his suggestion, she realized that Ciara had exited in the direction of the woods rather than the cottage. "Perhaps you have a point. Alright then, I would enjoy a short walk by the lake."

As they threaded their way through the gathering, Martha did not take his arm, partly because the size of the crowd demanded that they navigate it single file, but also because strolling the grounds arm in arm would send a message she did not want to send. Martha Quinn and Darius Weathersby were not a couple. They were dear friends who took comfort in each other's company in a way she did not feel needed to be announced, explained or justified to anyone.

"I noticed Mrs. Awalte was not among the crowd this morning," Darius commented as they followed the dirt path along Cassadaga Lake. "Is she in Buffalo?"

"She is. With Michael gone, she fears for the people in the asylum." It was not necessary for Martha to explain what she meant by that comment. Darius knew of their efforts to defend those with special gifts from unfair persecution. Defending their new-found religion was another thing they had in common, sort of. While Martha and Alva came to the aid of the gifted, Darius Weathersby exposed those who claimed special abilities they did not possess.

As Modern Spiritualism took root, charlatans flourished, eagerly willing to help the bereaved connect to their dearly departed loved ones for a fee. Darius had been taken in by one such swindler when he first came to the religion and was determined to expose those low enough to take advantage of the grief-stricken.

"Will you join her when the season here has ended?"

Martha did not answer right away. Rather, she took a moment to appreciate the beauty around her. The sun was shining, and there were geese on the lake honking lazily as they navigated around the clustering lily pads and cattails swaying in the gentle breeze. "No, my place is here." Having lived so long among the Spiritualists, she could not return to a place where her talents as a physician and a healer were not wanted or appreciated.

"I am glad. I have grown to think of you as part of this place. It would not be the same without you."

"I daresay Cassadaga has found a place in Ciara's heart as well. She will stay for a while, I think," Martha told him.

"Your nephew's children must be pleased to have their grandmother here for a visit. I imagine your household is quite busy these days. I have rented one of the new cottages should you need a quiet cup of tea later this evening."

"That sounds lovely. Perhaps I'll take ye up on your kind offer." The conversation dwindled as they strolled along, each comfortable with the silence as they made their way back to the House of Boughs.

* * *

Prudence and her daughter had reached the out-skirts of the crowd when Patsy ran abruptly away from her mother and towards a Seneca man who was approaching from the other side. "Mr. Jo! Mr. Jo! Over here," the child called, waving her arms in the air.

Jo Whiterock acknowledged the child and her mother with a wave of his own and picked up his pace in their direction. He strode comfortably through the sea of wool coats and trousers. At a distance, he appeared to blend in with the crowd. However, closer scrutiny revealed the differences between this man and the others. Many of the Seneca men wore their hair cropped, as was the fashion among the whites, but Jo wore his long black hair bound by a leather thong at the nape of his neck. His coat and pants were made of broadcloth, unlike the finer wools worn by the other men. It was not just his appearance that set him apart from the other men. Exchanging just a few words with the man revealed a humble wisdom that prompted immediate respect. Jo Whiterock was a welcome visitor to the Cassadaga Lake Free Association.

The Free Thinkers had caught Jo's attention when they first started gathering near Cassadaga Lake over a decade ago. Unlike most of his people who were skeptical of this new religion, it seemed a folly of the wealthy whites and many of its followers appeared more interested in parlor tricks than they were a true spiritual experience. Jo was curious enough to get to know the few people who began to gather in the small hamlet of Leona. As the religion evolved, those true practitioners manifested many admirable traits. They had a regard for the sanctity of the natural world Jo had not seen before among white people. They seemed to want more than their Christian god could provide and were interested in learning what he could teach them. The Spiritualists wouldn't win over many of the Seneca, but they found a friend in Jo.

The more time Jo spent with the true Spiritualists, the more he came to appreciate their common interests. They did not dismiss as ignorance the idea that the river had a soul, as did the fish that swam in it, and the breeze that guided it. He told those who chose to listen of the importance of their dreams and of other good and bad omens in the natural world. He was pleased to find that the more time he spent with the Free Thinkers, the more people chose to listen. Today he had come to hear Darius Weathersby speak about finding the spirituality within and had been impressed with the man.

Jo had no interest in taking the stage like Dr. Weathersby or Mrs. Watson, although what he had to say was just as important as those speakers who drew hundreds, even thousands to the House of Boughs. He was sought after by people he considered to be true believers, those who were attracted to Spiritualism for more than the mere parlor tricks that dazzled so many. True Spiritualists didn't just come to Cassadaga to have a weekend away from the city or to consider themselves plucky for listening to defiant speeches from orators whom their neighbors back home thought of as heathens, or worse. True Spiritualists understood the connection between the spirits and the living world. Jo could tell them about that world.

"When did you get here?" Patsy asked him.

"Just this morning, little one," he told her.

"You promised to take me for a ride in your canoe." She spoke boldly to him, although she was usually shy around adults. The whispered curiosity about Patsy and her abilities had made her wary around strangers, but she had taken to Jo immediately. When he looked at her or spoke to her, he saw only the child, not the gifts.

"Yes, I did, and I will today if your mother will allow it." Turning to Prudence, he continued, "I would be happy to take you both out now." One of the drawbacks of camp meetings in Jo's view was that they sometimes attracted thousands of people. Large crowds placed a heavy burden on the lake, which was popular for swimming and boating during the camp season. There had even been steam powered boats this year, which were talked about with enthusiasm by the other campers. A few years back, Jo had constructed a birchbark canoe in the tradition of his people with the help of Daniel and his sons who were interested in the craft. The vessel stayed near Daniel's property, in a popular picnic area called Lily Dale. With most of the water enthusiasts attending the lectures, the lake was currently quiet and peaceful.

"You are kind, Mr. Whiterock, but if you take us out now, you'll miss seeing Mrs. Watson speak," Prudence cautioned.

Jo smiled, looking back toward the crowd surrounding the House of Boughs. "I know Mrs. Watson well." Elizabeth Lowe Watson had been fascinated when Jo spoke of the matrilineal society of the Seneca and the overall respect shown toward women among his people. He counted her as a friend. "She will have the attention of her audience for an hour at least, which will allow the lake to show us some of its secrets."

Prudence weighed Jo's easy smile and the pleas of her daughter against the consequences of starting dinner preparations an hour later. As much as she appreciated the interest Mr. Whiterock had taken in Patsy's wellbeing, she could not risk her new position in Dr. Quinn's house by engaging in leisure activities when there was work to be done. "Another time, sir. Patsy and I got chores that need doin'." Turning to her daughter, Prudence said, "You go on now, and I'll be right along." Patsy knew better than to complain or argue and went off without a word, but her disappointment was evident in the slope of her shoulders and the slowness of her pace.

"The spirits in her are strong," Jo commented, watching the child leave. It was his way of speaking of a life force controlled from within, the same gift the Spiritualists referred to as animal magnetism. It was the best way he could express what he meant and not give up the secrets of his own people. Patsy was powerful; he had seen it immediately when they met. She was not a wielder of *otkon*, what the whites called witchcraft. Jo's own mother was thought to possess strong *orenda*, a power that could be channeled to do almost anything. Jo was said to possess the same gifts. There was always the potential for a person possessing such power to abuse it. His people feared those who wielded *otkon* just as the whites feared their witches. He recognized the power with which Patsy had been blessed and he would help her to understand it.

It was a relief to Prudence to have her daughter among people who did not fear her. She could see in Jo someone who would help her daughter. It hadn't escaped her attention that women spoke to men differently here, more directly. Still, she considered her words carefully. "Mr. Whiterock, Patsy seems to have taken a shine to you and I am grateful to see the child with joy in her heart again." The other Spiritualists, while good intentioned, saw Patsy's abilities as something they sought to study and understand. Jo already recognized these gifts and knew their power. Prudence wanted his help, but was unsure how to ask for it.

Jo could hear the concern and uncertainty in her voice. "There is much I can teach her." He had overheard whispers of Patsy's abilities as if they were something dangerous and beyond control, like a raging wind. He suspected that was because her own fear caused these gifts to escape uninhibited. She was only a child and he could see the peace within her. He could teach her not to fear her gifts. As a child of color, his people would welcome her and share with her wisdom they would not divulge to any white person.

"Thank you." Prudence was too shy to ask Jo when they would see him next and was relieved of the effort as Felicity Nolan approached.

"Hello," she signed. Turning in the direction of Patsy, who hadn't made much progress toward her destination, it appeared to the outside observer that she just stared at the child from behind for a minute. Patsy stopped, turned to face Felicity and smiled, indicating something more had transpired between them. Communicating with only her thoughts was a gift Felicity could use with similarly gifted people who did not know sign language. With Patsy, it became a fun secret that the two shared. Whatever was communicated lifted the child's spirits, and Patsy skipped the rest of the way home.

Felicity turned and had a short discussion with Jo entirely in sign language, which Prudence did not understand. She could not help but admire the ease with which the man spoke with his hands. Turning back to Prudence, Felicity used the spoken word. "Aunt Quinn asked me to invite Mr. Whiterock to supper this evening." After a few quick words about the Nolan's contribution to the meal, she went on her way.

Prudence looked at Jo, who smiled back. "I guess we'll be seein' you later, then."

"Until then…" Jo gave a short bow and then walked back in the direction of the crowd.

* * *

Elizabeth Lowe Watson, a New York native, but lately of Santa Barbara, California, was a trusted friend to the Spiritualists. She had made the trip back east in honor of the incorporation of the Cassadaga Lake Free Association and to speak on the topic of women's rights. An outsider might have been surprised that Mrs. Watson drew an even larger crowd than Darius Weathersby had. The gathering in and around the House of Boughs looked as if it had already doubled and carriages were still filing through the entrance gate as she was getting ready to take the stage.

"Dear God, what unholy gathering have we stumbled upon?" Neala Ahearn questioned her husband as they pulled up to the line of carriages on the narrow road outside the gate.

"I can't say, but I'm that surprised to see such a collection of people here. I was unaware the Free Thinkers were so large in number," Darragh Ahearn answered. "I daresay, it will be no easy task to find the child in this crowd."

Neala had managed to convince her husband that the colored child Patsy had stolen the crucifix that had been carved by Darragh's father. The keepsake had traveled all the way from Ireland and was the only remaining link to that place and the man who had made it. Neala and her husband had left Inis Mór shortly after they were married, seeking a more stable life on the mainland. The Ahearns later followed a cousin to America in 1839 and settled in Boston, Massachusetts. It had been Neala's wish to move to Buffalo some years later. With her children grown, she wished to partake of the excitement and glamour the city between the lakes had to offer.

They had been settled in Buffalo less than a year when the family treasure went missing. It was the intention of getting the crucifix back, not the allegation of witchcraft, that had motivated the man to accompany his wife to Cassadaga. Darragh was unaware that Neala's intentions differed from his own or that the child they sought was connected to Ciara Sloane and her sister Martha.

Neala was determined to see both Patsy and Martha locked away before they could cause the Ahearns any more harm. She was willing to risk her husband making the trip to Cassadaga if she could be rid of Martha once and for all. The possibility of Ciara catching the eye of Darragh again, should he meet and recognize her, wasn't a concern to Neala. Seeing Ciara among these godless Free Thinkers, he would surely realize he had chosen wisely when he took Neala as his wife.

"To be sure, I'll not spend a minute longer here than is necessary," Neala assured him. "One of these heathens must know the whereabouts of that Quinn woman."

Chapter Eleven

Neala Ahearn blew out an exasperated sigh as she followed her husband through the tightly packed crowd around the House of Boughs. What any woman had to say that would draw such a crowd, she couldn't fathom. The shade of the large maple trees offered little protection from the afternoon heat. They had inquired where they might find Alva Awalte or Martha Quinn and were met with quizzical looks from just about everyone they spoke to. Many were annoyed by Neala's questions while Mrs. Watson still had the stage.

There were a few among the visitors to Cassadaga who recognized the names of the women she sought, but did not know them personally. Those Spiritualists who were counted among the women's friends would never disclose the whereabouts of Martha or Alva to a stranger, let alone to a woman who, by introducing herself, had been identified as an enemy of the Cassadaga Lake Free Association. What Mrs. Ahearn didn't know is that the Spiritualists protected their own. Their neighbors and friends knew of Alva and Martha's efforts to protect the most vulnerable among them, like Patsy, and had heard the story of the child's incarceration in the insane asylum at the behest of Neala Ahearn.

By the time Elizabeth Watson had finished speaking, Neala was close to the stage, hoping to get a better look at the crowd from there. As the speaker passed by, Neala placed a hand on her arm to draw her attention from a group of admirers hoping for a word. "Pardon me, ma'am, but I do so hope you can help me. I am lookin' for a dear friend, Mrs. Martha Quinn. I understand she is among those gathered here today."

Elizabeth turned to the woman and smiled, wondering why anyone in this crowd looking for Martha would not address her as doctor. "I don't believe we have met. I am Elizabeth Watson," she said, extending her hand.

"I am Neala Ahearn. I've come all the way from Buffalo to speak with Mrs. Quinn or her companion Mrs. Awalte. Do you know them?"

"I'm sorry, but I do not. I do hope now that you are here, you will participate in all that Camp session has to offer. There will be music and I believe Mr. Raines will have his steamboat out on the lake shortly."

Neala and her husband had split up during their search and so she stood without protection with Mrs. Watson as a rather imposing Indian walked directly toward them. She had heard frightening tales about the Indians and had no wish to meet one up close. "No, thank you ma'am. I must find my husband if we are to get to Fredonia before suppertime." She hastily retreated as the large man approached.

As Neala disappeared into the crowd, Elizabeth closed the short distance between herself and Jo Whiterock. "Did you hear that?" Elizabeth asked him.

"Some of it. She seeks the child." Jo had observed the strange woman approach Elizabeth. Her posture was rigid, rather than relaxed, like someone using harsh words, and he noticed the subtle changes in Elizabeth's own body language as they spoke. Jo had managed to overhear some of their conversation as he drew closer.

"I fear you are right. We must warn Martha."

"I will go and make sure that Patsy stays hidden," Jo told her. "You must fetch Martha."

Mrs. Watson spied Martha and Darius in the crowd and hurried toward them, anxiously fending off well-wishers along the way. She quickly drew the pair aside and delivered her news, pointing in the direction she had seen Neala Ahearn travel in search of her husband.

Martha entered her house shortly after, with Darius behind her to find Jo, Patricia, and Prudence in the kitchen. Patsy was safely tucked away on the second floor. "Where is Ciara?" she asked after briefly introducing Darius to everyone.

"She met us by the lake and returned with the boys to Daniel's," Patricia told her. "She doesn't know about Mrs. Ahearn."

"That's just as well," Martha commented, relieved that Ciara was unaware thus far of the trouble that had followed them from Buffalo.

"We must get ye out of here while there are yet enough people here to hide your escape." Martha told Prudence. Turning to Jo, she said, "They'd be safe among your people."

"They would, but it is a long journey for a small child, and I have only one horse," Jo reminded her. The Cattaraugus territory, where Jo and his Seneca relations lived, was about 25 miles east of Cassadaga, more than three days away on foot with a woman and a child in tow. They might shave half a day off their travels by going straight through the forest, but that would mean they would be sleeping in the rough. He explained this and waited patiently while the others discussed the details.

Martha looked at Prudence, whose expression gave away nothing of the fear inside her. "Would ye take wee Patsy with Mr. Jo? The Seneca will welcome ye and Mrs. Ahearn wouldn't dare follow ye there."

Prudence knew the safest plan was to head to a place where Mrs. Ahearn would fear to follow, and the Cattaraugus reservation was just the place, but in the short time she had been living among the Spiritualists, Prudence had thought herself finally come home. There was no life for her that didn't see her serving others, though here she was visible to those she attended and there was hope of a life beyond servitude for Patsy. These were not things she wanted to give up, though she would without hesitation to keep her daughter safe.

"It is just for now." Jo assured her, understanding the grief hovering just under her fear.

"Of course," Martha agreed. "This is your new home and when it is safe, we will see ye return here for as long as ye like."

Prudence released the breath she was holding and smiled. "You folks have been so kind. Patsy and I can never repay all you are doin' for us." She looked around at the kitchen, a bushel basket of peas that needed shelling catching her eye, and she made to get up and tend to it.

Martha took the basket and set it back on the table. "Jo, would ye please go over to Daniel's and tell him we'll have to cancel the supper for tonight." Turning to Prudence, she said. "Go to your daughter and explain that ye must leave here soon. I'll make sure ye have somethin' in yer belly before ye go."

"I'll stay," Jo told her, "if the angry woman comes here…" He didn't have to say that Neala feared him and would not come in the house if he was present.

"He's right," Darius agreed. "I'll go to Daniel's."

As Darius made to leave, Ciara entered the front door. They had not yet been introduced and he only smiled and gave a short bow as he hurried out. "What's amiss, then?" she asked, looking at the faces around the table.

"Nothin' to worry about, sister," Martha told her. "We'd a little problem, but we've put our heads together and solved it." She took a deep breath and reluctantly told Ciara of the Ahearn's appearance in Cassadaga.

"Ye must go with them!" Ciara told Martha, panic evident in her voice.

"They will be safe with Jo, and I would only slow them down," Martha argued.

"I'm not feared for their safety; I'm feared for yours."

"Sister, ye need not worry for me. Once Prudence and the child are safely on their way, Neala Ahearn will go back to Buffalo."

Ciara stood up straight and looked her younger sister directly in the eye. "Martha, I am beggin' ye to go with them. Ye're not safe here."

Not wanting to be in the middle of an argument between the two, Prudence went up to her daughter, and Jo removed himself to the front porch. When it was just the three sisters in the kitchen, Martha asked, "What is it about the woman that frightens ye so?"

Ciara herself drew a deep breath and blew it out slowly. "There is much ye don't know about this woman, sister." This was a story best told over a pot of tea, so Ciara put on the kettle.

* * *

Ciara was unaware that she had been spotted by Neala making her way back from Daniel's and was followed to Martha's cottage. Before Neala could formulate a plan to approach the house, she saw the big Indian exit and take a seat on the porch. She ran back toward the House of Boughs in search of Darragh. "We must fetch the constable straight away," she told him, breathless.

"You've found them, then? Do ye think we need the constable?" However, Darragh readily agreed when he was told of the guest currently occupying the seat on the porch of the Quinn cottage and they were back in little more than an hour with Constable Mueller in tow.

* * *

Ciara poured three steaming cups of tea, placing one in front of each of her two sisters. "Neala Ahearn was once called Neala Cleary and we were the dearest of friends on Inis Mór. Do ye recall Neala Cleary?"

Patricia answered first. "Aye, now that ye mention it, I do. Come to it, I can't believe I didn't recognize the names."

The older sisters began to exchange memories of Neala Cleary and their childhood on the small island. For Martha, their words unlocked images stored in the deep recesses of her mind. She registered Ciara reminiscing about a particular day spent gathering on the beach. Soon Ciara's voice receded to the background as the memories of that particular day on Inis Mór came flooding back in vivid images she could see in her mind's eye.

She and Patricia were gathering carraigin moss further along the rocky shore, a favorite task of both girls. The algae could be boiled in milk and then strained and when sugar was added, it made a jelly similar to tapioca. Martha stopped to savor the memory when she observed the older girls further up the beach.

Neala lagged a bit behind Ciara as they walked along the shore gathering driftwood for their fires, and whatever might be nice to add to the soup kettle. Her basket seemed heavier than normal, although it wasn't nearly full. The pair had been diverted from their task by the approaching currach. They could easily make out the fishing boat and the tall gangly lad who had nearly capsized it trying to stand and catch the girls' attention. "I daresay, ye best wave back before they all drown," Ciara advised her friend, unable to contain her mirth.

"Joseph Grady will get no such encouragement from me," Neala countered, "fool that he is."

"Ach, give the lad a chance. He is kind and he would do anything for ye," Ciara argued as she watched

the fishing boats come in. Behind Joseph and his brothers was Thomas Ahearn, and his son, Darragh. The third boat belonged to Ciara's uncle Patrick.

"Now that Darragh is a handsome lad," Neala commented, watching as the Ahearn's vessel began to overtake the other two on its way into shore.

"Aye, he is that, but he knows it, so he does," Ciara told her.

Martha came out of her reverie to answer her older sister's question. "Aye, now that ye mention it, I do recall that day. I'd've never guessed the woman who followed us here was Neala Cleary." Martha had been toddling around after Ciara and Neala since she could walk. When she thought back to that day on the beach, she remembered that she had sensed a change in their friendship since Neala's ma had passed. Martha had always been quiet and observant, holding more in her mind than she would reveal with words. At the time, she didn't understand what she saw or felt, but could readily determine that Neala's intentions toward Ciara had changed. Martha closed her eyes, trying to bring herself back to that day. She could see back to that time from the same perspective as she had originally, through the eyes and mind of a child.

The older girls had stopped gathering to watch the boats come in. Martha couldn't hear them, but she could tell they were comparing the lads coming in from the sea. Just then she realized that Darragh Ahearn was the problem. When Martha watched Darragh, she felt the joy in his heart, and it was directed at Ciara. Ciara did not appear to have any connection with Darragh, though Neala did. Neala felt for Darragh what he felt

155

for Ciara. While Neala was not outwardly acting differently, Martha knew that she felt differently toward Ciara, like how Martha felt when Patricia got to ride in the currach to Inissheer with cousin Patrick, but Martha could not. It bothered her that her oldest sister seemed not to realize this. Neala didn't want Ciara to be the joy in Darragh's heart. She wanted Ciara to leave, so that Darragh would look at her. As the boats drew nearer, the bad feelings Martha sensed from Neala grew. Indignant on behalf of her sister, Martha dearly wished a wave would rise up and knock Neala off her feet. No sooner did the child finish the thought, then did the sea rise up and take Neala to the ground. Martha only smiled, unaware of any connection between her thoughts and Neala's soggy misfortune.

If Neala hadn't looked a sight to the lads coming to shore, soaking wet and furious, they might have noticed that the wave hadn't touched Ciara, who couldn't have been standing more than a few feet from her friend. Only the hem of her dress was wet. They might also have noticed the small child sitting further up the beach giggling. Martha's snickering turned to a full-blown belly laugh when Neala glared at her and trudged up the beach, dripping like the seaweed clinging to the branches in her basket.

Martha remembered the incident as if it had happened yesterday. Smiling, she recalled the childlike satisfaction she felt seeing Neala soaked to the skin and fuming mad. It was that day she realized that Neala was in love with Darragh Ahearn. Another incident came instantly to her mind, one she doubted Ciara even knew about, so she told her.

Patricia had been tasked with seeing Martha and their youngest sister Katie safely to cousin Jeanne while Ciara and her mother were occupied with the washin'. Wee Katie did so love to wander from the road and Patricia had gone to fetch the child when Martha noticed Neala leaving her cottage and setting out along the road ahead, her pace slow and her head down, the gathering basket dangling from her arm. Martha saw her straighten up and walk a little taller when Darragh Ahearn approached. "Good day to ye, Darragh," she beamed.

"And to ye, Neala. Have ye seen Ciara this mornin'?" He knew the girls often went together when they were sent to gather from the sea or the hills.

"I haven't. Is there somethin' I can do to help ye?" She knew Ciara had stayed home to help with the chores there, but dared not tell Darragh, thinking he might seek her out.

"I thank ye, but no," he answered, disappointed. He held a posy of stringy wildflowers at his side which had caught Neala's attention.

"Would ye walk with me to the beach?"

"For a bit, I suppose." He casually dropped the posy to the ground since he was unable to give the flowers to their intended recipient.

"Such a beautiful posy. Would ye just toss them aside?" She reached down and picked up the bouquet. "May I?"

Darragh shrugged indifference as Neala sniffed appreciatively at the posy.

"I remember that as well," Patricia said. Surely ye couldn't have been angry at her for takin' the posy. The look on Darragh face told her plain as he tossed it aside who it was meant for. There was no mistakin' it."

"Aye, I must confess that I was pleased she had seen the look on his face." Martha turned to Ciara. "She knew well enough Darragh had no interest in her, but she didn't want ye to know that." Ciara looked confused and Martha shared her memories of the following Sunday.

As the small group of parishioners filed out of the church, Neala pushed through the crowd, knowing that Joseph Grady would be looking for her. Out of the corner of her eye, she noticed Darragh Ahearn making his way toward the Sloane family, who were still exiting their pew. She turned abruptly to catch up with him, nearly knocking over old Mrs. Donohue behind her. When they were close enough to be heard by Ciara and her family, Neala called for Darragh's attention. "I did so enjoy the posy yesterday," she told him.

Martha heard the comment, although Ciara, who was reaching for her shawl, hadn't. Darragh Ahearn hadn't given Neala a posy. He only had eyes for Ciara; everyone else on Inis Mór knew it, even if Ciara didn't. Martha noticed that Joseph had come up behind Neala and had also heard the remark. It grieved him to see Neala fussing over Darragh. Anyone who cared to look could see it. Darragh seemed befuddled at her comment, anxiously looking in Ciara's direction. Martha wished she could just push Neala away from Darragh. As the thought entered her mind, Neala jerked back like something was pulling on her dress. Joseph stepped forward to steady her and she collapsed in his arms. Neala tried to avoid the stunned looks on the faces of those around her as she pushed out of Joseph's arms and put herself to rights. The look that got her attention, however, was the one of outrage worn by Martha Sloane.

"That was you!" Neala hissed at the small child. Martha merely stared at her, daring Neala to make the accusation loud enough for others to hear.

"Can ye believe she actually accused me of makin' her fall?" Martha laughed at the absurdity of it.

"Truth be told, sister, she blamed ye for a lot," Ciara told her.

"I was but a wee babe then. What harm could I have possibly brought her way?"

This was the secret Ciara had kept for decades, the secret that had forced her family to flee Ireland, and she was glad to finally be rid of it. "She thought ye were a child of the Sidhe, a witch even."

"What? Surely nobody took her seriously?" Martha looked at Patricia to refute such an outrageous claim. The expression on her sister's face prevented Martha from asking any more questions. "There's more to tell, I take it?"

"There is." This time it was Ciara who saw the events as clear in her mind as if she were watching a show on the stage, and her young self one of the actors.

The widow Donohue walked slowly down the hill into the cemetery, leaning heavily on her cane. She made her way to the section overlooking the sea, stopping in front of the small stone marker that stood vigil over her husband's grave while she made the sign of the cross.

"There's the widow Donohue," Ciara said to Neala as they walked passed the cemetery. "We should see her safely home when she's done." The hill leading up to the front gate was steep and difficult to negotiate. It would take more than her cane to get the Widow Donohue safely home. The girls entered the cemetery quietly, wishing to give the woman privacy while she prayed over the grave of her husband.

They could hear her voice laden with grief as she spoke to her dead husband, "Oh, dear Seamus, had ye chosen the life of a farmer ye'd be with me today. Ye should have listened to wee Martha. I did tell ye, did I not, on the day that babe was born, she'd be a powerful seer like her great gran before her, for she was born behind the veil."

Ciara froze in her tracks. She remembered that day last year when Seamus Donohue drowned. Ciara and Martha had come to fetch young Patrick's wife, Jeanne, when old Seamus and his wife came through the gate. Seamus intended to borrow Patrick's currach. His was in need of repair and he wanted to determine if the seabirds were nesting on the other side of the island. As he made to leave, Martha got very still, then, without warning she began to wail, begging the old man not to take the boat out. He patted the child on the head to assure her he would be just fine and went out anyway. Seamus ignored the pleas of his own wife, who believed the child had foreseen a horrible tragedy. On his way back in, the vessel was overtaken by a wave so large, the usually stable and steady currach was lifted up and Seamus was knocked into the sea. When the boat drifted back to the shore without old Seamus, they knew the worst had happened.

Ciara hadn't thought about her sister's outburst, nor had she been aware that there had been talk among the villagers afterwards. None of them knew about the caul covering her sister's face at birth. The widow had warned them not to discuss it outside the family. Then again, things like that had a way of coming to light, and gossip could travel on the island faster than the sea breeze at times. Perhaps word had gotten out.

Neala gasped behind her as she overheard the widow's remarks. She quickly put the details together in her mind and then was rattling off all the misfortunes that had befallen her when Martha had been nearby. Neala looked stunned, muttering, "It was her! She did all those things; I knew it!"

"No, ye don't understand. She's just a babe," Ciara insisted.

"Ye were there the day yer sister was born, yet ye've never told me she was born behind the veil, and me yer dearest friend. Did ye not hear Mrs. Donohue's own words just now? The child will be a powerful seer, like her great gran before her. Yer ma must have been stolen for a faerie bride. Ye know well they are given secret spells upon their return! Martha is a child of the Sidhe. Do ye deny it?" Neala demanded. Ciara's stunned silence was evidence enough to Neala that she had kept this secret. "Ha! I knew it." Neala stormed out of the cemetery.

Ciara was speechless. She knew the lore of which Neala spoke. A woman stolen as a faerie bride would be returned when her beauty faded. As compensation, the returned woman was given secret spells and herbs that could kill or cure, and have power over man for good or evil. A child of the faeries was also thought to have malevolent powers. Neala was trying to explain her misfortunes at the expense of Mary and Martha Sloane.

Mrs. Donohue approached Ciara, having witnessed the entire outburst. "Oh, my dear, ye must get home now and warn yer da, for that child is surely on her way back home to tell her own."

"I don't understand, Mrs. Donohue; the caul is not a sign of evil and Martha is a wee angel."

"Listen here, lass, ye know not of what ye speak. Now do as I tell ye."

"I don't understand," Ciara insisted. "How could Neala think wee Martha is a child of the faeries?"

"'Tis not my place to tell ye." Mrs. Donohue insisted, but the desperate look of confusion on Ciara's face forced her to reconsider. "My own mother did tell me of your great gran, Branna Sloane. A powerful seer was she, and no mistake. Kept our people safe, so she did, knowin' when a storm would hit, and when the rains would come, and the winds would blow. She did warn the men one day to come in early, for an evil storm was brewin'. Well, Neala's grand da didn't come in with the rest, and didn't he get caught in it? He was all but dead when his body washed ashore. The fever did take him some days later. There were whispers after that: did Branna bring about the fever because he defied her? For what purpose, I ask ye? 'Twas foolishness, still, but there were some that believed the rumors. Grief will blind a person, to be sure."

Ciara had never heard that her gran was a seer or that there were some who blamed her for Declan Cleary's death. She argued with Mrs. Donohue in disbelief.

"Branna was an old woman by then and passed of the lung fever not long after Declan. 'Tis a small island, and we all depend on each other, don't ye know. With Branna in her grave, the bad blood between the Clearys and the Sloanes faded. There hadn't been a seer born to the Sloanes until wee Martha came along."

The old woman placed her gnarled hands on Ciara's shoulders and looked her dead in the eye. "Come lass, there's no time to waste. Yer da knows the tale I've told ye, and he knows the danger the wee lass will be in when word spreads that she's a child of the Sidhe left here to do mischief."

Martha had listened to her sister's tale in complete disbelief. "Do ye mean to tell me, they all thought me a faerie child? What fools." The truth was that Martha had never really stopped to consider whether she had actually caused each of Neala's mishaps. When the wave knocked Neala over that day on the beach, it had seemed to Martha more like a wish that had come true, rather than a direct action on her part.

"Not straightaway they didn't," Ciara told her. "But ye know the stories of the faerie folk were feared on the island. It was thought that a child of a Sidhe and a mortal mother grew up strong and powerful, but with evil and dangerous natures. Once Neala told her da what she heard in the cemetery, he became convinced as well. After that, they blamed everything on ye. It seems the bad blood between the Clearys and the Sloanes never did go away, it just simmered under the surface. If the washin' was still out on the line when the rain came, somehow it was yer doin'. It got worse over time. Neala's youngest brother came near his death with the fever, and they blamed ye. After a while, any time something bad happened, others would find a reason to point their finger in yer direction."

Martha had few memories of the stories of the Sidhe. She was only four when she left Inis Mór, and it seemed that the faerie folk had stayed in Ireland because she could not recall hearing their stories growing up in Buffalo. "Surely people could not seriously attribute all their bad luck to me!" Again, she turned to Patricia hoping for a different answer.

"Saints preserve us! I had put it out of my mind until now. I suppose I came to think of it as a bad dream," Patricia confessed. "The whispers of folk who would stop talkin' when we came by…Ma tellin' us to keep ye safe when we went gatherin', and then her not lettin' ye out of her sight at all."

"'Twas a small island and the Clearys made their accusations with conviction." Ciara told them. "It made no difference to them that ye were a kind and peaceful child with a quiet nature. They saw what they wanted to see and managed to convince others of it as well. Fear is like fire: it spreads just as fast and does just as much damage. After a while, Pa thought it no longer safe to keep ye here."

"Do ye mean to tell me that we left Inis Mór because of me?" Martha sat there in disbelief as Ciara recalled the events that had motivated her family to leave the island for good.

Ian Sloane held his pipe in hand, although hadn't brought himself to light it. He stared into the fire, so lost in his thoughts, unaware his wife had entered the room.

"Well, that's wee Katie down, for now," Mary announced, having spent the last hour trying to settle their youngest child. She looked at her husband and could tell events of the day still weighed heavily on him.

"She's none the worse for wear, is Martha," Mary stated, with more confidence than she felt.

"Aye, 'tis true enough, until it happens again," Ian cautioned. Young Timothy Cleary had followed Ian's daughters to the beach. He had been teasing Martha along the way, calling her a witch.

"Do ye know what they do to witches?" he jeered. "They're set afire."

Ciara had tried to chase him off, but the lad persisted. He laid hands on Martha and made to throw her into the surf. As he was pushing her toward the water, he hissed in her ear, "...or we could just toss ye into the sea so ye can return to yer own kind!"

Patricia and Ciara tried to pull him away from the shore, but he was a strong lad. Martha was in tears and she wished a strong wind would just blow him away. Just then, the sea breeze kicked up, blowing Timothy's hair into his eyes. He loosened his grip just a bit to push the strands away. Martha felt his hand slacken. She stomped on his foot with all her might and broke free. The wind continued to whip the strands of black hair in Timothy's face, obscuring the girls as they ran up the beach and headed for home.

"*Our daughters are no longer safe here,*" Ian told his wife. *He reached over to the table beside him and picked up a letter. "I've written to Alec in America." Ian's cousin had settled in Buffalo, New York, as a printer. It was a prosperous business in the burgeoning city and he had been trying to lure members of his family in Ireland there for years. "We will leave as soon as we are able."*

Ciara had heard her parents talking that night. "So ye see, sister, we couldn't stay there knowin' yer very life was in danger."

Tears began to well up in Martha's eyes as she realized all that the move had cost her family. "Ma and da died on the voyage here, and wee Katie as well."

"Now ye must not take the responsibility for their deaths." Ciara was fighting her own tears. "Tis likely we would have come to America anyway. Cousin Alec had written to da a few times, and I'd heard he and ma talkin' about it before all of this happened."

Martha did not look convinced. "All that we went through when we first arrived is because of me."

"Ye know well that's not true!" Ciara's voice rose, desperate to relieve her sister of such guilt. "We've had a better life in Buffalo than we would have had in Ireland, or have ye forgotten all our countrymen endured during the Great Hunger?" Ciara's voice softened a bit. "This is why I've never spoken of it before. I'll not have ye carryin' this burden around. I know it's hard, but ye must think of the present danger. Should Neala find out who ye are, there's no tellin' what she'll do. Ye must go with Jo and the others. Neala fears the Indians too much to follow ye there."

Martha forced herself to focus on the threat before them and to consider Neala Ahearn's appearance in Cassadaga in light of what she now knew. She put the pieces together in her mind quickly. "Ciara, I was a child then; we all were. Should the woman realize who we are, what could she do to me now? It was Darragh she was really after. She was more than a bit jealous of ye, to be sure, and in the end, she got what she wanted. I doubt she ever had any real fear of me."

Ciara stared at her sister in disbelief. "I never had any interest in Darragh, surely she knew that."

"'Tis likely she did know that, but ye were the one who had captured Darragh's heart. He would never look at another as long as ye were there," Patricia told her. "It was plain for all to see, except ye, evidently."

Ciara reviewed the details of the memories they had just recalled and suddenly was able to see what she had missed all those years ago. The thought that all they had lost leaving Inis Mór could be laid at her feet crashed upon her like the angry sea. She began to weep for the life they all lost on Inis Mór, the deaths of her parents and her youngest sister, for all they had endured when they first came to Buffalo, and for the loss of her beloved husband.

Patricia looked at both of her sisters, tears streaming down her own face. "The blame lies with Neala and no other," she said with conviction.

Ciara wiped the tears from her eyes, considering her sister's words. The dawning realization of all Neala Ahearn had cost them forced the fear of her aside and replaced it with determination.

"Aye. Now what are we going to do about it?"

Chapter Twelve

Jo could feel their approach like a storm. First there was a change in the air around him, followed by a distant thunder. Although he could not yet see her, he could sense that the angry woman was afraid, and her rumbling could be heard as she told the constable of the menacing Indian guarding the Quinn cottage. Jo rose to warn the others.

Jo came into the cottage to find both Martha and her sisters drying their tears at the kitchen table. "The angry woman and her husband are on their way, and they are not alone." "The constable?" Martha asked, and Jo nodded. She turned to Ciara, "Away ye go upstairs and warn the others. She might recognize ye, but she won't know me." To Jo she said, "Up in my chamber there is a tree just outside the window that is easily climbed. I'll distract the constable and ye can get them down and through the woods to Daniel's."

Jo nodded. There was no need to articulate the rest of the plan. They would use the canoe to cross the lake and wait in the woods for one of the men to bring Jo's horse. It would be safest to begin their journey at night, when the camp and surrounding village had settled into sleep. Footsteps could be heard on the front porch as Jo hurried up the stairs.

"She knows us, I think," Patricia told Martha. "On the day ye left to come here, she came to the door lookin' for ye. She asked if my given name was Patricia. I don't know why she would have done that."

"That may be so, but she doesn't know that we know her." Martha took a deep breath and went back into the kitchen and waited for the knock on the door. It came only seconds later, but she still entered the room and cleared the tea cups before she went back to answer it. "Just ye stay here. I'll handle this."

"Constable Mueller, how may I be of help to ye today?" Martha asked upon slowly opening the front door of the cottage

The Constable did his best to peer beyond the doorway to determine if Martha was alone, but she followed his gaze and moved to block the entrance from his view. "Mrs. Quinn, may we come in? This gentleman and his wife have a rather important matter to discuss with you."

His smile was strained and the hostile energy surrounding the trio was palpable to Martha. Constable Mueller was no friend of the Spiritualists, and his visits to the camp were largely unpleasant. He detested the large number of people that came to Cassadaga during the camp season and, while they were always law-abiding gatherings, he looked for any reason to break up the crowds and send people back to the city. There was no hiding the gleam in the constable's eyes now that he had a serious complaint to investigate.

Martha moved forward, forcing them to back away from the door. "I see no reason not to conduct our business on the porch. 'Tis a lovely day, after all," she said, ushering them out.

Reluctantly the others each took a seat. "What is it I can do for ye, Mr. Ahearn?" Martha looked at him directly, trying to see in the man who sat before her the boy she had known, and it made him uncomfortable and he looked away. Still, something must have jogged his memory because he looked again as if he was surprised to see her. She realized that the hostility that was radiating off the other two was absent in him. He was here seeking justice, nothing more.

All eyes were on Martha, and so nobody saw the scowl on Neala's face. She immediately recognized the woman before her as the defiant child she had known. Sure, Martha hid her contempt for the constable behind good manners, but Neala saw through her now just as she had all those years ago.

"So, you know this man?" The constable asked before Darragh could answer Martha's question.

"I met Mrs. Ahearn a few weeks ago in Buffalo, but no, I do not know this man." Martha wasn't lying. There appeared to be no trace of the lad she remembered and she wondered if he recognized her. She looked enough like Ciara that it could strike some sense of familiarity in the man, but his expression gave nothing away. "May I assume this has to do with the child, Patsy?"

This time Neala spoke up. "The child stole from us!"

"Mrs. Quinn, we have no wish to trouble ye," Darragh interrupted. "We just wish our property returned to us."

"Patsy and her mother are not here," Martha told him calmly. "However, I did speak to them in Buffalo and was assured that the child did not take yer crucifix."

"'Tis a bold lie, for I saw her with the sacred cross in her hands with my own eyes. Not an hour later, the place on the wall where it has hung since we arrived in Buffalo was empty," Neala insisted.

Darragh placed a hand on his wife's arm both to placate and silence her. "'Tis a family treasure, made by my own da and carried over from the old country. We want it back, is all."

While Prudence had told her daughter that they must leave immediately, she withheld the fact that the Ahearns had come all the way to Cassadaga in pursuit of them. Neala's voice could be heard as they shimmied down the tree, first Jo, and then Ciara. Prudence helped her daughter out of the window and on to a sturdy branch.

"Mama, she's here!" Patsy's eyes were white with fear.

Prudence tried to remain calm. "Child, you must move. We got to go now. Pay no mind to the folks on the porch. Dr. Martha will take care of them."

"She's here." Patsy repeated in a small voice, white knuckles clutching the tree branch.

Patsy had moved down most of the tree with her mother just behind when she froze. The tree began to shake violently and the rustle of the branches against the cottage was loud enough to be heard in the front of the house, drawing the occupants off the porch to investigate.

The tree towered above the cottage and the leaves could be seen shuddering from the front lawn. Neala took in the scene: one tree shivering like a dog left out in the cold and the others around it completely still. "'Tis her! I'm sure of it! She set the pots and pans boilin' over as if she were the devil himself! This is her doin' sure enough," she insisted, pointing at the tree. "She should be locked away!" Neala grabbed her husband's arm and pulled him around to the back, leaning heavily on her cane as she went.

"Just where do ye think yer goin'?" Martha called loudly as she chased after them, with the constable at her heels. It was a short jaunt into the woods and she prayed silently the others had time to disappear into the trees.

The minute the tree started to shake, Jo jumped up grabbing the nearest branch with one hand, swinging himself up to grab Patsy with the other. With the child safely in his arms, he jumped back down. Motioning toward the side of the house, he directed Patsy and Prudence toward a large lilac bush that would conceal them. To Ciara he said, "Draw them into the woods," and then he was off in the direction of the bush.

Ciara prided herself on always choosing comfort and practicality over fashion. Wearing the fuller cut skirts of the previous decade and sensible boots, she was able move through the uneven terrain of the forest faster than she might have if she had conformed to more form fitting clothing. However, no amount of fashion common sense could eliminate the sweat streaming down her face and neck as she escaped into the late afternoon heat, which was not significantly diminished by the forest canopy.

"They've run off into the woods!" Neala shouted, walking as fast as the cane supporting her would allow toward the clearing behind the house. She could see someone trotting off into the dense foliage. "We must go after them!

Jo knew it was a gamble to assume this deception would work, sending the constable and the Ahearns in false pursuit of he and his companions into the forest, but it was one he had to risk. Fleeing through the trees with a child in tow would be cumbersome and loud. They could be tracked easily and would likely be found. Instead, he waited a few minutes for the search party to get deeper into the woods and then set out on foot to the road toward Daniel's house.

Their pursuers were a sight, to be sure. The angry woman stumbling over fallen branches, clutching her husband's arm, while the portly constable struggled to keep up. There were no other houses in that direction; they would find their way to Daniel's eventually, but Jo hoped Ciara could keep them busy until he could get Patsy and her mother to safety. "Just walk normally," he told them as they headed out toward the road.

"We still headed to Mr. Nolan's?" Prudence asked, resisting the urge to pull Patsy closer to her. The child was still frightened, but she didn't dare draw attention to them.

Jo nodded. "If we keep a steady pace we should arrive well before them."

Prudence was afraid to ask what might happen should they not. Patsy began to slow down and her mother noticed that the child was walking with her eyes closed, and head bent in fierce concentration. "Move along, child," she warned. Patsy continued at the reduced pace for just a few more seconds and then returned to her mother's side.

They nodded and smiled at a few people along the way, appearing to passersby as if they were casually going about their business. The fifteen minutes or so to

Daniel's house was uneventful and they arrived to find his sons filing out the door along with their father, whose attention was drawn toward the tree line. The crackle of broken branches and rustle of the undergrowth indicated approaching footsteps. Turning toward Jo, he said, "Quick, get ye down to the lake and we'll handle this."

Ciara emerged from the woods. "They'll not be far behind me," she told them, winded from the journey. Turning to Jo, she added, "Ye must hurry."

Jo ushered Patsy and her mother to the banks of the lake, where they would be obscured by thick brush that surrounded it. The canoe would be seen easily from shore if they started out now, so they waited patiently for their pursuers to arrive, find nothing amiss and then leave.

"Away into the house with Felicity," Daniel told his mother. "I'll handle this."

"Ye've a plan? Ciara asked. "How did ye know?"

"The lass," Daniel said. "She warned Felicity." He tapped his forehead with one finger, indicating that the child hadn't used the spoken word.

Daniel could see Constable Mueller making his way toward the clearing behind the house. Darragh Ahearn was further behind helping his wife, who looked as if she might collapse at any moment. He turned to his three sons. "Okay, lads, just like I told ye." Each of them nodded. "Alright then, off ye go. Straight to yer auntie's and not a word along the way to anyone."

The brothers deliberately moved slow enough that they could still be seen as the constable emerged from the woods. "Constable Mueller, what brings ye to Lily Dale?" Daniel asked.

The constable had removed his handkerchief and took the time to mop his brow before he answered. "Good afternoon, Mr. Nolan. We are in pursuit of thieves, who we believe were in hiding at the home of your aunt. They absconded into the woods and we tracked them here."

"Thieves? Here? My aunt wouldn't harbor criminals, and well ye know it," Daniel argued.

Constable Mueller gave Daniel a brief summary of the Ahearn's complaint, all the while fanning himself with his hat. The Ahearns had emerged from the woods panting heavily from their efforts.

"It seems to me my auntie told ye that the people yer lookin' for were not there."

"There was sorcery at work at that house, Mr. Nolan," Neala insisted, "of that I am sure."

Daniel listened as she told him of the bewitched tree, managing to show the perfect mix of exasperation and amusement in response to her accusations. "Ah, that would be my lads, I'm afraid. They ran off earlier to play a prank on their Gran, here from Buffalo. They snuck in from the woods and scampered up the tree in their auntie's back yard to lay in wait." He added a brief chuckle as he continued. "They jumped from the branches and scared the life out of her. Ma chased them through the woods all the way back here. 'Tis likely them ye saw."

"What I saw sir, was a single tree shaking violently, while all the others around it were still," Neala insisted.

"I'm that sorry, ma'am. 'Twas just my lads jumpin' from the branches," Daniel assured her.

Constable Mueller looked doubtful. "Where are your sons now, Mr. Nolan? I would like to speak with them."

"Ah, but ye just missed them," Daniel said, pointing toward the road. "They're away back to their auntie's to confess their sins and apologize for causin' such a ruckus. I can try and call them back if ye like."

The boys could be seen further up the road, but were clearly out of calling range. "No, that won't be necessary. I'll have a word with your mother, though."

Daniel shook his head. "She's not inclined to receive visitors just now."

"I'm afraid we must insist. A crime has been committed, after all," Neala asserted.

Daniel ignored her and directed his comment to the constable. "Ma will not thank me for sayin' this, but she's no' a young woman to be chasin' the lads 'round in this heat." To Mr. Ahearn, he added, "Sir, ye must see that ye've made a mistake."

They were standing outside the protection of the trees with the sun beating down on them. In the late afternoon heat, it became more believable that the boys were responsible for the disturbance in the tree. "Aye, perhaps we have. We're sorry to have troubled ye."

"'Twas no trouble," Daniel assured them. "'Tis easier goin' if ye take the road on the way back."

"Darragh Ahearn, ye know as well as I do that three lads could not have been responsible for what ye saw with yer own two eyes!" Neala was furious as they headed back to their carriage.

"Neala, darlin', 'tis so hot, I can't say for sure what I saw. Ye've sent the poor constable back to the woman's cottage to question the lads. Should he learn anything useful, he'll send word."

"It was that Indian! He must have helped them escape," Neala argued. "If we find him, they'll not be far behind, to be sure."

"For Christ's sake, woman, ye don't even know if they were here in the first place! Now I've brought ye here, as I promised I would, and we've spent the better part of the day lookin' only to be told the folks we seek are not here."

Neala had the knack of being able to summon tears whenever it suited her purpose, as she did now. "That old wooden cross is all we have left of yer da. I'm only after gettin' it back for ye." She made the sign of the cross as she continued to speak. "Ye were not there to see that child work her sorcery in our own home. She is evil, I tell ye, and she must be locked up."

Darragh had the look of a man who knew he would regret his next words. "What would ye have me do?"

"We must find the Indian, I tell ye. If we find the Indian, we shall find the child."

"We'll start lookin' again first thing come mornin' if we must." Darragh held up his hand in an uncharacteristic gesture meant to tell his wife that he would hear no more argument. "Ye'll not like to hear this either, but yer not so young to be chasin' folks around in this heat, and neither am I, to be sure. Come the mornin' we'll go lookin' for the Indian."

Chapter Thirteen

"If ye could 'ave seen the look on Constable Mueller's face when I told him he'd just missed the boys." Martha smirked as she told Darius of the Constable's adventures in the Leolin Woods earlier that afternoon. "I'm that ashamed I didn't offer the man a cold drink, for he looked as if he could use one after traipsin' through the woods for the second time."

Indeed, the afternoon's antics had Ciara exhausted as well. Patricia had sent word with Darius that she and Ciara would stay at Daniel's house for the evening, a message he was pleased to deliver in person. "I wouldn't have either. He's caused more than his share of trouble for our community. Perhaps your breach of etiquette will force him to think twice about how he treats the Spiritualists."

"'Tis kind of ye to excuse my own rude behavior. I suppose it's true enough that Constable Mueller is no friend to us. Still he's a sight better than some of the others who have sworn to uphold the law in Chautauqua County," Martha said.

They were each lost in their own thoughts for a minute. Finally, Darius spoke. "You've had quite a day and it's left you with plenty to think about. I won't be offended if you need the evening to yourself."

Martha smiled and moved closer to place her hand over his. "Don't be daft. I'm glad yer here. If I were alone, my mind would certainly go to places it shouldn't." She had told him of her conversation with Ciara and the reasons her family had left Ireland. "I'm glad Ciara has the wee lads to distract her tonight; to be sure she'd be doin' the same were she here."

The silence returned and stretched out for a bit longer. Darius knew she had things to say and was willing to wait for her to put thoughts into words.

"All those things that happened to Neala, the things she said I did... As if I could summon a wave from the sea to hit only her..." Earlier in the afternoon Martha dismissed the idea outright. Now she wasn't so sure.

"Surely you know it is possible," Darius told her. His voice was gentle, giving her the chance to accept the idea. "From what you have told me, you were upset each time something happened. You were a small child, and would not have had control over your abilities, just as Patsy has not yet learned to temper hers."

"I would never intentionally hurt anyone."

"Of course not, and Mrs. Ahearn, or rather Miss Cleary, wasn't hurt; she was just embarrassed."

Martha remained unconvinced. "I certainly can't do such things now."

"Are you certain of that?" He answered her raised brows with the same gesture. "Think about it. You were so young, and the year you left Ireland was very traumatic. You lost half of your family, lived in the poorhouse, and nearly lost Ciara. You didn't remember any of your childhood in Ireland until today. Perhaps the strain of those events locked your abilities deep within you."

"'Tis much to think about, to be sure, but not tonight. I've got other things on my mind just now." Martha smiled as she leaned forward and kissed him to end the conversation and because she wanted him.

Perhaps the most profound revelation of living among the Spiritualists was that she could ask a man for what she wanted from him, be it physical release or emotional support. More inspiring was that she always got what she asked for. Most men saw women as domestic servants whose job it was to bear and raise their children, keep the home and obey their husbands. Martha had considered herself a fortunate woman to have married Johnny, who both respected and adored her. That there was liberation beyond what she had shared with her husband was an unexpected gift.

Men like Darius Weathersby were a rare breed. His physical attraction to Martha was different than her beloved husband's had been. His desire was not born out of love, but out of attraction. He admired many of the same things in Martha that Johnny had, only just in a different way. She felt the same, and thought it might be attributed to the fact that they had both already found their one true love, and that person was gone to them in this world. Bound up in Johnny's love for her was need and fear: the need to protect her, the need to cherish her, and the fear that she might be harmed or taken from him forever. Darius appreciated Martha in the present. Fear and need were not factors in his feelings, the way they had been with his own wife.

This relationship based on want instead of need emboldened Martha to explore her own desires and seek what would satisfy them. To her great pleasure, Darius was a willing participant in her journey of discovery. With the house to themselves, they were content to remain entwined where they were, casually removing each other's clothing as the need to seek flesh increased. What Martha sought Darius willingly gave. Their attention became more focused. Tongues and fingers explored, appreciative grunts and groans guiding their way. It went on like this until they both were breathless. The idea that she need not be concerned about the noise was also liberating. In the city, Martha had lived in a multiple family home, where what went on in the chamber was easily heard by the rest of the household. Now moaning and gasping brought a new level of intensity to her climax.

Neither of them could talk for a while, but were content to lay naked in each other's arms. After a while, Darius laughed out loud. "What do ye find so funny?" Martha asked, pulling the sleeve of his shirt from the back of the sofa and wiping the sweat from his brow.

"It's a good thing your house is set off the road. Anyone passing by might think we were killing each other!"

Martha chuckled at the idea of some passerby rushing into her home to offer aid against an intruder and finding the two of them naked on the sofa. Sure enough the Spiritualists were promiscuous by Victorian standards, but they were not exhibitionists. "'Tis true, ye were noisier than usual. Perhaps I shouldn't have done this." She ran her hand up his thigh, delighted to find he could easily be aroused again. "You'll have to restrain yerself this time."

Darius kissed her soundly if only to remove the cheeky smile from her face. "When I'm done with you, they'll hear you all the way across the lake!"

* * *

In the hour just before dawn, Prudence and her very sleepy daughter were well on their way with Jo Whiterock headed for the Cattaraugus reservation. They had made it across the lake and remained safely tucked away in the forest until Darius came with provisions and Jo's horse. Prudence was grateful to be astride the horse with Patsy nodding off in her arms, while Jo led the large beast through the dense forest on foot. A tense silence had settled over them leaving Cassadaga and the quiet of the woods was unsettling as they traveled. Prudence wondered when it would be safe to talk, and when it was, what she would say to this Indian she barely knew. The silhouettes of the trees were slowly becoming visible against the sky as the night began to fade.

"The angry woman is no match for Dr. Quinn," Jo commented, breaking the hours long silence now that they were safely away from the camp.

"I reckon you're right, but that doesn't mean she'll just give up and go home, either." Prudence adjusted the dead weight of her sleeping daughter before continuing. "It doesn't sit right with me just leavin' Dr. Quinn to deal with that woman and her husband."

"It's really fear that is driving the woman." Jo had overheard much of what Martha had Ciara had discussed. "She has a troubled history with Dr. Quinn and her sister. She sees them as a threat."

"Fear can make a person do foolish things, even dangerous things."

"This is true, but fear can also make a person cautious," Jo argued. "In the city, surrounded by her people, the angry woman found her courage. She is not among her people here." With her husband's good name and the law behind her, Neala had been able to make considerable trouble for Patsy back in Buffalo. The previous day's events indicated she would be unable to do the same in Cassadaga.

"I wouldn't be so sure of that. These folks got plenty of money to be sure. Seems to me, they are her people," Prudence argued.

Jo considered her words. He had found over the years that the Spiritualists could be divided into three groups of people: the true practitioners and believers who were seeking a real connection to the spirit world, the deceivers who pretended to have answers to the questions the true believers were asking, and the followers who just latched on to what they perceived as a fashionable trend. He couldn't reasonably argue that the latter two groups weren't a potential threat, so he didn't try. "Would you have us go back? The trouble between Dr. Quinn and the angry woman started long ago and far away, when the doctor was just a child. The angry woman can't harm her now, but the same is not true with your daughter. The angry woman comes to accuse her of theft and take her away." Jo stopped walking and looked up at Prudence, "The constable can't arrest Martha for accusations from her childhood, but he can take a colored child accused of theft away from her mother."

Prudence felt the weight of those words. Dr. Quinn had placed herself in harm's way to help two colored people she barely knew. Never before had anyone lifted a finger to help her. The power of that realization left her mute.

"Dr. Quinn has her allies in Cassadaga if she needs them. Our job is to see your Patsy to safety," Jo reminded her.

Jo's comments brought to the surface another source of anxiety. They were headed to the Seneca reservation. Prudence couldn't help but wonder if they had escaped one spider's web only to be ensnared in another. Jo was the only Indian she knew. Would the Seneca people welcome a child like Patsy? Prudence knew very little of their ways and didn't know how to voice her concerns to Jo. She desperately wanted to put her mind at ease, but did not want to appear ungrateful. "And what will your people make of a young colored child who can shake the leaves off a tree without lifting a finger?"

It was not a simple thing to put her mind at ease. The Seneca feared witchcraft just as the whites did, but Patsy was not a witch and Jo was confident his people would see that. "Your daughter does not want the burden her gifts carry."

His words were simple, yet Prudence understood their meaning and was grateful for someone to finally see Patsy as she did. She had the heart and mind of a child. She needed to be among people who would see her as a child first. Was it too much to hope for that the others on the reservation would accept her for what she was?

"She will be safe with my people." Jo hoped this remark would lay Prudence's fears to rest. He had seen in her eyes a wariness of people that likely went back to her days as a slave. Some day they would exchange stories of their pasts that would undoubtedly include suffering at the hands of the whites. For now, they would both see that Patsy's suffering came to an end.

Chapter Fourteen

"I should be on my way before your sisters come back," Darius said, rolling over and reaching for his trousers, which had been tossed carelessly over the bed post. In the hours before dawn they had made their way up to Martha's chamber.

Martha rose and began to dress as well. "Ye could stay and meet them."

Darius smiled. "It would ruin your good name and mine if they were to find me here so early in the morning. Why don't I come back later and you can properly introduce us?"

There was no shame in their relationship, but Martha was unwilling to cast a shadow over it with what she knew would be her older sister's disapproval. "Aye, yer right."

They finished dressing in silence and were walking down the stairs when the door opened at the back of the house. Martha hesitated for only a second before she raised her chin just a bit higher and continued walking calmly down the stairs. Martha was handing Darius his coat on the landing when her sisters entered from the kitchen and took in the scene before them.

Patricia gasped and turned around to retreat to the kitchen. Ciara stared at Martha, her expression giving nothing away. "Ah, I see that yer up. I'll just go get the breakfast sorted." She turned to leave, but stopped when Darius spoke to her.

"Mrs. Nolan, in all of the adventure of yesterday, we've not formally met. I'm... My name is Darius Weathersby and I... What I mean to say is..."

Ciara might have voiced her disapproval, or simply just let the man stumble over his words for a little while longer, but she knew he meant something to Martha and could not bring herself to condemn them. "Mr. Weathersby, I can see that ye care for my sister, and she you. Would ye stay for breakfast so we might get to know each other better?" It pleased Ciara that he looked toward Martha, who nodded briefly in approval before he answered.

"I am deeply honored to accept your kind invitation."

The sisters also exchanged a look that told Martha that Ciara would not hold back in her inquisition and that told Ciara that Martha would listen to her sister's reservations about such an unorthodox relationship, but that nothing would change. Ciara turned and withdrew back into the kitchen, where exclamations and harsh whispers could clearly be heard from the other side of the door. Martha placed her hand over her mouth, attempting to contain her mirth.

"Dr. Quinn, you never cease to impress me," Darius said, turning to hang his coat on the coat rack at the foot of the stairs and to hide his own smirk. "We're all but caught in the act and you are amused." Now he laughed outright, bringing her in and kissing her soundly on the mouth.

"Dr. Weathersby, there's no shame in the affection that we share, and I'll not pretend otherwise," Martha insisted, and then kissed him such that they might have returned to her chamber if her older sisters were not just in the other room.

"Is that what we share? Affection?"

Martha's smile became shy. They had not put their feelings into words, mostly because neither seemed to need such reassurance. She reminded herself of that and raised her chin to look him in the eye. "Aye, among other things."

He dropped his head and brushed his lips along her jawline. "Other things, yes." His smile was warm when he raised his head to look at her again. "We share a very special gift, Martha Quinn, and I am grateful for it every day." He backed away, turned slightly and folded her arm around his. "Now let's go and face your sisters."

* * *

By the time the Ahearns had arrived back in the campground they found the number of people significantly reduced.

"Most folks have gone back to the city," a young man told them.

"What of the Indian?" Darragh asked him.

"You mean Jo?" Darragh nodded and the man continued. "He returned to the Cattaraugus territory yesterday."

"Was he alone?" Neala asked.

"I expect so, but I can't say for sure, ma'am."

Darragh thanked the man for his time and then turned to his wife. "Dearest, ye've heard the man. The Indian's away home, and likely travelin' alone. Now let's be on our way as well. I don't like the look of the sky." Indeed, the clouds had rolled in on their way Cassadaga that morning.

Neala had made up her mind that she would see Martha and the colored child behind bars. With the child out of reach, she set her sights on Martha. "Darragh Ahearn, that Quinn woman is not to be trusted. She helped the thieves escape yesterday and well ye know it. I'll not leave here until she's arrested for her interference."

Darragh took a deep breath and let it out slowly in the hopes of finding an argument that would persuade his wife to let this go and return to Buffalo. "'Tis just a wee cross and we've taken enough time to see it returned to us. We must give this up and go home or we'll be caught in the storm to be sure."

It was the tone of his voice that helped her to decide. He was pleading with her rather than issuing a directive. "I'll not give up!" She turned and began walking briskly in the direction of the Quinn cottage.

* * *

Prudence made her way toward the small clearing where they had decided to camp for the night with an armload of twigs and bark to start a fire. It was a chore she did not want Patsy to undertake. The child was unfamiliar with the forest and Prudence did not want her to wander by herself away from the camp in the event anyone from Cassadaga had pursued them. Jo was seated against a fallen tree skinning the brace of rabbits he had snared for their supper and Patsy was watching with interest. She had been born and raised in the city where meat was sold in the butcher shops, not snared and skinned by those who intended to eat it. The conversation between man and child was easy, and Prudence quietly set the pile of wood at her feet so that she could watch the two of them.

"Mrs. Ahearn has the butcher come right to the door," Patsy told Jo. "That's what the well-to-do white folks do. Ma would go to Behringer's butcher shop on Elm Street for our table. Do you know where Elm Street is?"

"No, I have never been to the city." Jo smiled at the look of surprise on the girl's face.

"No matter. I expect you wouldn't like it much."

"Why is that?" Jo asked.

"It's crowded and smelly. Folks aren't very kind there. Everyone here is pleasant and says 'good day'. Folks in the city don't talk to folks they don't know, like folks they pass on the street. Do your people say 'good day' to folks they pass on the street?"

It was a difficult question to answer. Strangers did not often pass through the Cattaraugus territory and the Seneca had just cause not to trust those who did. It was fair to say that a stranger would be greeted, but whether the greeting was friendly or not depended on the stranger. Jo told her that and she seemed satisfied with the answer.

Prudence knew she should enter the camp and start the cookfire, but it was a joy to watch her daughter so relaxed with this man. She wondered if he had children of his own. She knew he no longer had a wife. She had put him out years ago, which was her right, when he started spending more and more of his time with the Spiritualists. He did not share the disregard for the Free Thinkers that most of his people had, and so had not been taken by another woman for a husband. Although that was not a story he willingly shared, it seemed to follow him whenever he came to camp.

Chapter Fifteen

Maude looked up from her screen when she heard the back door open.

"I thought ye might be needin' a break, but I can come back later if ye like," Dory inquired as she came out carrying a tea tray.

Maude saved her work, and put the laptop on the table beside her. "Thanks, I should probably stop for a little while." She arched her back, then stood to stretch properly.

"Perhaps a wee stroll is in order. The tea will keep for a bit, if yer interested."

Maude raised her arms above her and then bent forward to touch her toes. "Oh, I think that is a great idea," she agreed, reaching her full height again. "Where to?"

"If we cross the field over there and walk down the hill to the road, we'll come to a lovely wee beach. I played there often as a child. To this day, when I've somethin' to sort through I go there and listen to the water make its way to the shore. I'll show ye the way and when ye feel ye need a break again, ye can find it for yerself."

"Sounds perfect. Please, lead the way."

As Maude followed the old woman, she was amazed at just how confidently Dory negotiated the uneven terrain of the pasture. She could hear the ocean just beyond the wall, but wasn't at all prepared for what she saw when they descended the hill. The view was exactly what she had seen in her mind's eye when she wrote the scene of the girls gathering driftwood on the beach when Martha was a child. Looking out on to the beach, she could see bits of driftwood the older girls might have gathered, and the rocky area in which Patricia and Martha had harvested carraigin moss.

The cemetery was right there overlooking the sea. They had approached the other day from the road that wound around from the front of Dory's house. The cemetery was high on a hill, and while the sea could be seen, the beach could not. There was no question about it. Maude had been here before in another life. She could feel it. An inexplicable sensation passed through her body. It was not quite a jolt, but not as subtle as a tingling either. This was where all the trouble that had sent the Sloane family across the Atlantic started.

A series of violent waves crashed on the shore, as if to offer confirmation of that supposition. It made Maude jump back, although they were still on the road, nowhere near the surf.

"Ah, the sea will give ye a fright now and then." Dory's comment brought Maude back to the present.

"I didn't expect the waves to be so… aggressive. Still, it is beautiful. I can see why you like it here. I would think just watching the raw forces of nature would go a long way toward putting any problem in perspective."

"Aye, the sea's as good as a tonic, to be sure. 'Tis why I never left and likely why I've lived so long," Dory told her. "The island has a way of keepin' those of us who were meant to stay, and sendin' off those who weren't. My dear husband loved this spot as much as I did. He asked me to marry him right here, so he did."

They were silent for a while, and Dory seemed far away in her thoughts for a few moments. "Now my James - young Jamie is named for him, don't ye know - came from Inis Meàin, the middle island. His mother was a Quinn, another of the old families there, so he was born and bred to the life same as me."

At first Maude thought she hadn't heard the woman correctly. "Did you say Quinn?"

"Aye. James' ma was Megan Quinn. The Quinn's go back more than two hundred years on Inis Meàin, to be sure," Dory told her.

Maude could not believe what she was hearing. In her books, Megan Quinn was Johnny's sister. Not the same Megan Quinn, certainly, but it made Maude wonder where she got that name from. Could it be that Johnny had spent a portion of his childhood only a few miles from where Martha was born? "Martha Sloane, the youngest of the sisters to come to Buffalo married a young man named Johnny Quinn. Johnny had also come from Ireland not long before her. He had a sister named Megan. Is Megan a family name, do you know?"

"Well, imagine that, the two of them travelin' all the way to America before they found each other!" Dory spoke as if it were true, and that the Johnny Quinn, who Maude at one time had thought she made up, was really from one of the Aran Islands. "Let me see now… James' ma was named for her great gran. The name may well go back further than that."

"Mrs. Griffin was showing me a record of births in the Sloane family bible. Would a member of your husband's family have had anything like that?"

Dory tilted her head back a bit and considered the question. "We've a few boxes in the loft of the barn, sent over when James' sister passed. They've been there more than twenty years. We never did go through them. 'Tis a bit dusty up there, but if ye don't mind that and the occasional spider, ye're welcome to have a look."

Having found herself once again in what Don called a "uniquely Maude situation," she had mixed feelings about this interesting twist of fate. Any other researcher would have immediately sprinted back to the house and rummaged through the spider-infested loft in search of the Quinn family bible, but Maude would overthink her good fortune as she always did.

How would knowing for sure that Johnny Quinn was born on Inis Meàin change anything? If confirmed, it would be another interesting piece of her past, but Maude couldn't figure out how it would help her understand the message from Mary Sloane and the story unraveling in her dreams and on her keyboard. Would the story she was writing be changed by this new information? That was the critical question.

It seemed that Maude was going to have to accept that somehow she could access her past life memories while she was in her writer's trance. Would confirming this information change what she might have written? Johnny was long dead both then and now, so maybe this information wasn't relevant to her quest at all. Maybe it was just another part of the overall history of her lives. As Dory said, they crossed an ocean and still found each other.

Dory waited patiently while the argument continued in Maude's head. Still unsure of what to do with this information, Maude said, "I think I'll wait until Don can help me."

"Aye, well, it will go faster with the two of ye." Dory agreed. "Our tea is getting cold. Shall we head back?"

As they walked back to the house, Maude wondered about Dory's childhood on Inis Mór. "You said that James was from Inis Meàin. So, the house belonged to your family?"

"Aye. We've raised the finest calves in all of Ireland for more than two centuries," Dory told her proudly. "To this day, if ye speak of the Donohue's on the mainland, folks recall my own da, and his father before him."

"Donohue? That name sounds familiar. Do you have other family on Inis Mór?" Maude asked.

"Not anymore, no, and more's the shame of it." Dory tilted her head, as if trying to locate a sound on the sea breeze. Her smile was one mixed with pride and exasperation. "That'll be my Jamie comin' and yer man along with him." She pointed to the road, which could be seen from where they stood in the pasture. Two figures made their way along, singing at the top of their lungs, such that their tune was carried over the field and became louder as each party traveled closer to the house.

Dory and Maude reached the house before the men, and could hear easy chatter and laughter had replaced their tune as they made their way up the drive. "They've become fast friends, so they have," Dory commented. "'Tis no surprise. Jamie always was an easy goin' lad who could find someone willin' to share a pint."

"Well, Don is the same way. Now there'll be no keeping him out of the pub!"

When the two men had made it up the drive, Dory excused herself and Jamie went to do the afternoon chores in the barn. Don seemed well pleased with himself and Maude couldn't tell if it was because he had made some new friends or because he had made it back from the pub on his own steam without injury or insult. Don always was happy to share a pint. "You look like you had a fun day," she speculated.

"That I did. How about you? Did you get a lot done?"

"I did. Do you think you can manage another short walk? I have a lot to tell you." When Don agreed, Maude went in to stow her laptop and apologize to Dory for bailing out on the pot of tea. Don seemed more alert as they set out the same way Maude had just come, and she told him what she had learned on her short walk with Dory.

Standing on the beach, Maude stretched out her arm and gestured around the general area between the shore and the cemetery up on the hill. "Did you see any of this when we were in the cemetery? I'm asking because I wrote about this very beach today. I could see it in my mind as easily as I can see it now."

Don looked around. "I don't see how I could have. I didn't notice it just now until we were at the bottom of the hill.

"That's what I thought, too. It appears you were correct in your assumption that I'm channeling the past while I'm writing." She went on to tell him how the story was unfolding.

"Okay, so that's a good thing, right?"

"The jury is still out on that," Maude told him. "That's not all I learned today." She took the next few minutes to tell him about Dory's family connection to the events they were trying to unravel and about the Quinn family on two of the Aran Islands.

"So, who are you most concerned with right now, the Quinns or the Donohues?" He asked, showing a remarkable lack of curiosity for someone who just found out that his ancestors in a past life may have lived a stone's throw from his wife's ancestors in that same past life. That was Don. He was willing to put his own interests aside to help Maude process all that she'd just learned.

"Well, I don't see how Johnny has anything to do with why we're here. He'd left Ireland before Martha did, and he was dead by the time her troubles with the Ahearns in Buffalo began."

"That makes sense, but I am more concerned about the Quinns."

Maude turned to her husband and was embarrassed to admit to herself that she was surprised. "Of course you are. I'm sorry Don, I keep forgetting that this is your journey, too." She stopped and faced him, taking both of his hands in hers. "I was really worried after the incident at the harbor with Lester that you would be done with all of this. This whole business has been unusual to say the least. It has disrupted our lives and our livelihood. We're keeping secrets from the rest of our family and our friends." She reached up, took his face in her hands and gently kissed him. "I am so grateful that you're willing to stay on this path with me, that you understand the things that I don't and that you push me forward when I need it. This whole trip to Ireland was your idea. I think you were meant to learn some things, too. I forget sometimes that it's not all about me."

Don smiled and pulled her into his arms. With his chin resting on the top of her head, they just stood there for a few minutes. "Maudie, when I met you and realized I wanted to spend the rest of my life with you, I knew it would be a wild adventure. Without you I'd be sitting in the workroom up to my eyeballs in broken lamps."

"C'mon, let's go sift through the contents of the loft and see what we find." With a final squeeze, Maude let go, took her husband by the hand and headed back toward Dory's house.

There was sufficient daylight left that with the double doors of the loft open, there was no need for flashlights. "I wonder how they got these boxes up here," Don asked, looking around. They had climbed a rickety ladder to find three boxes large enough to have been cumbersome to hoist up.

"Who knows, but they're here now. Let's get started." Maude took one box and moved it over toward the open loft door so she could better examine its contents. Don took the second, heavier box and settled down on the floor next to his wife.

"Oh my god! I don't believe this!" Maude reached in and pulled out a stack of letters bound by twine like those Fianna Griffin had showed them. "There's a box full of these!"

Don lifted the lid and peered into his box. "Looks like I hit the jackpot, too." He reached into the box and carefully pulled out a small leather-bound ledger. "It's a journal." Don examined the first few pages, then skipped to a few pages in the middle, and finally looked at the last page. "Don't get too excited; it's some kind of farmer's journal. It's in Gaelic, but it looks like the person recorded rainfall, and maybe some breeding records too."

"Still, that's pretty interesting. Are all of the volumes the same thing?"

"Looks like it. There's no bible in here. How about yours? Is there anything other than letters?

Gingerly lifting three more stacks of letters out, Maude found a few old photo albums. "This is really amazing. It was worth coming up here even if we don't find a family bible."

"True, but we are running out of daylight and we still have one more box to look at." He placed the ledger back in the box and went to swap it out for the next one.

"Don, look at all these letters. They could tell you so much about your family. Aren't you the least bit interested in at least looking at when they date back to?"

"Of course I am, but we don't have that kind of time right now. We still have over a week before we have to go home; we can look at them another day. Let's start with the bible, if there is one, and decide where to go from there."

"Okay, you're right." Maude reluctantly placed the photo albums back in the bottom of the box, but she held a stack of bound letters in her hand, gently fingering through them looking for any reason to untie the twine and read one.

"Okay, look at the letters if you must, but I'm going through this final box. It feels as heavy as the last one, so it probably has some books in it too." He looked over at Maude to see if his description of the contents of the final box had motivated her to put down the letters, but she was already untying the string.

"This stack is from the 1920's." She made this assumption based on the date of the first letter, and that the return address on the remaining correspondence was all same. With a slight frown, she tied them up neatly and returned them to the box. There were many other stacks and she carefully sorted through them looking for the oldest looking of the lot.

"Yup, books, as predicted," Don reported. The first few he pulled out were novels by Irish writers he had never heard of. They were from the 1940s and 50s. As he worked his way to the bottom of the box, the volumes got older. "Wow, this is an interesting one. It's poetry, by the looks of it, all handwritten, but no author." He flipped carefully through the book. "Looks like it is written in Gaelic."

Maude looked up from what she was doing. "How do you know it is poetry if it's written in Gaelic?"

"There are only a few stanzas on each page. We'll have to ask Dory who the poet in the family was, although, this book is much older than the rest, so she may not know who wrote these either." He looked over to find all the letters bound neatly and returned to the box. "No luck on the letters?"

"No, they are also written in Gaelic, and look to be after the turn of the twentieth century. You're right, they can wait. How about you? Is there a bible in that box?"

Don set the book of poetry aside from the others and examined the last two books in the box. Both were novels. "Well, this was a dead end."

"I'm sorry, Don. I know you were hoping to learn something about Johnny's life before he came to Buffalo."

"Well, I'm glad we came up here to look. It would have been bugging me if we had waited. Besides, we don't know for sure that these things aren't relevant somehow."

"Well, there's lots of interesting data in those ledgers. I bet some grad student back home could get a master's project out of them."

Don had been placing the other books back into the box, but he was reluctant to return the book of poetry. Maude took it from him and opened it. "This looks pretty old," she said. There was no cover, just pages stitched together. "Let's bring it back into the house with us and see if Dory knows anything about it."

"Did ye find what ye were lookin' for?" Dory inquired.

"Not really, but you have some real treasures up there. Does everyone here keep so many documents from the past?" Maude asked.

"Aye, 'tis not unusual for those families that go back a long ways on the islands to have much in the way of family papers and the like," Dory told them.

"We did find what I think is a book of poetry, but it's written in Gaelic. I was hoping you might be able to tell us something about it. I can't find an author's name on it." Don held up the small book for her to see.

"Well, I'm happy to take a look. Just ye help yerselves to some fish chowder. Jamie'll do the same when he's brought the cattle in." Dory wiped her hands on the apron she was wearing before she took the book from Don. She reached in the pocket for her glasses and began thumbing through the pages while Maude and Don helped themselves to fish chowder and fresh baked brown bread.

Maude noticed that Dory handled the book like any other she might have pulled off her shelf, rather than the care due a rare historic document. Fianna had done the same with the Sloane family papers. Maude wondered if they did not realize that such historical documents needed to be handled delicately or if they simply didn't consider their own family collections to be rare treasures. The book was sturdy and able to withstand Dory's scrutiny, but Maude had to force herself not to caution the old woman to be gentle. She was relieved when Dory closed the book and placed it in the table.

"Aye, well, yer right that it's written in the Irish. I would translate it for ye, if only I could make out the words."

Her comment made Maude smile. It seemed that the handwriting of the past in Ireland was just as difficult to read as it was in the U.S.

"Ye could try Father Cleary. He's the island historian. He's after readin' all sorts of old things," Dory suggested.

"We found a notation in the Sloane bible that Mrs. Griffin thought he could help us with, too," Don told her.

"We're supposed to visit her tomorrow. I wonder if she would let us take the bible over to Father Cleary after." Maude asked.

"I don't see why not," Dory told her.

Chapter Sixteen

Maude and Don came down to the kitchen the next morning to find Dory in the middle of breakfast preparations, and Father Cleary at the table with a cup of tea in his hand.

"Ah, yer up, then. Wonderful. Look who's come to see ye!" Dory introduced them to the priest and above their protests that she not fuss, saw them seated with cups of coffee.

"Seems Fianna told him yesterday about the notation in the bible ye were wonderin' about, and he did stop by to have a look yesterday," she told them.

"We were hoping to call on you later this afternoon Father," Don told him. "Mrs. MacMahon thought you might be able to help us read this book. It's poetry, I think."

Father Cleary took the book, placed it down on the table, and turned toward Maude. "Fianna tells me ye're a writer."

Maude took a few minutes to tell him about her work and the research she hoped to accomplish on Inis Mór.

"So, ye know a bit of the history between the Clearys and the Sloanes?" He asked. His smile was sincere, but there was a bit of accusation underneath it. It was an odd question and it surprised Maude. His look was penetrating, as if to say this was family business she was after, and no business of hers.

How had Maude's interest in the Sloane family history prompted a visit from the priest? Had Fianna told Father Cleary that she had let Maude read the letter Ciara had written to Jeanne? How could Maude justify wanting to know more about a personal family matter, even if it was so long ago? Her Catholic guilt got the better of her and she didn't know what to do. Of course, this was a family matter, and it was an unpleasant matter at that. They had no way of knowing her connection to this story. Maude certainly wouldn't lie to a priest, but what would he think of her if she told him the truth? Before common sense could get the better of her, she plunged ahead, asking, "Are you familiar with Modern Spiritualism?"

Father Cleary nodded. "Aye, so yer a Spiritualist, are ye?"

Maude looked at Don, who gave her hand a squeeze and gave a quick nod of encouragement. "Not exactly." She took a deep breath and began to tell him of her connection to the Sloane family in Buffalo and of the message from Mary Sloane. "So, you see, Father, we are here trying to understand what it all means."

Father Cleary listened carefully, his expression the usual mask of a priest who had seen it all and judged nothing. When Maude was finished speaking he picked up the tea pot in the center of the table to refill his cup and took the time to add cream and sugar. He stirred the contents and then watched it swirl around. "'Tis quite a tale ye've just told. I should think yer books are very popular. Ye're a grand storyteller."

"Father, with respect, I am telling you the truth." Maude maintained eye contact until the priest turned to Don, looking for confirmation.

"I know this sounds unusual, Father, but Maude believes she has a familial connection to the information she is seeking, and so do I," Don told him.

Father Clearly stared at them both, and then turned toward Dory, who had thus far remained silent. "What say ye, Dory?"

Dory, who had taken a seat at the table when Maude began her story, sat up just a bit straighter and cleared her throat so that there would be no mistaking her words. "I believe them, Father. They have been guests under my roof these last few days and I know them to be good people."

Maude thought her words were generous, considering they hadn't been completely honest about their reasons for coming to Inis Mór. She was a bit put out that the priest directed his comments to Don, but was wise enough not to say anything. "I believe that ye believe what ye're tellin' me is the truth. I'm a priest, but I'm also an historian and a student of organized religion in general. In my opinion, Modern Spiritualism was born out of the failures of the Church. Spirit guides and guardian angels are much the same thing, so are prayer and meditation. How we interpret what occurs beyond our earthly lives can vary, but we share the belief that there is somethin' after we depart this world." He directed his next comments toward Maude.

"I'll not judge any person who seeks a greater connection to the divine."

Catholic guilt rose up like a tidal wave. Maude could not pretend to be religious, nor could she claim to be seriously exploring Modern Spiritualism as an alternative to the Catholic faith in which she was raised. There was nothing for it but to tell him the truth. "Father Cleary, I was raised Roman Catholic, but beyond seeing our sons through confirmation, we are not religious. This business with the Sloane family just…happened. I started some research twenty years ago in fulfillment of the requirements for my doctorate. That is what put me on this path. I'm not sure where it will lead, but I'm prepared to see it through to the end. If it leads me to a more spiritual life, I would be open to it, but I'd be lying if I said that's what I'm seeking."

The priest was silent for longer than Maude was comfortable as he weighed her words. "Ye've heard folks say that things happen for a reason, have ye not?" he asked her. Maude nodded and he continued. "Part of yer journey may indeed be meant to bring ye back to a more spiritual life, as ye put it." He directed his next question to Don. "And what about ye, sir? Have ye found what ye've been lookin' for?"

Don answered with confidence. "Yes, I have."

"Aye, I believe it," Father Cleary told him.

There was a look exchanged between the priest and her husband that left Maude wondering what understanding had passed between them. Don had answered his question in the affirmative, but there was still so much about the Quinn family he did not know. What was he looking for that he had already found?

"Well, Mrs. Travers, I can tell ye what I know. I can't say how it will help ye, but I'll do it just the same."

"You know about the relationship between Neala Cleary and Martha Sloane?" Maude felt like she had passed a test of some sort and could now be told all the family secrets, but she was still surprised that Father Cleary would have any details from so long ago.

The priest chuckled. "Yer history is so short in the States. To those of us here on the island the year 1835 is like yesterday compared to the time our ancestors first settled this area. Here we spend more time around the hearth than the telly. The stories that make up our own histories are oft times more compelling. Aye, I'm familiar with the trouble that passed between the families."

"To start with, the notation ye saw in Fianna's bible with reference to Martha's birth record was a page number." Father Cleary continued. "It was difficult to make out without a magnifyin' glass. That page referred to the place in the bible where they pressed the caul. Martha Sloane was born behind the veil. Do ye know what that means?"

"Yes, I was able to determine that the other day in the cemetery," Maude told him. "I didn't know it at the time, but a friend was able to do some research and tell me what it meant."

"Ye were able to determine that, were ye now? What else did ye learn?" Father Cleary asked her. Dory had been sitting back quietly in her chair, but now she moved forward, eager to hear what Maude had to say.

"Mrs. Donohue, the widow Donohue, had delivered the baby. Ciara and her younger sister Patricia were there as well as their cousin, Jeanne. The birth was a difficult one. They all seemed shocked by the membrane that covered the baby's face. Now that I think about it, Mrs. Donohue asked for a bible."

There had been a slight gasp from Dory as Maude told what she had learned that day in the cemetery and how she had learned it. "Saints preserve us! Ye've a powerful gift yerself," she told Maude.

"I'm beginning to realize that," Maude admitted. "Father Cleary, is the caul still in the Sloane family bible?"

"Aye, babes born behind the veil are said to have special gifts. The caul itself is thought to be good luck. They'd have placed it on a wee bit of cloth and placed it in the bible for safe keepin'. Part of the reason Martha's story has survived is because of that tiny bit of cloth pressed between the pages."

Maude listened as he relayed a similar story to the one she had written the day before. She gave Don's hand a squeeze under the table. Powerful gifts indeed. "So, is a child of the Sidhe and a witch the same thing?" Maude asked. "It seemed to me that people alternately accused Martha of being both."

Father Cleary hadn't used the term witch in his telling of the tale, and didn't feel the need to ask Maude why she was making such a distinction. "Now, the legend of the faerie folk goes back centuries here on the island," Father Cleary told them. "There's more than one person who's stretched a bit of faerie lore to explain what seemed to defy rational explanation. In her mind, they were the same thing."

"Do you think she really believed a four-year-old girl caused her misfortunes?" Don asked.

"Aye, I do," Father Cleary told him. "The legends of the Sidhe make for good storytellin' these days, but back then, folks believed what happened in the stories. What's more, they believed the faerie folk lived among them. There are folk today who still leave a bit of ale in their glass at the end of the night for the faeries who will visit whilst they sleep."

Maude thought it strange that Father Cleary did not mention Neala's interest in Darragh Ahearn and how that might have played a role in the events that happened so long ago. He would have heard the legend from the Cleary descendants, so perhaps they were unaware of her true motives. Still, Maude had heard enough from the priest to be convinced that what she had written yesterday had actually happened.

"Do you think Martha was capable of doing those things?" Maude asked him.

"Aye, now there's a question." That was all Father Cleary was willing to say on the topic. He would not add fuel to an old fire by offering his opinion of the matter. "Now let's have a look at this book, shall we."

It seemed the topic of Martha Sloane's abilities was closed. Maude decided she would not continue asking this line of questions. The widow Donohue had been right all those years ago: it was a small island and they all relied on each other. Once the Sloanes left Inis Mór, any ill will between the Cleary's and the remaining members of the Sloane family would have ceased over time. Best to keep it that way.

Father Cleary was more careful in his handling of the pages of the old book than Dory had been. "Well, if the author is a poet, he's a terrible one," he noted. "Look here, he's included his name in the first one. It's Sean Quinn. This isn't poetry, but I wouldn't call it a journal either. 'Tis more just..." He paused to search for the right word. "'Tis more like reflections. Mr. Quinn is a romantic to be sure."

The book had thirty pages and the entries on each page were short, so Father Cleary took the time to read them while Dory served Maude and Don breakfast. Maude forced herself to eat, but she kept an eye on the priest as he turned each page, his expression giving nothing away. The twenty minutes it took for him to read through to the end seemed to drag on forever. There was a smile on his face when he placed the book on the table.

"It appears young Sean was in love with Mina Donohue. Most of these pages talk of his hopes of askin' for her hand in marriage." Father Cleary turned to Dory. "Who is Mina, then?"

Dory thought for a moment. "She'd have been the daughter of Thomas, and the grandaughter of Seamus."

"Seamus?" Maude blurted out. "I wrote about a Seamus Donohue yesterday. I also wrote about his wife, but I don't actually know her name. I just referred to her as the Widow or Mrs. Donohue because that's what they called her when the trouble between Neala and Martha began."

Dory responded as if Maude's comments were nothing out of the ordinary. "Ah, that would be Anna Donohue. Indeed, she was a widow, but not for long, for Seamus was killed at sea in, oh, let me see…" She lowered her head in thought. "'Twas around 1834, I believe, and Anna passed just a few years after."

A shiver ran down Maude's spine. Dory had just confirmed what Maude wrote about the death of Seamus Donohue. It was amazing that the old woman could recall her family's history with such clarity. Maude silently acknowledged her good fortune that the tradition of oral history was still strong on Inis Mór.

"So, Anna's daughter married into the Quinn family?" Maude asked Father Cleary.

"Aye, she did that. The lad wrote of their weddin' day here on Inis Mór. 'Twas a fine ceremony. The sun was shinin' that day, and all the folk from the village turned out to wish them well."

"Were you able to get a sense of when this was written?" Don asked. "There were no dates that I could see." Don had been hoping for some connection to Johnny Quinn.

The old woman thought for a moment. "The Donohue women were forbidden to marry before their eighteenth birthday. 'Tis a family tradition and I did marry my dear James the day after my own eighteenth birthday. So, let me see, Mina would have married around 1833, I should think.

"Father, does Sean mention anything about a young relation named John or Johnny?" Don could see that Maude was shaken by the knowledge that what she had written the other day so closely resembled the actual events during the time leading up to the Sloane's departure from Inis Mór, but for once the need to find out about his own kin during that life overrode his need to provide her reassurance.

"Mr. Travers, do ye possess the same gifts as yer wife?" Father Cleary asked him.

"Not that I'm aware of, why?"

Father Cleary turned the pages so that Don could see them and pointed to a passage. The only word Don could recognize was *Ian*, which he knew was Gaelic for John. "Well, 'tis true enough that young Ian, or John as ye call him, was a cousin of Sean and was indeed there that day." Father Cleary chuckled as he continued the story. "The wind was high on the mornin' of the weddin' and the crossin' from Inis Meàin was rough. The poor wee lad was sick all over his Sunday best. He stood with his ma at the back of the church, and neither was happy about it."

"That was our Johnny, Maude, I'm sure of it." Don nearly jumped out of his chair, but instead reached for his wife's hand and gave it an enthusiastic squeeze. "All the people of the village turned out to wish them well. The Sloanes would have been there, Maude. Johnny and Martha were both in the church that day."

"Well, isn't that a sweet love story," Dory remarked. "To think, they may not even have laid eyes on each other that day, but they'd find each other again on the other side of the ocean. To be sure, the Lord works in mysterious ways."

This revelation left Maude speechless. Don was smiling at her, certain that what he had told her was true. In her books, Johnny was eight and Martha was four when they met at the poorhouse. She recalled writing in her first novel that he had been watching them from around the corner of the building when they arrived at the poorhouse. She had assumed it was because the three sisters looked so much alike. Could it have been because he recognized them? He would have been around six years old at the wedding of his cousin. Martha would have been around two. Perhaps he didn't so much recognize them specifically, but they had a familiarity maybe in the way they were dressed or spoke that resonated with him. Their memories of life on the Aran islands would have been difficult to recall both because of the young ages at which they left and because of the personal trauma they had each experienced.

Now that Maude thought about it, those traumas were nearly the same. They had each lost their parents and their sister. Although Johnny's sister hadn't died, she was bound out as a house servant on a nearby farm, but he was still separated from her. Maude dearly wished that they were back home at the kitchen table with an open bottle of wine between them so that she and Don could stay up into the wee hours of the night talking about what all of this meant.

"Maude." She was pulled out of her thoughts by the sound of her husband's voice.

They were all looking at her, expecting what, she couldn't say. "This is a lot to process," she replied, mostly because she didn't know what else to say.

"To be sure, the Lord has a reason for revealin' this information to ye," Father Cleary told her.

"Well, it brought ye to the island, to us," Dory added. She smiled at Don, "and here it seems we're practically kin."

"It seems to me that ye have found out a great deal," Father Cleary told them, "but perhaps ye have not found what ye are lookin' for just yet." He stood from the table. "I thank ye, Dory."

The kitchen was quiet after Father Cleary left and Dory was occupied with the washing of the dishes, a job for which she refused help. Maude and Don sat sipping the last of their coffee. When the silence stretched on too long, he said, "We have a few hours before we are supposed to visit Fianna. Why don't we take a walk?"

"Oh, I'd forgotten all about that," Maude confessed. Turning to Dory, she asked, "Do you think it is okay to visit her in light of our discussion with Father Cleary? I realize now that we were asking her to discuss personal family business. I hope she isn't upset with us."

"Ach, no. It's just seein' as though 'tis Cleary family business as well, she would have wanted to have a word with Father Cleary, is all."

Maude looked as if she was disappointed to hear this, and truth be known, she would have liked a reason to put off the visit until she had some time to think about what they had learned from Father Cleary and Sean Quinn's book of reflections. Don suspected as much. "C'mon, we have some time to talk this through. Let's take a walk."

Chapter Seventeen

Maude directed her husband across the cow's pasture so that they would end up at the small beach they had visited the day prior. They walked hand in hand, both occupied with their own thoughts. When they reached the beach, she stopped to take off her shoes and roll up the cuff of her jeans. Don did the same and they padded around in the cold surf for a while in companionable silence.

At long last, Maude broke the lengthy silence, venturing, "I have no idea what I'm going to say to Fianna when we get to her house."

"I'm more concerned with the fact that you don't seem to know what to say to me right now."

"What is it you want me to say?" Her tone wasn't defensive, but his remark had taken her by surprise. "There is a lot here to process, Don. At first, I was excited to learn that Martha and Johnny might have been in the same place, and maybe even interacted before they met at the poorhouse, but now I wonder where that piece of information fits in this whole thing."

Don didn't seem to have a response, so she kept talking. "I feel like everything we learn here has relevance to the larger picture. These families are as interconnected now as they were back then, but that's not what's on my mind just now." She stopped and turned to face him. "In less than a day I have found out that just about everything I wrote since I arrived here actually happened. It has me thinking about what else I have written, and also what I have not written. I didn't originally write about the real reason the Sloane family came to Buffalo. I also didn't write that Johnny was from the same region in Ireland as Martha, or that it's likely that they were at least in the same place at the same time before they met at the poorhouse. Why do you think that is?"

"I don't have an answer for you." Don walked out of the chilly water and motioned for her to follow. They continued walking up the beach toward some rocks that were large enough to accommodate them.

"I wish Charlotte was here," Maude said as she took a seat. "Maybe another ghost would make an appearance and tell her what all of this means."

"You may be on to something there," Don told her.

"What do you mean?"

"Well, that's exactly what happened. Another ghost did show up. Mary Sloane came to Charlotte and directed your attention toward Inis Mór. Maybe the fact that you didn't write about certain details of Martha's past troubled her enough to try to remind you of that time."

Maude's laugh had a nervous edge to it as she entertained visions of the ghost of Mary Sloane reading her books. "Do you mean that I was repressing these events? Why would she want to drag all of this up? The person I was then is long gone."

"Try to think of her as a spirit guide who only has your best interest at heart," Don suggested.

Maude considered his words. "I do remind myself of that occasionally. I have to believe that at the end of all of this, our lives will be changed for the better."

"They have already changed for the better," Don told her.

Maude was reminded of the look that had passed between her husband and Father Cleary after he had asked if Don had found what he was looking for. "Maybe for you. What is it that you think you have found?"

There was no need for her to explain the question, Don knew what she was asking. "I found what I was looking for the day we met. Being on this journey with you has only confirmed what I already knew. Learning that it has been this way across many lifetimes is just gravy."

Maude was not prone to tears, so she leaned in and kissed her husband before he could see her eyes fill up. She stayed in his arms, not feeling the need to say anything. Finally, she spoke, when she was certain her eyes were dry and her voice was steady. "I can face whatever we learn on this journey as long as we're together."

Don gave her hand a squeeze. "I'll be right there with you, be it alongside you or nudging from behind."

Maude noticed as the sun peeked out from behind a cloud that it was a bit higher in the sky than when they arrived. "Do you think Fianna would be upset if we cancelled on her with such short notice?"

"It would be rude to even consider that. I'm sure she went to some trouble in the kitchen in anticipation of our arrival. Why do you ask?"

"Well, it seems to me that the fastest way to get some answers to my many questions is just to keep writing the book. Between my conversation yesterday with Dory and our visit from Father Cleary this morning, I'm comfortable believing that what I end up writing has already happened. I was thinking of grabbing my laptop, finding a comfortable place to sit and seeing what happens."

Don was intrigued by the idea. "Why here?"

"I'm not sure. It's just a feeling I have. It seems like this is where the trouble began. Maybe I'm wrong, but I feel connected to this place."

Don had noticed that Maude grabbed her backpack before they set out. Now he realized that she was hoping for the opportunity to sit here and write. He considered the possibility of getting some answers against offending Fianna, who may also have more valuable information to offer. "I have an idea. Why don't you stay here and I'll go and visit Fianna?"

"That's a great idea. I can meet you in the pub later for dinner and we can exchange notes."

Maude was settled against a large rock far enough from the surf that she wouldn't get wet when the tide came in. The overcast sky would keep the glare off her screen, and she hoped it didn't spell rain, either. For a while she just sat there, looking out over the ocean, allowing the sounds of the sea birds and the crashing waves to clear her mind. It was helpful to read the last chapter she had written, and as her focus switched to the screen, the sights, sounds and smells of the beach began to recede and were replaced by those of Martha's kitchen in Lily Dale, where breakfast preparations were underway.

The scene was a bit awkward seeing as Ciara and Patricia had entered the house not a quarter hour before to find their sister all but in the embrace of Darius Weathersby. The man was now seated at the kitchen table, while Martha set the dishes and cutlery around him and Ciara rummaged in the pantry for butter and honey. Patricia made no attempt to disguise her discomfort and sat at the opposite end of the table with her hands folded neatly on the table and her lips compressed in a tight line.

The sounds of the birds going about their morning routine in the woods just behind the cottage could be heard above sizzling bacon. Ciara fussed over the cast iron skillet, taking more time than was needed to remove it from the stove. While she had made up her mind to be kind to Dr. Weathersby, she would have answers to her questions nonetheless. If Michael had been there it would have been he who determined if Weathersby's intentions toward Martha were honorable, but he was not there and the responsibility was now Ciara's. "Will ye be stayin' on here now that the visitors have left?" she asked him.

"For a while, yes. I have rented the cottage until the end of the month."

"This time of year, Darius travels quite a bit," Martha interjected. "He lectures at many of the other

Spiritualist Communities around the country." The truth was that Martha had considered joining him in his travels, but she hadn't had an opportunity to raise the issue, and so thought it wise not to mention just yet.

"Where do you call home, Dr. Weathersby?" Patricia asked in her best authoritative teacher's voice.

Darius was spared the need to answer the question when a knock came on the door. "Who could that be at this hour?" Ciara asked as she moved to answer it. As the words '*Oh dear God!*' came out of her mouth, the others stood and followed her out of the kitchen. From the parlor window, they could see Neala and Darragh Ahearn standing on the porch.

"Ladies, why don't you go back to the kitchen and let me handle this." Darius moved ahead of them toward the door.

"No," Martha told him. "'Tis time we confronted this woman once and for all. Isn't that right, sisters?"

"Aye, I have a few things to say to Neala Ahearn," Ciara agreed.

Martha waited until Darius and her sisters were seated in the parlor before opening the door.

"Mr. and Mrs. Ahearn, what can I do for ye so early this morning?" This time, Martha stood aside and allowed them to come in.

"Mrs. Quinn, I do apologize for the hour. We're wantin' to be on our way back to Buffalo ahead of the storm this mornin' and just hoped to have a quick word with ye before we're on our way." Darragh was clearly uncomfortable calling on the house so early in the morning.

Martha looked beyond them and noticed the overcast sky. Darragh was right; a storm was not far off. "Aye, well then, come in and state yer business so that we can get back to our breakfast," Martha told them.

The three of them entered the parlor and Martha made a quick introduction to Darius, who rose to greet them. "I know ye've already met my sisters." Ciara stood and looked directly at Neala. "That would be Mrs. Ciara Sloane Nolan and Mrs. Patricia Sloane Thomas, late of Inis Mór. Oh, and I am *Dr.* Quinn. Martha Sloane Quinn. Ye may recall we had a younger sister, Katie Sloane, but sadly God took her on the journey to America all those years ago. Ye do recall when my family fled to America, do ye not?" Martha maintained eye contact, waiting for them to search their memories and recognize the names.

Neala said nothing, but Darragh knew them immediately. "Saints preserve us! Ciara Sloane, after all these years, and Patricia and wee Martha, too. We were that sorry when we heard of yer parents and wee Katie." Turning to his wife, he said, "Can ye believe it, my dear? Ciara Sloane here in Cassadaga and isn't she the very image of her young self!"

Darragh's kind words infuriated his wife. "Dear god, husband, have ye forgotten why they left the island? Wee Martha here was a child of the Sidhe to be sure, and she did use her evil powers to do me harm. Ye may have forgotten, but I haven't!"

Martha spoke. "I am the daughter of Ian and Mary Sloane and no other! I'm also not a fool. I know what you did all those years ago, even if my dear sister doesn't." Martha's remarks were met with stunned silence.

Darragh's heart had been broken when Ciara left Inis Mór with her family, and although he had never said so, he hadn't believed the rumors about wee Martha. "Dear sweet Martha, let me apologize for my wife. I never did believe ye to be a faerie child." He turned and glared at Neala, whose outrage over his remarks only grew.

"Ye doubt me, do ye? Have ye lost what little sense ye had, man? The very reason we are here is to find the other witch who stole from us. Who did she come to for aid? Who took her in and hid her from us?" Neala thrust a pointed finger in Martha's direction. "*She* did!" Then she directed her venom at Martha. "Where have ye hidden that dreadful creature? She's away with the Indian I expect. Ye've got everyone under yer spell, so ye have."

"Now listen here, Neala," Patricia said, moving between the old woman and her sister. "I've had just about enough of yer accusations. That child is no more a witch than is my sister! Ye will leave her in peace."

"I'll have what's mine and I'll have the both of them in shackles!" Neala was shaking, but whether it was out of fear or anger, only she knew.

"Go on and get it then if ye think she stole from ye," Martha told her. "Ye are right, she left with our friend Jo yesterday, with an escort of ten other Seneca men." A bit of exaggeration seemed appropriate in the event the Ahearns considered pursuing the child. "She'll be safe in the Cattaraugus territory soon enough. There isn't a constable in all of New York who will set foot on the reservation to retrieve that child. Just ye go there and make yer accusations. See how far ye get."

"I knew ye would protect her!" Neala shouted. "Ye witches, both of ye! The constable may fear the Indians, but he loathes the Free Thinkers. I'll have ye arrested for aidin' a criminal!"

"'Tis you that's lost yer senses, Neala," Ciara told her. "For we've told ye more than once that the child has done no wrong by ye. Now be gone, or yer dear husband will learn the truth about ye!"

"Would ye let her talk to me like that?" Neala's cane was no longer able to support her, and she grabbed her husband's arm for stability, nearly throwing him off balance as well.

Darragh tried to get Neala to sit but she refused. "To be sure there was trouble between the families back on the island, but that was so long ago. Surely ye can see past that now," he said to his wife.

"See past that now?" It was Martha who spoke up. "I thought ye a fool when we were young, but sure enough ye've grown into a right buffoon. I'll not be seein' past anythin', Darragh Ahearn, and neither will ye, for it was yer wife who started all the trouble on Inis Mór, and for ye, no less!" Darragh's eyes grew large, but Martha kept on talking. "I knew ye had eyes for our Ciara, and sure enough Neala knew it as well. She wanted ye for herself and she knew that wouldn't happen as long as Ciara was on the island. I was nearly drowned because of her spreadin' rumors. As if a wee babe could make the sea rise! We were forced to leave, and we lost ma, da, and wee Katie to the ship fever along the way. We'd no choice but the poorhouse when we finally got to Buffalo, all because Neala wanted ye, and here she is all these years later at it again. Didn't we just lose my sister's dear husband because your Neala had poor wee Patsy sent to the asylum?!"

Martha turned her attention to Neala, "Well, I hope the two of ye have been happy all these years. Did ye ever think what it cost to get him?"

"What it cost to get him, ye ask?" Neala moved unsteadily toward Martha. "I'll tell ye what ye Sloane witches have cost me and mine! For it was Branna Sloane who let the sea take my great grand da, and well ye know it! When ma got the lung fever, it was yer own ma at her side when she died, and me left to keep the house for pa and my four brothers. I'd no sisters to help with the chores, like ye did. The only way out of that house was through marriage." She turned toward Ciara. "The best man, the hardest workin' and kindest man was my Darragh, but he couldn't see me if ye were around. And then there was this one," she turned again and pointed in Martha's direction. "Ye were an odd one from birth, quiet, but always watchin' folk. Ye did yer best to make a fool of me whenever Darragh was around, so ye did. 'Tis no fault of mine that others began to notice the evil in ye."

Ciara was in tears. "Neala, I considered ye one of my sisters."

"Well, ye had plenty of those, to be sure, and I had none. My Darragh saved me from becomin' a spinster, for another year of keepin' the house for da and the lads and I'd have been worn down to nothin'. No man would have wanted me. I'll not regret a thing I did to get him."

"We were forced to leave our home," Martha said, in a voice so low it was menacing. "We lost half of our family because of ye." Rage such as she had never felt before invaded her senses, and she began to tremble with it, her voice growing louder. "Have ye any idea what it was like? We were orphans in a strange land, forced to live in the poorhouse. Ye are a wicked, wicked woman Neala Ahearn." Before Martha could say another word, the sound of thunder rumbled overhead, and a gust of wind blew through the window slamming the parlor door shut. The sun was completely obscured behind a wall of thick grey clouds and without the lamps lit, the room had grown considerably darker. They were all surprised by the noise and unnerved by the sudden change in the room.

"See there," Neala yelled, "that's her doin', sure enough!"

"Ye fool! Ye think I can summon a storm? Well, wouldn't every farmer in New York be delighted if that were true."

Neala turned to her husband. "'Tis her! I know it. Ye've seen now what she is capable of. Surely ye can't deny yer own eyes."

Darraghs eyes held pity in them as he tried to reason with his wife. "'Tis just the storm. Did I not tell ye we should have been on our way already? We can only hope it passes soon so we can be headin' home."

The rain was coming down hard now but Martha didn't care. She wanted them gone from her home. "Ye're a fool indeed, Darragh, if ye are thinkin' I'd offer ye a place to bide until the storm passes," she told him. "After what yer wife has done to me and mine, she's not welcome here another minute. Let her be soaked to the skin for all I care!" Martha was trembling with anger and Darius came up and ushered her over to a chair by the window.

"Ye got what ye deserved for all the trouble yer family has caused mine. Had I known ye'd come to America to offer aid and comfort to those like ye, I'd have seen ye burned myself!" Neala bellowed.

"That is enough, woman!" Darragh had said very little, stunned almost into speechlessness by Neala's revelations, but she had gone too far. "Ye had a hard life as a lass, and ye the only one to keep the house after yer ma passed on, but ye and I, we've done well for ourselves. How can ye hold such anger in yer heart?"

"How can ye ask me that when ye never had so much as a word to say to me, kind or otherwise, if *she* was there? I'd have been stuck in that wee cottage until death took me if Ciara had remained of the island. Ye'd have married her, do ye deny it?"

Darragh couldn't deny it, but Ciara could. "'Twas long ago, Neala, that ye and I were young girls. Perhaps ye have forgotten that I'd no interest in Darragh. If he'd have asked for my hand, I'd have refused him. I'd have told ye that if ye had thought to ask."

Darragh did not seem shocked or offended by Ciara's comment. When he answered his wife, his voice was gentle. "My darlin', I won't deny that Ciara caught my eye when we were young, but in the end, I married ye because I loved ye, not because Ciara left. I'd have realized that even if she hadn't gone, for I have loved ye all the years between then and now."

Neala had stood expressionless as Ciara spoke, but Darragh's words brought her to tears. Still, the desperation and uncertainty of her youth would not be so easily dispelled. "Ye'd have me just believe ye, me, weary to the bone and desperate to get away, and ye expected me to wait until ye refused him." Turning from Ciara toward her husband, her tirade continued. "Ye are truly a fool, Darragh Ahearn, if ye have seen the evil done here with yer own eyes and refuse to accept it. I see that all these years have passed and nothing has changed. I've only myself to rely on." With a sweep of her cane, she cleared herself a path and rushed out of the house with the agility of someone half her age. The others had been stunned by her abrupt departure, but were spurred into action by a clap of thunder and the sound of harnesses rattling as the carriage took off into the storm.

"She's run off!" Darragh was in a complete state of panic. "She's never driven a carriage in all her years." He ran for the door.

"You won't catch her on foot," Darius cautioned. The few year-round cottages in the Spiritualist community boarded their horses at a stable about half a mile away. It had been recently built to accommodate the influx of horses during the camp meetings. Normally Alva's team would be there, but she was away currently. Martha would have simply rented a horse and carriage if she had need of one.

"She'll have gone to fetch Constable Mueller," Patricia predicted.

"I can't just sit here and wait," Darragh insisted. "The team will be easily spooked in this weather. She could be hurt." He was out the door before anyone could talk him out of it.

"He's a fool," Patricia said. "He'll catch his death out there in this weather."

"We'd be bigger fools to go after him." Martha's voice was entirely without sympathy.

"Sister, have ye any shred of yer Christian self left? He's an old man and not to blame for what happened to us," Ciara reminded her.

"Now listen here," Martha told her sisters in a tone that made them forget she was the youngest of the three. "I've lost enough of my family because of that women. I'll lose no more."

"I'll go after him," Darius said, already moving toward the hall to retrieve his coat.

"Thank ye, Mr. Weathersby," Patricia said before Martha could argue with the man. "Do be careful."

Darius gave Martha a look meant to reassure her. "I'd best be off. He'll not have gone far."

* * *

The rain was coming down hard. Darragh moved at a brisk trot, squinting against the water pouring down his face. Thunder echoed through the sky and the lightning bolt that followed provided a brilliant flash of light. Over the pounding rain Darragh heard a loud crack followed by the shriek of panicking horses. Neala was in trouble. He continued at a flat out run.

At the bend in the road a tree had fallen and spooked the team of horses. Neala was desperate to regain control as their panic forced the beasts backward.

She didn't see Darragh run up along the side of the carriage. The horse reared up as he tried to make a grab for the reins, knocking him down. Still panicked, the team spun around seeking to bolt in the direction opposite the fallen tree. Neala had been tossed off the bench and was on the floor of the carriage clinging to it, having abandoned any idea of trying to calm the horses.

"Darragh!" She could see him flat on the ground as the carriage turned.

Darius had set out from the house at top speed and came upon the scene just as Darragh had been knocked to the ground. He approached the team from behind as they began to turn and catapulted himself into the carriage, nearly kicking Neala, who was still on her knees. He pushed her aside and made a grab for the reins as the team bolted toward the open road.

"Darragh!" Neala screamed as she saw him lying on the road motionless. "Ye must help Darragh!" She began grabbing at Darius' hands, trying to turn the racing team around as he struggled to control them.

"Are you mad, woman? You'll kill us both!" He elbowed her hard until she relented, not daring to take a hand from the reins. It took another quarter mile to calm the team down. He stopped and quickly asked her whether she was okay and Neala responded with a brisk nod. Without another word, he turned the horses around and headed back toward the downed tree and the man who had fallen near it.

Darius pulled up, handed Neala the reins and jumped out of the carriage. "Stay here." He ordered.

Darragh was lying face down in the mud. "It's his head," Darius called, gently turning the man over and wiping his face clean. There was a deep gash at the top of his skull. It looked like the front edge of a hoof might have struck him as the horses tried in their panic to turn around. It was hard to ascertain the extent of the bleeding in the hard rain. Darius could see that he was breathing. "Can you hear me sir?" Darragh nodded. "Let's try to get you to your feet, then."

The man was dead weight and completely sodden, so it took a few tries to get him upright. Finally, Darius managed to get him up and into the wagon. They were quiet on the way back to Martha's cottage, but Darius was too focused on keeping the edgy horses under control to notice how odd it was that Neala had remained in the front seat of the carriage rather than riding in the back next to her injured husband.

Martha and her sisters met the carriage as it pulled up. It took all three of them and Darius to get Darragh into the house and on to the bed in the ground floor chamber. Ciara went to fetch towels while Patricia saw to make Neala as comfortable as possible in her drenched clothing.

"The wound is grave," Martha told Darius. "His skull is fractured." Ciara had come back and handed each of them a towel. "I'm afraid there's nothing I can do," Martha told her quietly.

Darius looked out the window and noticed that the rain had stopped. "I'll fetch Mrs. Ahearn. She should be with him." He exited and Martha receded to a corner of the room to dry herself as best she could, leaving Ciara at the bedside.

"Ye are a sight for sore eyes, Ciara. I'm that sorry for all the trouble we've caused ye, then and now," Darragh said, the words struggling to come out.

It had been a shock to see the man Darragh Ahearn had become, prosperous but not at all the arrogant lad she had known. Looking down on him now, in his final moments, she could only squeeze his hand and smile. She could think of no words that would comfort him and yet still ring true.

Martha approached, and he smiled like a proud father, as if her hateful words toward him had never been spoken. "Wee Martha a doctor, and a Quinn forbye. A fine family, the Quinns of Inis Meáin."

Any conflicting feelings Martha had for Darragh vanished with that comment and she could only stare at him dumbfounded. It was Ciara, after a few speechless moments, who responded. "Johnny Quinn lived in Buffalo. We don't know where his kin were from."

"Ah, well, there's Quinns on Inis Meáin, to be sure." Darragh had no further explanation to remove the stunned expressions on both of their faces. "Ye remember them, don't ye? I'm sure ye do."

Neala stood in the doorway, watching as the two women she hated most in life sat idle with her husband. She glared at Ciara, but directed her hostility at Martha. "Ye'll just let him die, and ye a doctor. That's proof enough yer a witch!"

Darragh turned to his wife, the effort it cost plain on his face. "Darlin', there's none who can keep me from the good Lord now. Will ye spend what little time I have left fightin'? Come to me."

Ciara and Martha stepped out of the room to give them their privacy. "How long?" Ciara whispered.

"Not long," Martha answered.

About an hour later, Martha went to check on them. She opened the door to find Neala weeping over the still form of her husband. "He's gone. My dear sweet Darragh is gone. I blame ye, Martha Sloane. Ye did all of it. The storm, the fallen tree, the horses, all of it! Ye are evil to the core!" She rose as if she had more to say, but the look on Martha's face made her pause.

Martha could only stare back at her. She would not argue when a man had just lost his life. Furthermore, she would not tell Neala that her husband's death was her own fault. Martha despised the woman, but she wasn't cruel.

"Mrs. Ahearn, I am very sorry for your loss." Darius had followed Martha to the chamber. "You will have to make some arrangements to transport your husband back to Buffalo. Allow me to offer you my cottage for the evening, so that you might rest." Without waiting for a reply, he moved past Martha to gently usher Neala out of the room.

"Take me to the constable! This is her doin' and I'll have justice!" Neala insisted.

"You've had such a shock. I'll send for the constable to come to you," he assured her as they left the house. "You need to rest just now." To everyone's relief, she didn't argue further and allowed herself to be ushered out. Darius looked briefly behind him, finding Martha. She knew he would seek out Daniel, not only to deal with the constable, but also to help in getting Neala Ahearn and her husband's body back to Buffalo.

The encounter had left the sisters drained. Martha was silent, her cup of tea untouched. Confronting Neala had left her with more questions than answers. "Imagine thinkin' that I can summon a storm. That woman belongs in the asylum, to be sure!"

Ciara looked up at her sister. "Are ye entirely sure ye didn't?"

"Have ye lost yer senses as well?" Martha countered.

"Sure enough, I have my wits about me. My eyes work just fine, too. Ye didn't see yerself, sister. Ye were boilin' mad, and no mistake. Who's to say the skies didn't darken because of it? I could feel the anger comin' off of ye. It was surely powerful enough to slam a door shut."

Patricia's expression was carefully neutral. She had no intention of getting between her sisters on this topic.

"But I did not wish any of that to happen. It just happened." Martha still was not convinced she had caused any part of the storm. "The sky was already overcast when I woke up this mornin'." Was anger really that powerful? Could this happen again? These were questions she needed answered, but was afraid to ask.

Ciara's next comments made Martha wonder if her own sister also possessed Felicity's ability to hear people's thoughts. "Seems to me this is somethin' ye should speak to Alva about. Promise me that ye will."

"Aye, I promise." Martha had not wanted to discuss the Quinns of Inis Meáin, but now the subject seemed preferable to the current topic of conversation. "I don't remember Quinns on the islands."

"I do," Ciara replied. "Now that I think on it, I remember Sean Quinn married a lass from Inis Mór. We were at the weddin', though I doubt the two of ye would remember. Ye were so young." Patricia and Martha both looked uncertain, so Ciara continued. "There was a wee lad at the back of the church, the smell of sick about him. He was called Ian, I think." She closed her eyes, trying to see if the lad in the church bore any resemblance to the boy she had met on the day they were admitted to the poorhouse. "It was him! Dear God, it was Johnny at the back of the church that day on Inis Mór!"

Chapter Eighteen

Maude closed her laptop, wondering if what she had written was true or if she was only spinning what she already knew. Worse yet, either outcome was equally disturbing for different reasons. If she had been able, once again, to extract accurate details of the past from her mind, it would force her to accept this new gift and then overthink the ramifications of it. If what she wrote was a fabrication, she was no closer to understanding what had brought them to Inis Mór in the first place.

The sky was still grey and it was hard to tell how late in the day it was. Her watch was still set to Buffalo time and she had to do some quick math to determine that it was approaching four o'clock. Don had likely finished his visit with Fianna and was seated on a stool in the pub. It took a few minutes to restore the circulation to her limbs and work out the kinks in her back. "Note to self: no more writing on the beach," she said out loud while packing up her laptop.

The surf continued rolling in, unperturbed by Maude's anxiety. She stood there watching it, hypnotized by the sound of the sea. Just the crossing from Inis Mór to Galway would have been dangerous for the Sloane family, if her experience on the ferry was any measure. They would have likely taken two boats to transport a family of six and their belongings. Maude looked over the horizon towards Galway, certain she would see two currachs rowing in that direction. She had visions of the past before when kayaking around the Buffalo River, but they came unsolicited and unexpected. "Oh well, it was worth a try," she said to the gull that was investigating the seaweed near her when all she saw was a few modern sail boats. Perhaps not all her gifts could be tapped on demand.

"How did it go?" Don asked his wife when she entered the pub. There were a few patrons sitting at the other end of the bar and another playing the tin whistle at a table in the corner.

"I'm not sure, but I have a lot to discuss with you. How did your talk with Fianna go? Was she upset that I wasn't with you?"

Don motioned to the bartender and ordered a refill for himself and a pint for Maude. "She would have liked to have seen you, but wasn't bothered that you weren't there. She did make me promise we would both come to see her again before we left."

When the bartender brought over the two pints, he brought with him a coddle of pork sausage, rashers, and root vegetables in broth, and placed it in front of Maude. "I figured you'd be starving," Don told her. "You know Fianna stuffed me like a Christmas goose, so eat up and we can talk when you're through."

Maude smiled as the savory steam wafted up from the bowl. "You know me so well, Don Travers. I have a better idea." She reached for her backpack and pulled the laptop out. "Why don't you read what I wrote while I eat and then we can talk."

Maude took her time with her soup and the plate of brown bread that came along with it. "I don't know how I'll go back to eating regular bread when we get home," she told Don, who nodded and shot her a quick smile while he kept on reading. By the time Maude wiped the last piece of bread around the bowl to remove what couldn't be scooped up with her spoon, Don was nearing the end. She glanced over to see what page he was on. "Two pages to go. Looks like I have time for a quick trip to the toilet." Maude made sure she used the correct term. They had both found it odd that when they first arrived in Ireland, their requests for the location of the restroom or bathroom were met with sly grins. After all, one did not rest or bathe in a public facility, so what was left but the toilet?

Don was done reading by the time she returned. "It looks like you got a lot done today," he told Maude.

"Well, I moved the story forward, but I can't be sure that any of this really happened."

"I would think that, after the confirmation you had from Dory and Father Cleary about what you wrote yesterday, you would be more confident that what you write is an accurate depiction of the past."

"Don, I'm a social scientist. I can't accept that, just because I have done it before, I am able to write about the past each time I sit down to the keyboard... not without proof."

"Well, it's a good thing I have some proof here with me." Don reached for a file folder sitting on the bar next to him and handed it to his wife.

"This is Ciara's other letter! She let you borrow it?"

"Yeah. Fianna felt bad sending Father Cleary over to the MacMahon's this morning without any warning. Evidently there is an unspoken code here on the island about sharing family history when doing so involves rattling the skeletons in the closet of another family as well," Don told her. "When I finished reading the letter, I knew you would want to read it for yourself, so she said I could borrow it."

Maude was so grateful for the casual way these islanders thought of their family documents. There would be no borrowing such a letter were it in a museum, library, or private collection at home. She examined her hands for any residual breadcrumbs and wiped them on her jeans for good measure before removing the letter from its envelope.

Mrs. Patrick Sloane
Oughill
Inis Mór , Ireland
September 30, 1880

Dearest Cousin,

So much has happened since I wrote you last. I did receive your letter of 15, July just a few days ago. We have grown so used to a reliable post here in America, I often forget that 'tis not so easy to get correspondence to and from the island. I did find out for myself that Neala Ahearn and her dear husband have been living in America for some time, although they had only recently moved to Buffalo.

The trouble to my family caused by Neala, both past and present, was recently laid at her feet, and her dear husband there to bear witness to her sins. I must confess I did not see that her home life was so dire when we were younger, although she never confessed such news to me either. 'Twas her desperation to be rid of her father and brothers that lead her to malice all those years ago. I search my heart daily trying to find compassion enough to forgive her. I confess to you, dear cousin, that I've yet to find it.

It grieves me to have to tell you that our dear Lord claimed Darragh in a storm-related accident earlier in the summer. I cannot in good conscience hold him responsible for the trouble caused by his wife back then or now and so have prayed that his soul finds peace.

There is yet good news to report. Patsy, the child who fell victim to Neala's hostile accusations, and her mother were living for a time with the Seneca Indians. You'll recall I've written in the past to tell you of the Indians. They are on their way back to Cassadaga where they will take up residence in Martha's wee cottage at the edge of the woods. I was well pleased to hear that Prudence, the child's mother, had wed Jo Whiterock of the Seneca tribe. Jo is a great friend to us and we wish them well.

The most important news I have to tell you, dear Jeanne, is that our Martha is on her way to Inis Meáin, even as I write this letter. 'Tis quite the story I have to tell you, cousin. We met Big Johnny Quinn as a lad on the very day we went to the poorhouse. All these years have passed, and we have just a few weeks ago learned that Big Johnny was Ian Quinn, the cousin of Sean Quinn of Inis Meáin who took Mina Donohue to wife.

You may recall Sean and Mina were married on Inis Mór. Can you believe that Martha and her beloved Johnny were both present in the church that day, although both too young to realize it? I've been wondering' for a while how it is we never knew it. Sure enough, the poor lad had more than his share of hard times when he first came to America, having lost his parents, and nearly dying from a putrid leg, and you know well what happened to us during that time. I suppose none of us could bear to look back, much less talk of, where we came from. Martha wrote to Sean Quinn to introduce herself as Johnny's widow and inform them that she was coming. I did beg her to wait with me in Buffalo for a reply but the whole affair with the Ahearns left her rattled and she was eager to be away. You should expect to hear from her yourself once she has become acquainted with Johnny's kin. I beg you write and tell how she fares. I know she will as well, but I have never been separated from my baby sister by more than a day's travel and I will look forward to any reports of her wellbeing.

As for me, dear cousin, I am back in my home in Buffalo, near enough to my son and his family and expecting Patricia to join me as soon as she can make arrangements. It is our hope that Martha will find what she is searching for on Inis Meàin, and return to us so that we will all be together again, though I have the suspicion that she will not. Please remind her often that we love her and that we desperately want her back here with us.

With love,
Ciara

"She came back to Ireland," Maude said as she placed the letter carefully back in its envelope. "I wonder if she stayed here."

"She did. Fianna was able to tell me that she is buried on Inis Meáin," Don reported.

"I wonder why she stayed?" Maude wondered. "I would think it was difficult to be separated from her sisters." Maude drained her glass, which she had placed far from the letter while she was reading for fear of spilling it on the old document. "Come to think of it, I wonder why she didn't return to Inis Mór? She still had family there who would have known her."

Don took a long sip to drain his pint, and motioned for the bartender to bring another round before he answered that question. "It had to be a shock to remember what happened there. Maybe the memories were just too hard to live with."

"I suppose living in New York also stirred difficult memories. Maybe staying on Inis Meáin allowed her to leave her painful past behind?"

"I expect you're right," Don agreed. "As you may have figured out by now, Martha's story is sort of a legend among the Sloane and Quinn families. A woman doctor and member of the board of the Cassadaga Lake Free Association, she was a celebrity to the people on these islands. They wouldn't have known any women who had accomplished such things. Fianna told me that when Martha left Buffalo, she continued to practice medicine on Inis Meàin, but she didn't practice anything related to Modern Spiritualism."

"That's odd because she moved to Lily Dale in the first place to learn more about her gifts," Maude mused out loud.

"Yes, but think about it. The family was forced to leave their home because the rumors about her powers made it unsafe for her to live there any longer. After they left, her parents and sister died and they were forced into the poorhouse. You could argue that even in adulthood, her gifts made her life very difficult. That feud with the keeper of the insane asylum resulted in Johnny's death." Don shuddered at the thought of that revelation, which had caused he and Maude considerable duress. "Neala's accusations against Patsy surrounded Michael's death. Just about all the deaths of the people she loved were somehow tied either to her abilities or someone else's. Fianna thinks she moved to Inis Meáin for a fresh start. Once they knew she was Johnny's widow, they gladly took her in. Even if they were aware of the trouble that had occurred on Inis Mór, they were removed enough from the situation that they wouldn't likely have been bothered by it all those years later."

"So, she went to Inis Meán to get away from her gifts?"

"It looks that way," Don agreed.

* * *

The next day Maude and Don set out on Brutus and Cecil to Fianna's house to return the letter. The smell of baking bread greeted them as they entered the house. Maude suspected they were in for another feast, and silently wished they had walked the few miles to her door. She was not looking forward to riding home in a food coma.

When they were seated and the tea had been poured, Maude apologized for her absence the day before. "I also want to thank you for all of your help. I realize that this is your family business and that I am a stranger. I really appreciate your willingness to share what you know."

Fianna took a sip of her tea before responding. She placed the cup back on the saucer and looked at Maude directly. "Well, ye are family after all, are ye not?"

The casualness of her remark and friendly smile did not deceive Maude. She had not been honest with Fianna, or with the MacMahons about her reasons for wanting to know more about Martha Sloane's life on Inis Mór. It was time to fess up. "I'm guessing you've spoken to Father Cleary. I am sorry for not being totally honest with you. I hope you understand that it was not my intention to deceive you. I just assumed you would not believe that I was Martha Sloane in a past life. There are still days that I don't believe it myself."

"Aye, well, ye were a stranger to us. I suppose ye'd 'ave had no way of knowin'."

"No way of knowing what?" Don asked.

There was a brief silence before Fianna answered that question, as if she hadn't yet made up her mind to be completely truthful with them. "Well, ye wouldn't have known that Martha's gifts have been passed down in the family and that I am also a seer. I did not learn of your secret from Father Cleary. I learned it from Mary Sloane. She's been with ye since ye arrived on the island."

Maude had wondered why a Catholic priest had so readily accepted her explanation of the reasons she had come to Inis Mór. Fianna had done more than talk to him about the entry in the family bible. It relieved some of her guilt to realize that Fianna had been keeping things from her, too. Perhaps now they could have a real conversation. "Are you able to communicate with Mary Sloane?"

"Aye, I guess ye could call it that. 'Tis not like we have a conversation, like, but I am able to take her meanin' from the things she shows me."

"Father Cleary knows you are a seer. Do other people on the island know of your gifts?" Don asked.

"'Tis not somethin' I keep secret, but neither do I make it a point to tell folks. 'Twas more useful in the old days, when they still used currachs to fish the waters. Remember, electricity came to the island decades later than it did the mainland, so we had no radio or telly. I could provide important information about the weather the fisherman couldn't get for themselves. Now I'd as likely be ignored if I were to try and warn someone of a storm. Who needs a seer when ye have the weather report? These days those who seek me out are tourists who want to know if they'll find riches or their true love."

Maude detected that same twinge of sadness she had picked up from Dory. They grew up on the island in much the way Martha and her sisters had, although it was a century later. Dory and Fianna had been left behind while the other residents of the Aran islands went willingly into the twenty-first century. Perhaps the other villagers had no use for Fianna's gifts, but Maude did. "You said that Mary has been with us since we came here. Is she here now?"

"Aye, she is." Fianna pointed beyond Maude, indicating the ghost was standing just behind her.

"Would you ask her a question for me?" Fianna nodded and Maude continued. "Why am I here? Mary's message to me back home showed me Martha and her family leaving Inis Mór. I know now that they left because Martha's life was threatened, and while that was important to learn in terms of my understanding of her life, I'm not sure what it has to do with me now."

Fianna looked beyond Maude again, making a connection to Mary. "She says ye have the power to ask her yerself." Maude was confused and so the old woman explained. "She means ye can ask her and she'll tell ye." Again, Maude wasn't sure what Fianna meant. "Ye have the same gifts as I do. If ye ask the woman a question, ye should be able to understand the answer."

"I do?" Maude turned around, expecting to see the ghostly figure of an old woman standing behind her, but saw only the heavy draped covering the window. "Is she still here?"

"Ye can answer that question yerself," Fianna told her.

Maude checked behind her again and could not see Mary Sloane. "I'm afraid I can't. When I look behind me, I can't see anyone."

"Can ye feel her? Turn 'round and face me again. Sit back, take a deep breath and relax. Close yer eyes if ye think it will help."

Maude did as she was asked, and then waited for something to happen. "Am I supposed to feel something?"

Fianna smiled. "Sure enough, Mary was right about ye. Ye're tryin' too hard."

Maude closed her eyes tighter in an effort to concentrate, realized that also qualified as trying too hard, and then tried to relax. After a minute of sitting there, she opened her eyes. "I'm sorry, but I just don't get the sense that there is another person here."

"Maybe that is because there is not another person here," Don suggested. "Maybe she gives off an energy you're just not used to."

"Aye, just so," Fianna agreed.

"How am I supposed to become familiar with spirit energy?" Maude asked.

"I think maybe Charlotte can help you with that when we get home," Don suggested.

"That's fine, but what about now? I still don't know what Mary wants from me." She turned to Fianna. "I think it would be helpful for now if you could act as an interpreter."

Fianna's furrowed brow made her look as if she was in on something that Maude wasn't. "I'd be happy to, only she's gone now."

"Of course she is." Maude made no effort to hide the frustration in her voice. "I don't suppose she gave you an answer before she left?"

"No, she only showed me a wagon makin' its way along the bridge."

"Isn't that one of the images she showed Charlotte?" Don asked his wife.

"Yeah, and I also wrote that Martha remembered that day." Maude closed her eyes, searching her memory. "What did I write about that? I'll have to go back and check."

"Well, we could head back to the house and take a look before we grab something to eat at the pub," Don suggested.

Before Maude could agree, Fianna chimed in. "Oh, ye don't want to be goin' to the pub for yer supper. Here I've promised Dory not to feed ye, for she's after makin' ya a grand feast for yer last night on the island."

Maude and Don looked at each other, then at Fianna, before they asked in unison, "We're leaving?"

Chapter Nineteen

Fianna had confessed before they left her home that a few days ago she had seen that Maude and Don would depart Inis Mór the next day. "Ye're to visit Inis Meáin before ye go back to Dublin," she told them. Whether that had also been foreseen or was simply a directive, they didn't know.

When they discussed Fianna's mandate later that evening, Maude and Don were walking off the large meal that Dory had prepared in honor of their departure. Don suggested the reason they needed to go to Inis Meáin was to visit Martha's grave. "I agree that the scene that you wrote in your book about Martha's memory of the day she left is significant. Whatever the old woman told them as the wagon crossed the bridge was important."

"So, you are thinking that a visit to Martha's grave will help me bring those details to the surface?"

"That's what I'm hoping."

Maude was up early the next morning, anxious about their trip to Inis Meáin, and what they hoped to accomplish there. She took her usual seat on the back patio as the sun was coming up and allowed the sounds of the sea to soothe her. The door opened and Dory sat down next to her. "I'm glad to see that ye're up. I've a few things to tell ye before ye go."

Maude pulled her gaze from the sea and gave Dory her full attention.

"I'm not a seer like Fianna, but I've had a dream or two in my time that has given me pause for thought." The old woman had Maude's full attention, so she continued. "Last night Anna Donohue, yer widow Donohue, had much to tell me."

"I'm listening," It was all Maude could say.

"Well, Granny Anna- that's what I call her - Granny Anna was in my dream last night. At first, I didn't realize it, for all I saw was a wagon full of people makin' it's way toward the old bridge." Dory stopped talking when she noticed that Maude's eyebrows shot up in disbelief.

"Go on," Maude beckoned.

"As I said, a wagon makin' its way toward the old bridge, and a family ridin' inside. Granny Anna was chasin' the wagon, and the women aboard looked at her, but the wee lass sittin' there hid her face against her ma, startled as she was by Granny's approach. There she was, hobblin' alongside them as fast as her bent legs could take her. '*Tis a gift, Mary*,' she yelled up at the woman in the wagon. '*The child has a powerful gift. See that she puts it to good use.*' Well, sure enough, her hollerin' was frightenin' the wee lass who all but scurried her whole body under the protection of her ma's arms. Granny could see the child was feared, so she just looked at the woman hard, and the woman looked back. An understandin' passed between them and Granny walked away. Didn't I just wake right up, so I did. 'Twas Martha's family I saw, was it not?"

"The child has a powerful gift. See that she puts it to good use." Maude repeated Anna's words, trying to understand why the spirits from the other side continued to show her that scene. She looked at Dory who was staring at her, hoping for an explanation of her dream. "Martha spent most of her adult life using her gifts to help people, although after she moved to Inis Meáin she seemed to have stopped." Maude looked at Dory. "Is that it? Was Mary upset that Martha stopped using her gifts to help people?"

Maude repeated the question later that morning to Don when they were on the ferry headed to Inis Meáin. "How old do you think Martha was when she left Buffalo and returned to Ireland?" he asked.

Maude thought about it for a moment. "She'd have been in her late forties. Why?"

"Well, you're also in your forties. You're close to the age she was when she decided to give up her gifts."

"I don't understand what you are getting at," Maude told him, resisting the urge to remind her husband that she was in her early forties.

"Well, Martha lived many years beyond her forties, and never used her gifts again, from what we have been able to surmise. Maybe Mary Sloane doesn't want the same thing to happen to you."

Maude looked doubtful. "My weird dreams are nothing compared to Martha's gifts," she argued.

"You have skills beyond dreaming about the past. Both Charlotte and I have been telling you that you would have more control over your abilities if you would put forth a little effort. Look what you have learned since we have been here. Your writing also allows you to recall the past. You can connect with the past by simply being in the same location where important events have occurred. The thing is, you resist these gifts, like Martha did later in her life. Maybe Mary Sloane doesn't want to see that happen again."

"Don, Martha used her gifts to heal the sick, protect the persecuted and help people work through their grief. I can write about the past. It is not the same thing."

"How do you know the limits of your abilities? You may have gifts of which you're completely unaware. Martha was an adult when she realized her full potential and she let the fear of others keep her from continuing to use her abilities for the greater good. Think about it, Maude. There were indications from birth that Martha was extraordinary. You *were her*! Don't you think it's reasonable to assume that you may have other gifts as well?"

Maude continued to look skeptical, but Don persisted. "Mary Sloane directed you here, and look what you have learned since you arrived. I think that you needed to understand Martha's story so that you can understand your own. Mary went to great lengths to make sure that you understood her message."

"So, what are you saying? Should I give up our business and my research and set up shop in Lily Dale?"

"Not necessarily, but you should ask Charlotte to help you to understand your abilities better. There are workshops at Lily Dale, or private sessions if you are more comfortable with that, that can help you to identify your gifts and develop them."

Maude couldn't help recalling her discussions with Dory, Fianna and Father Cleary when they said their goodbyes. Although their words differed, the sentiment was the same. Each of them made her promise that she would embrace her gifts. It was as if they all had known what Mary's message was all along and were just waiting for Maude to catch up. She had been lost in those thoughts and looked up, surprised that Don had stopped talking and was staring at her as if he was expecting a reply. "I'm sorry, I drifted away for a minute there, what did you say?"

"I said we would figure this out together." Don placed his hand over hers on the railing as they watched the boat cut across the choppy waves toward the shore.

Inis Meáin, the middle island, was less than four square miles, so Maude and Don set out to the cemetery on foot. There were a few people at the pier offering tours of the island, or suggestions for lunch. They asked about cemeteries on the island and were pointed in the direction of Cill Cheannanach, a church dating back to the 9th century. There they would find the old cemetery that served those who died before the 1940s. The rugged landscape offered familiar challenges and they longed for Brutus and Cecil while ascending a particularly steep hill. The sky was overcast and the air was chilly. The climb at least warmed them up for a bit.

The old cemetery did not disappoint. It featured weathered headstones inscribed in Gaelic, or simple stone markers protruding from the ground. It was nearly impossible to read anything on the headstones. There was a young man on the opposite side of the cemetery. "Excuse me," Don called as he made his way over to the man. "Are you from here?"

The man looked at them, considering what Don was asking. Inis Meáin had the fewest visitors of the Aran Islands, and while many of its two-hundred or so residents spoke English, they did not interact with tourists often. "I am," the man said finally.

"I'm Don and this is my wife Maude. She is a writer and we have been on Inis Mór doing some research for a book."

The man shook hands with both of them. "I'm called Roger. What brings ye to the old cemetery?"

"We are looking for the grave of a woman named Martha Quinn. She left Inis Mór as a child with her family, and moved to America. She and her sisters became prominent residents of the city in the mid- to late-nineteenth century. We learned that she moved back here and is buried in this cemetery," Maude told him.

"Quinn, ye say? There are no more Quinns on the island." The young man pointed to the far corner of the cemetery. "Them that passed before 1940 would have been buried over there; the others would be in the new cemetery down the road."

"There are no Quinns left on Inis Meáin?" Don asked.

"Aye, the last of them died before I was born, a woman I believe. Most young people don't stay. There's not much to keep us here."

"Did you stay?" Maude asked.

"For now. I attend university in Dublin. I'll likely move on when I'm done," Roger told them.

"What are you studying?" Maude asked.

"Architecture."

There would be no jobs in his field on this tiny island and it made Don sad to think he would leave one day soon. "Thanks for the help and good luck in Dublin."

"I'm sorry," Maude told her husband as they made their way to the other side of the cemetery.

"I know you were hoping to find some of Johnny's family here."

"Well, I'd be lying if I said I wasn't. This is another small island with a long history. Who knows what we may have learned." He couldn't keep the disappointment from his voice.!

"Well, we can do some searching while we are here. Dory's sister-in-law died here. She's likely the person Roger was talking about. She must have had children. Maybe we can track them down."

"Yeah, maybe, but right now we are looking for Martha. There are only a few headstones with inscriptions, and they are pretty weathered. Do you see any word resembling her name?"

Maude was already on her knees examining the headstones. "No, but there is only one with the year 1912 inscribed on it, so I'm guessing this is hers." When it became evident to Maude that many of the characters she created for her books were real people, she asked a local genealogist to see what she could find out about each of them in the historical record. Abby Stevens had given Maude a flash drive with multiple files on it. In Martha's file was an article from a Lily Dale newspaper called the *Sunflower* from the year 1912. Maude never opened the file because she knew it was an announcement of Martha's death.

Maude pulled the grass away from the base of the stone, revealing the date for Don to see. "So, assuming this is her, now what?" She asked.

Don pulled his wife up and into his embrace. He kissed the top of her head before he let her go again. "Why don't I leave you two alone for a little while."

As Maude watched her husband walk toward the ruins of the church she noted that Roger had left the cemetery. She sat back down, unconcerned with the cold, damp grass. The idea that Maude had been Martha in another life became even more difficult to grasp faced with the physical remains of Martha's time here in Earth. It helped to think of Martha more as an ancestor than as a former version of herself. "What would you say if you were me and I was below this headstone?" Maude asked. "Maybe all of this was easier for you to accept." There was no response to her words, so Maude just sat there for a few minutes.

"Your mother has gone to great trouble to bring me here," Maude continued. "It seems we are both a bit of a disappointment to her. Well, that is not fair. She would have been very proud of you I'm sure. I guess it's me she's disappointed with. You had good reason to turn away from your gifts, but I guess I have no excuse."

Maude shifted her legs around so that she was sitting alongside Martha's stone, with her chin resting on bent knees. "Having these gifts, whatever they may be, doesn't make me any less me." She was speaking more like she was on a couch in a therapist's office. "I can still be an anthropologist, small business owner, wife and mother while I'm figuring this out. Heck, I can still be all of those things after I have figured all of this out."

There it was, the thing that had been holding her back. Maude assumed that embracing her gifts would somehow turn her into a different person. There would be no denying that her life would change, but she would still be the same person. That revelation gave her the courage to think about moving forward. "I'll call Charlotte when I get back and together we'll make a plan."

For a while she was quiet, staring out toward the sea, content in the knowledge that whatever she became would not take away any of who she already was. "Oh, you're back," she had sensed a person approaching and looked up expecting to see Don. There was no other person in the cemetery, but she still had the feeling that someone was there with her. Maude closed her eyes and took a relaxing breath, and then another. "Mary, is that you? I'm new at this. If you are here, please give me some sort of sign." Just then the sun peeked out from behind the clouds and Maude was filled with a sense of peace and joy. It was as if her heart was full. She could feel it; it was not an uncomfortable pressure, or tightness, but a feeling of happiness filling her up to bursting. "It is you. Thank you for finding me. I hope you will stay with me as I continue on this path."

As the sun moved once more behind the clouds, Maude realized that Mary had gone with it. She was overcome with a sense of relief and tears began to fill her eyes.

"Hey, what's wrong?" She hadn't seen Don approach. He fell to his knees, folded her into his arms and held her while she wept.!

"She was here, Don." Maude looked up at him with red and swollen eyes. "Mary was here. I could feel it."

Chapter Twenty

"Flight attendants take your seats and prepare for departure." The words barely registered as Don nodded off. They had driven back to Dublin from Doolin, where the ferry had deposited them after their brief visit to Inis Meáin. The flight home the next morning was at eight o'clock so they were up early to return the car and take the shuttle to the airport. Maude had put on a set of earbuds and was scrolling through the list of inflight movies, but Don had planned to sleep for as much of the flight as he could. The picture in his head as he nodded off was of the beach at Inis Mór. The waves came rolling in and he could see a man sitting in a currach by the shore.

"Would ye care to go out with me?" the man asked Don.

"Sure," Don pushed the boat into the surf and then jumped in, taking up the other set of oars. *Negotiating the choppy sea took all their concentration for a while.*

"I used to get terrible seasick," the man told him. "Not anymore."

Don looked out over the ocean. The water was calm and the sun was shining. They both raised their oars and allowed the currach to drift on the current. "You're Johnny, right?"

"Aye."

"I'm dreaming?" The question was worth asking just in case he was actually dead.

"Aye."

"How is it that we're able to talk to each other? We are each other."

"Ye're dreamin'."

"Why are you here?"

"Ye have many questions. I may have some answers."

Unlike many people who might have found their mind completely blank when presented with an opportunity like this, Don had a long list of questions. "How did you not know who they were when you met at the poorhouse?" He was referring to Martha and her older sisters, but Johnny seemed to know that.

"They had the look of the island folk, to be sure, but we did not talk of our homes then. We never did. Many folks who came to America back then had hopes for a better future. With the old world behind, and hard road ahead, most of us just tried to get from one day to the next. We had our share of heartache along the way, to be sure."

Talk of hardship reminded Don of something. "I've got this weird birthmark on my leg," he lifted his pant leg to reveal a brownish red mark. "Is that really leftover from your life?" Rodney Wake had told him that we can sometimes carry the scars of past life forward into subsequent lives.

"Aye, and I'm that sorry. They did pour boiling water into my wound. I fear that mark will be with the next lad too."

"You mean that someday I might be sitting in this boat talking to the next guy in the next life?"

"Well now, that I don't know, but there will likely be, as ye say, a next guy in the next life," Johnny told him.

"What about my irrational fear of snakes? Do I have you to thank for that too?"

"Nay, although I had a fear of serpents as well. Perhaps that came from the lad before me."

That brought Don to a more important question. "As I understand it, we keep coming back until we get it right, so how am I different from you?"

Johnny smiled. "Well, ye're still here. That's the main thing, I suppose, and ye're braver than I was."

"How so?"

"Ye married a rare woman. Ye'll be there when she needs ye." There was a sadness in his voice.

Don wasn't sure what he meant by that and was afraid to ask. Would Maude face some kind of trouble down the road because of her abilities? He forced himself to say it out loud.

"Those gifts can be a danger in your time, as they were in mine, as they have been throughout time, perhaps for different reasons, though. Yer Maude is a strong woman, like my Martha. She doesn't think she needs your protection, but she does, more often from herself than from others."

Although Don would agree with the sentiment, he was unsure how it was being applied. "I think you'll have to be more specific."

"Most folks did not appreciate a woman with a keen mind and voice of her own in my day. Women often pretended to be less than what they were in the interest of a roof over their head and peace in the home. 'Twas my job to remind Martha who she was every now and again, when the strain of bein' who she was became too much. I think I could have done a better job of it when I was alive, and I fear that when I was not there to tell her at all, she gave in."

"I don't think I'll have that problem with Maude. That might be one area in which she has achieved in her life what Martha could not. She is a respected scholar and business woman," Don proudly told Johnny.

"Aye, that she is, but ye must consider what she is about to undertake. The gifts she seeks to develop are feared now as they were then. In your day, the fear is masked by ridicule rather than accusations of witchcraft. For a scientist like herself to be considered a joke among her peers would be hard to take. She will want to turn away from this path. Ye must see that she stays on it."

"I can do that," Don said. He could see the regret in Johnny's eyes. The man blamed himself for Martha giving up the use of her gifts. "It had to give you some solace that she was with your family at the end of her life."

"Aye, I'd have loved to have gone back there with her." More regret. "We'd have had a lovely visit, but we'd have returned. Buffalo was our true home."

"You never kept in touch with your family back in Ireland?"

"In the early days, we had all but forgotten our kin on Inis Meáin. Those were hard times, so they were. Later, after my sister Megan married and had a home of her own, she began to wonder about those we left behind in Ireland. I was too young to remember any of them, but she began to write to my cousin, Sean. 'Twas Sean's Mina who told Megan of Martha's past when she wrote to the family to tell them we had wed. Megan wasted no time tellin' me. Can ye imagine, we were born just a few miles from one another? I could hardly believe it."

"You knew about Martha's past? Why did you never tell her?"

Johnny laughed. "Well, she was hardly a child of the Sidhe, now was she? She'd never spoken of her life before Buffalo. I doubt she even remembered it. I'd no wish to awaken old ghosts." The currach had drifted far out to sea and the coastline was all but gone. Johnny dipped his oars in the water and steered the boat back toward the shore. "I'd not have risked her happiness for all the riches in Christendom. She was a rare woman, was Martha, but I'm guessin' ye know that."

When the boat returned to shore, Don exited without another word and began to walk up the beach toward Maude. As he got closer he could hear the captain once again. "Welcome to Toronto, where the local time is 12:07 PM and the temperature is twenty eight degrees. That's eighty-three degrees for our American passengers."

Don looked over at his wife, who had fallen asleep while watching a movie. She looked so peaceful. Had she dreamed of the past again? No matter, he would go wherever the dream led.

Epilogue

Neala Ahearn stood invisible once again under the tree outside the wrought iron fence of the Nolan house. It didn't set well with her to have Ciara Nolan coping well with the loss of her husband after she had stood by and allowed dear, sweet Darragh to die. She could not forget the look on his face that day, just before he passed. His joy over seeing Ciara again after all those years, and on his deathbed no less, was more than she could bear. Neala made it a habit to wander by the Nolan house regularly. The coroner in Chautauqua county had determined Darragh's death to be an accident, but the Sloane women weren't to be underestimated.

There were people in the drive, and a carriage loaded with two trunks. Perhaps Ciara was leaving. Neala's smile faded as she saw two of the Sloane sisters exit the house. She moved closer, unnoticed, as yet another farewell ritual was unfolding in the drive.

After exchanging hugs and promises with all her grandchildren, nieces and nephews, Martha was left with only her oldest sister to say goodbye. She turned to Ciara, who made no effort to hide the tears spilling down her cheeks. "Dear sister." Before Martha could utter another word, Ciara grabbed her in a fierce embrace. The effort to maintain control of her emotions dissolved and Martha began to cry, too. They had said all they needed to say the previous night. Martha hadn't ruled out the notion of coming back to America, but she hadn't promised she would either. Now they just held on, hoping the feel and smell of each other could be recalled when they had need of it.

Martha was spared having to take her leave from Robert and his family just now. They would take her to the train station, where she and Robert would travel to Albany to say goodbye to Patricia and her family. From there they would travel to New York City and board the ship that would take them to Galway. Robert would be by his mother's side when they met the rest of Johnny's family and he would see her settled among them before he returned home.

Neala stood by the gate, unnoticed as Ciara finally released her sister. As Martha took her seat in the carriage, Ciara ran inside, unable to watch as they rolled down the drive. The others followed her into the house. "Well, that's one of ye gone, at least." Neala wasn't sure where Martha was going, but she was pleased to have her leaving Buffalo. She also wasn't aware she had said the words out loud.

Martha turned and saw her standing at the edge of the drive. Neala straightened up to her full height and looked Martha right in the eye, unapologetic. Martha stared right back at her. If Neala had looked away, she might not have seen the subtle tilt of Martha's head toward the tree that stood a few feet away from the drive as the carriage pulled onto the street. Just then several birds flew out from its branches. Neala looked up as the bird's droppings landed right on her nose. It seemed as though it was raining bird droppings. She could feel them on her shoulders and hear them pelting her bonnet. "Ach!" Martha's carriage faded into the traffic heading in the opposite direction as Neala hobbled as fast as her legs could carry her back toward her carriage. "Ye did this!" She turned and yelled up the street before climbing safely inside.

Robert had been focused on maneuvering the carriage out on to the busy street and had not seen the exchange between the two women. He turned as Neala yelled up the street. "What's that all about?" he asked.

"I'm sure I don't know," she answered.

Making their way through the morning bustle to the train station required all of Robert's concentration, so they rode in comfortable silence. Martha's mind wandered back to her conversation with Darius Weathersby just before she left Cassadaga. They had nearly quarreled, though both ultimately made an effort to see that their last evening together would be something they both looked back on fondly.

"I shall miss this," Martha said as she lay naked in his arms.

"So will I."

"Ye are a handsome man, Darius, and I can name three women right here in Cassadaga who will be on yer doorstep the minute I leave." She was teasing, but then again, she wasn't. The relationship they shared had helped them both learn to live with devastating losses. Martha hated to think that Darius might fall into despair again when she left. Indeed, there were women interested in him and she hoped he might take an interest in one of them.

"Perhaps I should leave that very minute, too." He didn't mean to go with her, she knew that.

"Promise me ye will find someone that makes ye happy."

"You make me happy."

"I must go and meet Johnny's family. Ye know I must, and I'll travel easier knowin' ye are happy."

"If you want to be assured that there will be other women in my life, I suppose there will be, but I don't want what we have with anyone else. Don't misunderstand me, I never had any illusions that we would marry. I know you didn't want it, and neither did I, but we share a rare gift and I don't want to share that with another. I want that to be ours alone." He kissed her deeply and for a while they simply enjoyed each other's company.

"I shall miss ye," she told him again.

"Then don't go." Darius knew he was starting something by saying that, but he couldn't help himself. He hadn't fallen in love with her, and would have been able to let her go, but there was more to the reasons she was leaving.

Martha didn't want to have to explain herself again, so brought her lips to his, letting her regrets come out in slow, deep kisses.

Darius wondered if he should just leave it be, but he could feel the conflict within her and could not pretend it wasn't there. "If you had known about your family on Inis Meáin sooner, would you have gone then?"

Martha was quiet for a bit, unable or unwilling to answer the question. "I don't know," she finally said. "What does it matter?"

"I think you are running away. You have abilities you have only begun to explore. There won't be anyone to help you where you are going."

There was not a response to that statement that wouldn't start trouble between them. Finally, she said, "I know where to return when I'm ready to continue. Can ye accept that?"

They both knew that she wasn't coming back. Martha had begun to explore her gifts in the weeks since her confrontation with Neala Ahearn. The power of them frightened her. Darius had delayed his travel to provide what support he could. He was unable to convince her that she would be able to control her emotions and how they impacted her abilities in time. Martha was going to Inis Meáin with no intention of using any abilities beyond those she had learned in medical school. He answered her question anyway. "Yes, of course I can. I only want what's best for you."

As the carriage headed toward the train station, Martha wondered if she had lied to Darius. She had said she would never use her gifts to harm another person and yet Neala Ahearn would have a devil of a time cleaning her dress and bonnet. She giggled at the thought. No real harm was done, after all, so she felt her conscience was clear.

"What are ye findin' so funny?" Robert asked her.

"Oh, nothin' I suppose."

The carriage continued on and the train station came into view. Robert looked over at his mother. "The train's here. I guess we'll be off soon, then."

"Aye, so we will."

Acknowledgements

To my husband, Bob, and my son, Charlie, I thank you for taking care of yourselves, the dogs, the house and the business when I needed you to.

My profound thanks also go to Jackie Kishbaugh, Michael Supernault, Ashley Southworth and Lucy Russem for holding down the fort at work when I needed them.

My novels are inspired by my scholarly work and so I thank Drs. Joyce E. Sirianni and Douglas Perrelli for inviting me to join the Erie County Poorhouse Cemetery Project. It has been such a pleasure to work on this project. I have learned so much from both of them, and their friendship has inspired each of my books.

There were several historians who were incredibly generous in giving me both their time and their detailed knowledge of various aspects of Buffalo's history. Jennifer Liber Raines from the Western New York Genealogical Society is without a doubt the most gifted researcher I know. She provided me with countless municipal reports and period newspaper articles that helped me to understand where the Erie County

Poorhouse and Insane Asylum existed in the public stream of consciousness.

Cynthia Van Ness and her staff from the Buffalo History Museum provided me with enormously helpful primary and secondary source data including microfilm of the Erie County Poorhouse Inmate Records, period maps, and the City of Buffalo Directories. These data help put the story in a more accurate place and time.

Charles Alaimo from the Buffalo and Erie County Public Library helped me navigate period maps of the city so that my characters could move about on foot, horseback or by carriage as they would have in Buffalo during the nineteenth century.

Ron Nagy from the Lily Dale Museum and Amanda Shepp from the Marion H. Skidmore Library, in Lily Dale, New York, provided me with period newspaper articles and other primary and secondary source material on the history of Lily Dale and Modern Spiritualism.

Linda Lohr from the History of Medicine Library at the University at Buffalo was a tremendous help in tracking down articles from the Buffalo Medical and Surgical Journal and other historical references relating to medicine, medical care in Buffalo and the diagnosis and treatment of insanity during the nineteenth century.

I am so grateful to Dr. Diane Morrison for helping me understand infants born "en caul" and how such births were/are recorded in New York.

Mason Winfield has written several books on the Iroquois and their supernatural beliefs. He was also kind enough to answer my questions about the general relationship between the Seneca people and the Modern Spiritualists of Cassadaga during the nineteenth century.

Richard Wedekindt of Wedekindt Funeral Homes helped me to understand the funeral and mourning practices during the nineteenth century. He is an encyclopedia of the funeral industry in Buffalo, both past and present. He has compiled many volumes on the subject, which he generously made available to me. I am very grateful for his help and his willingness to return my phone calls and e-mails and for welcoming me into his home so that I could have answers to my many questions.

There is a real antique lamp shop located on Hertel Avenue in Buffalo, New York, called the Antique Lamp Company and Gift Emporium. John and Sue Tobin, the owners of this wonderful establishment, were very gracious and accommodating in answering all of my questions about their business and about the retail items mentioned in my books. I am also grateful for their continued support.

Thanks to my readers, Bob Higgins, Casilda G. Lucas, Jacqueline Lunger, Jackie Kishbaugh, Charlie Higgins, Emily Crist and Christine Hicks for helping me with everything from inner senses and local history to spelling and grammar.

About the Author

Rosanne Higgins was born in Enfield, Connecticut, however spent her youth in Buffalo, New York. She studied the Asylum Movement in the nineteenth century and its impact on disease specific mortality. This research focused on the Erie, Niagara, and Monroe County Poorhouses in Western New York. That research earned her a Ph.D. in Anthropology in 1998 and lead to the publication of her research. Her desire to tell another side of 'The Poorhouse Story' that would be accessible to more than just the scholarly community resulted in the *Orphans and Inmates* series, which chronicles fictional accounts of poorhouse residents based on historical data. The story could not be contained in one book and so a series has resulted including *A Whisper of Bones, The Seer and the Scholar, A Lifetime Again,* and this work, *The Girl on the Shore*, the most recent addition.

http://www.rosannehiggins.com/blog.html

https://www.facebook.com/pages/Orphans-and-Inmates/516800631758088

92689153R00169

Made in the USA
Lexington, KY
07 July 2018